Now What?

A LOVE STORY

AUTHOR OF *NOW WHAT? 52 WEEK JOURNAL FOR WOMEN*

Roz Brown

Now What? A Love Story
Copyright © 2021 by Roz Brown

ISBN: Soft Cover – 978-1-64318-093-9

Imperium Publishing
1097 N. 400th Rd
Baldwin City, KS, 66006

www.imperiumpublishing.com

Now What?

A LOVE STORY

IMPERIUM PUBLISHING
CREATE YOUR STORY

AUTHOR OF *NOW WHAT? 52 WEEK JOURNAL FOR WOMEN*

Roz Brown

Special Thanks & Acknowledgements

I would like to take this time to thank some very special people in my life. First is my wonderful editor Nancy Tucker. I'm so thankful that God placed you in my life, and I'm so grateful and honored that you'd take on such a task as editing my books. As I tell everyone, you make me look good on paper! You've been my ear when I wasn't sure what or how to write the story God wanted me to share. You're literally the first person to see the raw me on paper, and you still love me. Thank you for the wonderful ideas and perspectives that only an editor can give. I love and appreciate you.

To my friend Niki Manbeck, thank you for coming up with the idea of a story line for the Now What line. I certainly wouldn't have thought of it. Thank you so very much for our friendship, sisterhood, and partnership in the now what project, as well as the long conversations, the tears of joy and fear we shared of how in the world are we going to get this done. We held our breath as we waited on God to give us clear direction and purpose. Thank you for taking such a huge chance on me as a publisher. You could have given this opportunity to anyone, but you chose me! Thank you so much!

To my personal assistant, friend, and sister Rosie Davis, thank you so much for the morning phone calls, encouraging words, support, and love throughout these years. It has meant so much to me. When I've wanted to cry, you've been there, when I wanted to give up, you wouldn't let me, saying, "God has a plan for your life. You can't give up!" Thank you for believing in me when I didn't and couldn't believe in myself. Thank you for the road trips to get me to the book signings, speaking engagements, and other places God sent us. You were the proud chauffeur, saying, "God doesn't want you to drive to these events." Even when I protested, you still drove. I just want to say in comparison to all you do, thank you seems small, but I couple it with all of my gratitude and love.

Last but not least a thank you to Pastor Sean Brooks and wife Cindy Brooks. I couldn't ask for a better support team in ministry. The two of you have been my rock and shoulder to cry on when I've been at my weakest, always offering an open door for a phone call, email, or an in- person conversation. I know that this book would never have happened had it not been for years of prayers, continued support, and counseling from both of you. I have grown to depend on both of you for spiritual guidance. Thank you so much. As Cindy would say, "Trust in the Lord with all your heart; lean not unto your own understanding in all your ways acknowledge him (ACT LIKE YOU KNOW HIM) and he will direct your path."

Dedication

I dedicate this book to a very special woman who has been in my life for more than thirty years. You've been a friend, confidant, mentor, spiritual mother, sister in Christ, cheerleader, and so much more. When others had unkind words to say about me, you came to my defense. You've upheld my standard of living without apology and gave me the nickname Butterbean.

This book I dedicate to one of the most obedient, God loving women I know, Mrs. Joan Johnson. When we met some thirty years ago, you saw something in me that I didn't even see, a future of walking with the Lord! I would have never dreamt God would be using me in this capacity or any capacity to be honest; however, Joan you've been in my life through the tough, rough, good, bad, and the ugly as we'd say. We have made so many memories through the years. No one would ever know the fun God provided to two women who wanted to simply love Him and one another.

I think about all that we've discovered in our life like sinful cookies. Although they only cost $1.00, they were the best cookies ever. I remember the time you gave me a birthday party and my guest and

I rearranged your living room. You didn't even get angry but laughed until you cried. There are so many other adventures like Worlds of Fun with my children and your grandson, sharing a fish dinner with me and my children because I had no money to purchase food, and your paying for me to take my driving test so I could be independent. Oh, the stories I could tell! The life secrets we share, the word of God we both hold so dear to our hearts, the love for Jesus, and the many life lessons of obedience you've taught me have been so incredible. My life wouldn't be the same had I not had a friend named Joan Johnson, aka Butterbean #1, to share the journey with me.

Joan, aka Butterbean #1, I love you so very much, and I thank you for the years of kindness, support, child rearing tips and ideas, financial support, and lessons of love.

This book I dedicate to you!

Love Roz

Aka-Butterbean #2

CHAPTER ONE

The Story!

A lice said goodbye to her staff at the hospital where she was the director of pediatrics as she needed to rush home. The twins would be waiting since she had promised to help them get ready for their high school graduation pictures. What an amazing journey she had been on for the last nineteen years. Alice was one of the most intelligent women that Alex Davis, her husband, had ever met. He was tall and had sandy blond hair and green eyes. His skin was silky white. They had fallen in love when interracial relationships were still taboo, especially in the South!

Their now what journey had started long ago. They had followed God's leading from the very beginning, and He hadn't let them down yet. Alice's husband, Alex Charles Davis, was born into a family of physicians. His dad, grandfather, and great-grandfather all were physicians. Alice was born Alice Elizabeth Taylor into a family of pastors. Her dad, grandfather, and great-grand father all were pastors. Both families were well-known in their small community of Lyonsville, Georgia. Although Alex and Alice had been told their love was forbidden, they knew it was ordained by God!

Alice's thoughts took her back as she took the scenic route home to reflect on how this beautiful, wonderful, turbulent life of now what's began. She and Alex had tried to stay away from each other once they acknowledged their feelings for one another, but it was useless. They were either thrown together on a committee at church or shared a class or project at school. It seemed that no matter how hard they tried to stay away from one another, God was throwing them back together. Finally, one Sunday afternoon they were working on a project at church for the youth group. Everyone else had left for the day, and it was Alex and Alice's job to clean up.

Alex started the conversation, "Hey Alice!"

She turned around to face him. "Yes?" she answered.

"Could I have a word with you, please?" He gestured for them to sit down, and he continued. "I know that I have feelings for you, and I know how our parents, community, and others feel about interracial marriage. I also know that as hard as I've been trying, it seems God just keeps throwing us back into one another's lives. I've been praying like we said we would do, and I've asked God specific things, and he's answered them all with a yes, it's okay for us to date. However, I don't just want to date you, Ali." That was what he called her when they were alone. No one else had ever heard him call her this. It was his special name for her.

Alice looked at Alex and said "Al, which was her special name for him, I've been praying, fasting, and asking God to lead both of us, and I've come to the same conclusion. I don't want to live my life without you. My heart is yours, and I hope this journey God has chosen for us will be worth it." Then, she corrected herself and said, "I know it will be worth it because it's orchestrated by God. It won't be easy, Alex. I hope you know this. You could lose your inheritance and everything else."

Alex knew what Alice was saying was so true, but he didn't care anymore. He wanted to be with her, and more than being with her, he wanted to be a pastor and teach the word of God. He didn't want to be a doctor and never had the dream of being a doctor. It was his dad's dream for him. How would his parents take this news? They couldn't tell them yet. They would at least have to graduate from high school, and that was a few months away. They had both celebrated their eighteenth birthdays, making them legal adults, and they knew what they wanted in life.

Alex said, "Since we've made this decision, I think we need to pray together and ask God to bless, guide, and protect us. Also, we need an advocate in our corner, not just Jesus. We have him but need someone else who will help us through this journey."

They finished cleaning the fellowship hall and walked to the sanctuary hand in hand. No one was at the church, so they felt comfortable holding hands. They both knelt before the throne where a huge cross stood, and Alex led them in prayer, "God we love you and we love our parents. We don't want to disrespect them or you in any way. We've both been praying for over a year that you'd remove our feelings for one another if they were wrong. We've asked you to make clear your purpose and plan for our lives, individually or together, and we believe with all our hearts you want us together to serve you. We know this walk will not be an easy one, but your word says if God be for you, who can be against you. It is with that scripture, believing with all our hearts that you want us together, that we come and ask you to open doors, soften our parents' hearts, and change their minds regarding racial issues. Lord, we so love you and we lay our lives at your feet to do with us as you please. In Jesus' name we pray. Amen."

Alex looked at Alice and tears were streaming down her face. He asked her if she wanted to say anything, and she said, "No you've said it all." They locked up the church, walked to their cars, gave each other a hug, and sighed, now what?

CHAPTER TWO

Thinking Back the Story Begins!

Alice entered her dad's office at the church. "Dad, what are your thoughts about Alex Davis?" she asked.

Her dad looked up at her and said, "What do you mean what are my thoughts about him?"

"Well, do you like him? Do you think he's a nice young man? What do you think of him is what I want to know?"

"He is a nice young man with a bright future, his dad tells me he's going to follow in his family's footsteps and become a doctor. I'm sure he'll do well for himself and one day he'll make a nice young lady a good husband," was her father's reply.

"Thanks, Daddy," Alice replied and quickly left his office. She was way too nervous to tell him the truth.

She hurried down the hall and collided head-on with Alex. He saw how upset she was, and all he could do was hold her in his arms. He quickly pulled her into a nearby office so no one would see them.

"What is wrong?" he asked, with a concerned look on his face.

She took a deep breath and said, "I just got through talking with my father about you."

"What?" he said with a look of horror on his face. "I thought we agreed that we wouldn't say or do anything until after graduation, and that's still a few months away. We can't get our parents upset or even give them an inkling about how we feel. They will forbid us to see each other. You know my family has the money to send me away and maybe we'll never see each other," he said with a serious look of concern.

"I know. I didn't say anything. I just asked him what he thought about you, and he said you were a nice young man with a great future and you'd make some nice young woman a great husband someday," Alice said.

Alex took Alice into his arms and said, "You know there will never be any other nice young woman for me but you. I've loved you since the day I laid my eyes on you, and I'll love you until I take my last breath," he said, looking her straight in her eyes, glistening from crying.

She laid her head on his shoulder and said, "I love you more than words can say; I just pray God will continue to lead and guide us."

Alice felt a small rash on the back of Alex's neck. "What is this rash on your neck?" Alice asked. She also said, "You feel warm, Alex, are you feeling okay?"

"I don't know, maybe the rash is from the soap or shampoo I've been using. It's on my hand, too, but I've been putting some ointment my mom gave me on it for the itching. It should clear up soon," he said.

He assured her he was fine. They knew they couldn't leave the office together because church was filling up quickly, so Alice left first and ran into her best friend, Michele Ann Graham, who was one of the friends with whom Alice and Alex had shared the news about their love and devotion for one another.

Michele was a beautiful young woman. She grew up across the street from Alice, and their families were very close. Michele hated that her two best friends couldn't share their love because of racial tensions that were still going on in that day and age. She hated the injustice, and that is why she had decided to become an attorney. However, not just any attorney, she wanted to be a civil rights attorney.

Alice looked at Michele and said, "Alex is in there. We were talking, and I wanted to come out first so no one would see us together."

Michele walked right up to the door, opened it, and said, "Come out here right now."

Alex obeyed the voice of his good friend he called little sister. She said, "Alex, do you feel okay? You look like you don't feel so good. What's wrong?"

Alex said, "I have this nagging headache, and I'm kind of hot, but my mom gave me some medicine for my headache and she said it would help with my fever."

Both women said, "We don't want to catch whatever virus you have," and they all three laughed.

Alex said "I don't think it's like that. I've just been pushing myself trying to lose weight and picking up extra hours at the youth center helping my brother-in-law and sister out. I'm sure I'll be okay."

Just as they'd finished their conversation, one of the deacons of the church walked up to them and asked what they were doing there and why they weren't in Sunday school.

Michele was the first to speak. "Deacon Walters, we are on our way right now, and you have yourself a blessed and wonderful Sunday."

The three of them locked arms, and off to Sunday school they went. Having a secret and not telling anyone is one thing, but being in love and not being able to share it with loved ones is the most heartbreaking. Alex and Alice still longed to share the joy of God's gift with others.

Church ended, and the young people stood in the lobby of the church planning what to do after church. Just as they were making plans to go eat, Alice's father beckoned for her. She left the group and went straight over to him.

"Yes, Daddy, did you want something?"

He replied, "I wanted to talk with you about your question this morning. Was there more you wanted to say about Alex Davis?"

"No sir," was her reply.

"You know if you ever want to talk, your mama and I are always here for you. We love you and want only the best for you," was her dad's response.

"I know that," Alice said before she placed a huge kiss on his cheek. "Now," she continued with a please say yes look in her eyes, "May I go to lunch with my friends?"

"Go ahead, but don't blame me when your mama is upset that you didn't eat lunch with the family," he said with a wink and a grin.

Alice left without a word. She blew a kiss to her dad and gave a sign of I love you with her fingers. He knew he had a great daughter, but he knew she was keeping something big from him.

He met his wife with an open car door which had been a custom of his since they'd met in high school. He always rushed to the car to get her car door opened and ready for her. Through the years she had grown accustomed to this kind of loving treatment, knowing she felt like royalty around him. She was a beautiful black woman with curly hair and big brown eyes.

With a raised eyebrow to her husband, Mrs. Taylor asked, "Where is Alice?"

"She has gone to lunch with some of the seniors in the church high school class. That's why she drove her car today instead of riding with us to church," he said.

His wife, a wise woman, looked at her husband and said, "Tom, " which is what she often called him, although his name was Thomas David Taylor IV. "You know our daughter is in love?"

"What?" he said, with a look of surprise and horror all at the same time. "Who is this lover boy you are talking about woman. Tell me right now! I want to know his name. Alice is far too young to be in love, and we haven't met or heard about any boy."

Her mother laughed and said, "That's because it's a secret."

"Do you know who it could possibly be?" he demanded.

"I have my idea of who it is, but I'm not going to tell you because you'll just intimidate the poor boy as soon as you see him. No sir, I won't be sharing that information with you because you'll simply over react, plus I'm not completely sure. I just have a thought about who I think it is," she explained calmly.

Alice raced into the house, excited from spending the afternoon with her church high school friends, and especially being able to be with Alex. Although not many knew of their secret affection for one another, it was amazing to see him in his element of serving others, knowing in her heart that Alex would be a great pastor, husband, and father. Alex was a wonderful, faithful friend to all he knew, and Alice knew he was her best friend by far.

Alice's thoughts were interrupted by a stern husky voice.

"Alice," her father called.

"Yes, Daddy," she answered.

"May I have a word with you, young lady?"

Alice's face lost all color. Just hearing the sternness in his voice made her pray immediately, "Oh Lord, please help me to face this possible now what moment whatever it may be. Lord, I don't want to lie to my dad; I don't want to be in sin. I want to honor you in all I do and say." With that prayer she entered a beautifully decorated room of soft maroons and grey which her mom had meticulously and lovingly decorated for her husband.

Mrs. Taylor, a well-known home interior decorator, had first used her own home to practice her decorating skills before launching a now successful business. She was a sought-after home interior designer. In fact, many of the influential women in their town had called upon Mrs. Taylor's experience and expertise to decorate their homes and husbands' offices for them. It was Alex's mom, Mrs. Davis, who had first seen Mrs. Taylor's talents as they met one day to discuss a church tea for the women and where to host it. After seeing Pastor and Mrs. Taylor's home, Alex's mom insisted that they host the tea there.

"Dianne, your home is absolutely beautiful! It looks as though I just walked into a show room at one of the finest decorating stores in Georgia."

Dianne humbly smiled, thanking Joan Davis for her kind words.

"How did you ever come up with these decorations?" she asked.

"I studied interior design in college. It has always been a passion of mine to take something old and make it new. It reminds me of what God did for me taking my old flesh and making me new in Christ Jesus. It's just my way of giving back my gift from God to others. If you really think we should have the tea here, then I'm certainly okay with that." That was the start of a very lucrative business for Dianne Taylor.

Alice was still standing in the doorway. "Daddy, you wanted to talk with me?"

"Yes, your mom and I have noticed something about you lately, and we can't put our finger on it. We want you to be honest with us. Are you sure there's nothing you want to talk to us about or tell us?" he asked.

Alice knew her dad well, and she knew he was fishing for information, and he wasn't going to get the information he thought he was going to get. Just then a thought came to her that she hadn't yet shared with them, that she had been awarded a full scholarship to any college or university in the United States. She had planned to tell them right after school on Friday, but when her friend Michele invited her to go to the movies with her and some other friends, she totally forgot. And in her mind, she said, "If it's news you want, my dear dad, then news I'll give you."

She looked at her mom and winked slightly as not to let her dad on. Alice, with her big hazel eyes and warm smile, paused for the slightest of seconds to give her dad just enough time to work himself up. She then said, "Well, dad and mom, I'm…" and before she could get anything else out of her mouth, her dad jumped to his feet and began this huge speech.

"We knew it! You're in love. Your mother and I were just talking about this after church. Alice, you know we love you and want the very best for you, but you are just too young to be in love with anyone; in fact we've never even met this young man that you are crazy in love with. We know nothing about where he comes from, his family, or anything. I just don't think you needed to keep this type of information from your mom and me. If he is an honorable young man, why are you keeping it a secret and why hasn't he come to see me and talk to me? Is he someone from your school, our church? Who is he?" he demanded.

Just as he finished his crusade of cross examination, Alice looked at her mother and her mother looked at her and they both burst out laughing. They laughed so hard they both found themselves on the floor with Mr. Taylor standing over them, trying to have a stern look, but because of their laughter, he himself couldn't be as serious as he wanted to be.

He said, "I don't see what is so funny. Dianne, are you going to harbor lying and deceit in our house?"

Mrs. Taylor looked up from the floor at her husband and said, "Honey, I don't know what you're talking about. As far as I know, no one has lied or deceived you because you never gave her a chance to say anything."

He looked at his wife, and said, "You heard her. She said I'm…" and then he stopped dead in his tracks, realizing that his wife was right. Then, he began to laugh as well. He sat down on the floor with the two most important women in his life and said, "I'm so sorry. Please forgive me for ranting on like a fool. Please tell me and your mom what you were going to say before I went off on my tangent."

Alice smiled at her dad, reached over and gave him huge zerbert on his face, and said, "That's what you get for not letting me talk. As I was going to say, Friday they announced the winners of the Howard Reid scholarships, and I'm one of the recipients!"

Her mom and dad both hugged her and told her how very proud they were of her. They understood what it took for their daughter to have been chosen for this prestigious award. This scholarship was one of the largest scholarships given from the Howard Reid Foundation in Georgia. This foundation was created by Dr. and Mrs. Howard Reid for which the local hospital was named, The Howard Reid University Hospital of Georgia. The foundation was created after their only son, a doctor who had died of a sudden heart attack at age thirty-five. They wanted to create something to remember their son by, and they knew he would want to give back to the community. Each year the foundation chose three young people who had decided to go into a field to give back to the community such as medicine, social work, and ministry. To qualify, these individuals had to be at the top of their class and other challenging work that was required as well. The students had to be nominated by the school staff as well as receive letters of recommendation from community leaders.

Alice was beaming as her father and mother looked at her with pride.

"You've certainly made my Sunday afternoon," her dad said, and her mother interjected, "I concur, and all along we thought your attitude was about a young man."

Alice didn't lie. She just smiled and said, "I'm going to take a short nap before we go back to church tonight." Once she was in her room, she fell to her knees and prayed. "Thank you, Jesus, for interceding for me. Thank you that I didn't have to lie to my parents. Father, open their eyes and Alex's parents' eyes to your plan for Alex's and my life. I know they want the best for us and that they love us, but you've given Alex and me a plan that only you could have come up with, and we want to follow your will for our lives. Please, Lord, help them accept your truth, your plans for our lives. In Jesus' name, Amen."

Alice was up and out of the house early Monday morning. She needed to stop by the local donut shop and get her and Michele their favorite cinnamon rolls before class started. This was the last few months of high school and then she would be Mrs. Alex Davis. She still didn't know how they were going to break the news to their parents. What would all of this look like, what would their future consist of without the support of their parents? Both were very close. Alex had three sisters who adored him. She had no idea how they would react either but figured they would be on their baby brother's side, telling him to follow God. All three of his sisters were very strong women of God. The oldest sister was a leader of women's ministries in her church, the middle sister's husband ran a youth group home which was part of their church, and the youngest sister was a chaplin at the local children's hospital. Each was strong in her faith and in decisions to go in the direction that God had chosen for them, so Alice knew that Alex had some allies in his life.

However, Alice's situation was a horse of a different color. She was an only child, so she had no support in that arena other than her best friend Michele, who she had been friends with since kindergarten. She knew she had a friend who would stick closer than a brother to her.

What a now what moment she was living in right now. Alice's mother had taught her years ago about "now what" moments in life. She explained that they were those unexpected events that could take your breath away and keep you on your knees. She now understood she'd be living this now what moment for a life time. When she reached the donut shop, Alex's dad was waiting for his order to be completed.

"Good morning, Alice," Dr. Charles A. Davis said.

"Good morning Dr. Davis, how are you this morning?" Alice replied.

"I'm doing fine, just fine. Are you ready to graduate high school and start your college journey? You know this is the most important part of your life, choosing the career of your life, mapping out your footsteps. I was just talking to Alex yesterday and without saying anything he agreed with me that becoming a physician is the only choice he has." He continued, "I hear you've decided to join the ranks of us and become a physician as well."

"Yes sir, I've wanted to be a doctor since I was five years old when my parents gave me a kid's medical kit. I love helping people and making them better," she said. Then she said, "Dr. Davis, did Alex say he wants to be a doctor? I'm only asking because you said this is the most important journey of our lives, choosing one's future footsteps in life."

Dr. Davis looked at Alice and said, "Alex was born into a family of physicians, and that choice was made for him. Yes, I did say that young people have to choose their own journey, but that's only if your parents haven't already set you up for success, and we've done that for Alex."

Alice smiled and said, "I certainly pray that God will give Alex the same desire for his life as you have for his life. I understand you have a plan for your son's life and listening to him talk about your family's legacy of doctors at school, I know he's proud of the Davis family name. You have a very special son, Dr. Davis."

She stopped short of telling him your son wants to be a pastor, but she knew she'd be over stepping her boundaries and she didn't want to get Alex in trouble.

Dr. Davis said, "I'm glad to hear that Alex is proud of his family because we are proud of him as well. He'll make a great doctor one day."

Alice smiled and said, "He sure will," and with that she was out the door with her cinnamon rolls.

As Alice approached the school, she saw an ambulance and police cars. Her heart started to race as she wondered who had been hurt at the school. What could she do to assist? She quickly parked her car and ran toward the school. Just as she approached, Michele ran to her and said, "Stop!" Alice stopped dead in her tracks, frozen.

Michele said, "I need you to stay calm and listen to me carefully. There's been an accident at the school. Some of the boys were horsing around on the stairs. Alex was one of them. His computer bag got caught on his foot and he fell down two flights of stairs from the top level from the auditorium.

Alice knew exactly the place Michele was talking about. The kids and teachers were always talking about how steep those steps were and that someday someone was going to get hurt badly. She never would have dreamt in a million years it would be her beloved Alex.

"Where is he?" she demanded. "How badly is he hurt? Did he break a leg, is he even conscious?" she asked.

Michele took a long breath and began, "He's not conscious, Alice. I know he has a head contusion and probably several broken bones, including his legs. I heard one of the paramedics say he could be paralyzed from the neck down, but no one knows anything until he gets to the hospital and they treat him. Let's not start assuming things before we truly know the extent of his injuries."

Alice was now crying hysterically and just before she dropped to the ground, Michele caught her. "I'm sure glad you don't weigh much," her friend said with a smile.

Alice responded, "Thank you, Michele. Can I go to him, please? Take me to him right now. Oh Lord, please help Alex. Please, Lord, take care of him. You promised us a future and what future will I have if Alex dies," and she began to cry again. They didn't make it to the school in time for Alice to see Alex. The ambulance was pulling off from the school with its sirens blasting as they approached.

"No, no, no come back," were Alice's words as she and Michele stood watching it drive away.

CHAPTER THREE

Reality!

Alice and Michele reached the hospital a few minutes after the ambulance arrived. Alex's best friend, Sean Mitchell Brooks, met them in the waiting area of the emergency room. He was pacing the floor with tears streaming down his face. Alice knew it was bad for Sean to be crying. He was the star football player and the first mixed half black and half white kid who held the title of quarterback. His dad was white, and his mom was black. They were very prominent in the town of Lyonsville, Georgia. His dad was the honorable Judge Joshua Mitchell Brooks.

Sean was average height but looked like a body builder. He was fast on the field. Sean spoke between tears saying, "It was just a freak accident. I tried to catch him before he fell, I really did. God knows I tried, but I had to let his hand go or he would have pulled me over with him, and my weight alone would have certainly killed him." He continued "I was the first one to get to him."

Alice spoke first saying, "Everyone knows that you and Alex are like brothers. If anyone would give his life up for Alex, it would be you. You can't blame yourself. You know God doesn't and no one else is blaming you either."

Just as she finished her statement, Alex's dad and mom arrived. It was apparent that both had been crying and were visibly upset; however, because Dr. Davis was one of the physicians on staff, he could get more information than the average person. Dr. Paul Pearson came into the waiting room. He reached Dr. Davis and his wife Joan, and they hugged.

"Paul, tell me straight. What is going on back there?" Charles asked with a little authority but also in a humble and concerned way.

Dr. Pearson began with, "Let me just say that first he is not going to die, but he does have a long road ahead of him. He has a head contusion, but we don't think there is any brain damage at all. We are doing a CT scan on him right now. His left ankle is broken and there are some pretty severe fractures to the right leg. Right now he has no feeling in his legs. I don't want to say he's paralyzed because there is a lot of swelling and there will be more after we do the surgeries. He's awake and asking for someone named Alice. Do you all know who that is?"

Charles Davis was confused but answered, "Yes, she is one of his close friends."

Dr. Pearson said, "Is she here?"

It took Dr. Davis a few moments before he saw Alice, Michelle, and Sean over in the corner praying. He waited until he heard amen before he approached them.

"Alice," he said. She looked up at him and he could see she had been crying as well as the others.

"It appears Alex is asking for you. I'm a little confused that he'd be asking for you instead of me or his mom. I know that you, Sean, and Michele are all good friends, but it does confuse me that he'd be asking for you instead of a family member."

Alice stood before she spoke. "Alex and I are very close and in the last few months we've been working on a school project and maybe that is why he's asking for me."

Dr. Davis said, "I will allow it for now, but after this you may not visit him. I believe right now the best you and your friends can do for him is to pray. This is a family matter. You do understand, don't you?"

Alice never said a word. She just nodded politely and followed Dr. Pearson down the hall.

They reached the room where Alex was being prepped for surgery. He looked at Dr. Pearson and said, "May I talk with Alice alone, please?"

Once they were alone Alex said, "I love you and this is very hard for me to say, but if I can't ever walk again, I won't be able to marry you. Maybe this is God's way of saying we shouldn't be together. I don't want you bogged down with a man in a wheelchair. What type of life will that be for you?" He said it more as a statement than a question.

Alice had no idea how much time they had before Alex's parents would burst in the room and stop their conversation, so she knew she had to talk quickly. She began with, "I love you more than life itself and you know that, and marriage is till death us do part, right?"

Alex shook his head yes.

She went on, "Dr. Pearson said you're going to be fine, and they need to get you in surgery to work on your legs. We are not making this kind of decision until we have all of the answers. Do you understand me?" she said through gritted teeth.

Alex knew she meant what she said. He said, "Okay, my love,"

Alice reached down, took his hand, and said, "Furthermore, legs or no legs, I want to be your wife for the rest of my life, so I don't want to hear any more of that nonsense. Do I make myself clear, Alex Davis?"

He said, "Yes ma'am," as tears started streaming down his face.

She said, "I have one more very important thing to say. Your dad…" and before she could finish her statement, his dad came in the room.

"That's enough, Alice. As I said in the waiting room, I don't know why Alex asked for you instead of me or his mother, but you're not family, so I'm going to ask you to leave now."

He looked at Alex and said, "You need to prepare for surgery son. I've explained to Alice here that in the coming weeks it would be best that she not visit you because you need to get your rest and concentrate on getting better. You do understand Alex, don't you?" Again, it was more of a statement than a question.

Alex understood that this was what Alice was about to tell him before his parents entered the room. Alex nodded his head and gave Alice a look of don't be concerned I've got this. She understood. She took Alex's hand and said, "I'll be praying for you, Alex. Get well soon, and I'll totally take care of our school project, so don't worry about that at all."

Alice let go of Alex's hand and turned to leave the room when Alex called out her name. She turned toward him, and he said, "Thank you very much. I appreciate it more than you know."

Alice left the room, crying more over the fact that she knew Dr. Davis was not going to let her see Alex again. They didn't understand how much they loved each other, how much they'd planned for the future. In a few weeks she was supposed to be Mrs. Alex Davis, but now that may be on hold for a very long time. She reached her friends and told them what was said. Sean was the other friend who knew about Alex and Alice's relationship, but they knew he would never tell a soul.

It wasn't very long before Alice's father Pastor Taylor came rushing into the waiting room. He saw Alice and the others sitting in the corner talking. As he approached, he could see that his daughter had been crying and was very distraught and upset.

"Honey, are you okay?" he asked.

"Yes, daddy, I'm fine. Alex is being prepped for surgery. His mom and dad are with him now before they take him back," she said.

Her dad said, "Let me go back there quickly and pray with them."

He went back to the nurse's desk and asked where Alex Davis was. The staff knew Pastor Taylor. He was on the board of directors at the hospital and the head hospital chaplin as well. They directed him to the room. He knocked gently and opened the door.

Dr. Davis spoke first. "Hi, Pastor," is all he could say before he broke down in tears. Alex was still awake, but they were about to give him something to relax before he went into surgery.

Pastor Taylor began, "It's going to be okay. God has this."

Alex's mom didn't leave his bedside. They all joined hands around Alex's bed, and Pastor Taylor prayed, "Lord God we love you and trust you. We know what the doctors have said, and we know that you are the great physician. You have the final answer about Alex's condition, not the doctors. We're asking you, Lord, for complete healing for Alex. We are asking for no paralysis in his legs. We know that it's all in your hands. Whatever decision you make, Lord, we thank you right now for sparing Alex's life. We thank you that he has no brain damage, that he's able to speak clearly, and most of all God we thank you that Alex knows you as Lord and Savior for himself. Yes, Lord, we thank you and ask for your will to be done. If your will is not what we'd want, we ask that you'd give us the wisdom, knowledge, and understanding to accept your will, Father. We ask this in your precious son's name, Jesus Christ," and they all said, "Amen!"

They wheeled Alex into surgery. It seemed like an eternity before Dr. Pearson appeared before them in the waiting room. He came in, took his surgical cap off, and said, "I don't know what you prayed back their Pastor Taylor, but God heard every word. Alex is going to be fine. He may walk with a limp, but he'll be fine. He'll have a tough road ahead but with physical and occupational therapy, prayer, and hard work, he'll make a full recovery."

They all began to thank and praise God for answering their prayers. However, Alice knew this was the beginning of a long spring and summer as Alex's dad had made it perfectly clear that she was not to visit him. How difficult was this going to be? However, she knew she must not make waves and make it harder for Alex to heal. She'd keep him in her prayers and closer to her heart.

Sean was the first to ask the question, "When can we see him?"

Dr. Pearson said, "He's just getting out of surgery and will be in recovery for a couple of hours. He's going to be in a lot of pain when he wakes up after the anesthesia and the nerve blockers wear off, so I'd give him at least a couple of days."

Alex's dad interjected, "As I was telling Alice, I believe this is time for family and we ask that you give Alex some time before visiting with him."

Sean was not always Dr. Davis's favorite as he was always challenging the man on his views and the control he tried to have over Alex's life. Sean spoke up and said, "No disrespect to you, but we are Alex's family too. I know we are not blood relatives, but we are the next thing closest to him, and he'd want to visit with us if he were awake."

Dr. Davis stared at Sean and remembered he was in the hospital where his reputation was at stake, so he had to watch his words carefully. "I understand your friendship with Alex. In fact I understand that you attempted to catch him and failed. Is that right?" He said it as a questioning statement as not to blame but blaming all at the same time.

Sean knew what he was implying; however, Sean was equally as witty as Dr. Davis, just younger. Dr. Davis disliked that he'd met his match in a younger version of himself.

Sean replied quickly, "Yes, Dr. Davis, I did try to catch Alex, but I had to let his hand go to keep him from pulling me down with him. His injuries would possibly have been worse had I fallen on top of him."

Dr. Pearson stepped in at that point and said, "Sean is absolutely right. If he had fallen on Alex, he may have been paralyzed for life. I also heard that you were the one that reached him and stopped him from falling the rest of the way, which would have resulted in his death. This young man deserves your thanks, Charles."

Dr. Davis did not like those facts, but knowing the school's auditorium's layout, he knew it was true. Being a physician himself and seeing the x-rays and his son's injuries, he knew everything that was stated by Sean and Dr. Pearson was correct.

He then humbly stated, "I appreciate your helping Alex and saving his life. I know you two are very close, and in the appropriate time we'll let you all know when you can visit with Alex."

However, in his mind he had no intentions of letting any of them near Alex, especially Alice. He saw how they were looking at each other in Alex's room, and he was not comfortable with a bi-racial romance. His son would never make it with a black wife by his side in the southern community. If he was going to be a successful doctor, he would need someone like himself by his side. These thoughts were going through his mind, but he didn't see himself as a prejudiced or a racist man. He was a concerned and loving father who wanted the best for his son.

If he were prejudiced, he wouldn't be the member of a large church whose pastor was a black man. He wouldn't have a foundation for minorities that he had set up for the inner-city school children who would otherwise not be able to go to college or get free healthcare and clothing. No, he wasn't prejudiced, but there was an order, and it was up to him as Alex's father to protect him at all costs. Consequently, he would make sure that Alice kept her distance from his son.

Alice's father came to her and said, "Honey let's go. Alex will be fine, and you need to get back to school."

Alice said, "Dad, I drove Michelle here. I'll take her back to school, but I think I'm going to take the day off if you and mom don't mind."

Her dad knew she'd been through a lot today. He responded, "Just be careful. I'll see you later a home."

Alice drove the long way home so she could get her thoughts together. Truly she had no idea what she'd do if she couldn't communicate with Alex for the next few months. His dad had made it clear that she wasn't family and wasn't welcome. Alex was too ill to be bothered with this, so she would have to be the strong one to get them through it. She had to depend on her level head and the wisdom God had given her to wait this out. What doesn't kill you will make you strong she thought to herself, as her mom and dad had said to her often, but this was hard. This "now what" moment was life changing, and she didn't know if she could do it.

As Alice walked into the kitchen, her mother turned to her and said, "How are you doing?" That was enough to bring a flood of tears again. Her mom wrapped her arms around her daughter, knowing her daughter's secret that Alex was the man she loved and wanted to spend the rest of her life with. She knew this was going to be a challenge for Alice, but someday soon she'd have to share with her daughter that she knew her secret and that she could trust her not to share it with anyone, not even her father.

Alice's father entered the room and saw how upset Alice was. He had thought it was just the surprise of a good friend getting hurt and not knowing the outcome, but now that they all knew Alex would be fine, why she was so upset over this young man? He was a friend, simply a friend. As he thought it through, it dawned on him that maybe Alex was more than a friend, but he couldn't be! They'd never been on a date, spent any time alone, nothing, so he quickly dismissed that thought and just decided he had a very compassionate daughter who loved her friends and cared deeply for humanity. That was the way she had been raised.

Alice gained her composure and said with a happy voice, as not to give away her true feelings to her parents, "What's for lunch? I'm famished," and her dad smiled, knowing his little girl had bounced back, so he was right. She was just upset with the entire incident. Alex was nothing more than a close friend and classmate.

Her mother said, "I was just making some greasy oven cheese burgers, fried potatoes and onions, and a salad."

"Oh yes," Alice said, "let me take my bags upstairs and I'll be right back to help you set the table."

Her dad walked over to his wife and said, "Do you know how much I love and adore you?"

Dianne smiled and said, "I have a guess, but you can tell me anyway, Pastor Taylor? As she smiled at him, he wrapped his arms around his tiny wife and said, "This much," as he met her lips and she met his.

They stayed in that embrace for quite a while, not noticing Alice had entered the room. She quickly cleared her throat and said, "Get a room you two."

They laughed as they parted. Alice was used to their open affection toward one another. That was what she wanted for herself and Alex, a life time of love. Her parents had married young, too. They were freshmen in college when they tied the knot. It was a difficult time for them, but they'd made it. It was a lot harder for her parents in the fifties, but this was the seventies, and anything was possible now. They'd come a long way, but they still had a long way to go and she knew it.

They sat down to eat lunch, and her dad said grace over their food. As they ate, Alice shared with her mom everything that had happened. Her mom sat in silence, taking in every word her daughter said. All the while she was silently praying, Lord let your will be done. Please help these kids because they are going to need it!

It was almost seven p.m. when Alice woke up. She had gone to sleep soon after she ate that enormous lunch her mom had made for them. She had dreamed of Alex and how he was going to propose to her, and she dreamed that their families were okay with their decision to get married. The phone ringing woke her up, and she was saddened all over again because it was just a dream.

"Hi," a weak voice came across the phone. Even in a soft whisper of a weak voice, she knew his voice. It was Alex.

"Hi, how are you feeling?" she asked.

He said, "Like I've been run over a couple of times by the football team and then someone hit me in my head with a two by four."

Alice chuckled a little. Then, her mind started wondering how in the world he dialed a phone. "Alex, how did you dial the phone to call me?" she asked.

Alex handed the phone over and a husky voice said, "I dialed the phone for him, and I'm holding it up to his face. I promised him I wouldn't listen to the two of you making googly love talk over the phone."

It was Sean. He had gone back to the hospital after he knew that Alex's parents were gone for the night. He had explained the entire situation to Alex, even letting him know that he thought his dad was onto him and Alice. Alex wasn't pleased, but he and Sean had a plan.

CHAPTER FOUR

Breaking the Rules!

The week went by quickly although Alice hadn't gone to the hospital as ordered by Alex's dad. At eight p.m. sharp her phone rang, and Sean was holding the phone so she and Alex could have their nightly conversation. Sean was a great friend to Alex. They had been friends as long as Michele and Alice had been friends. The four of them were inseparable. However, Sean didn't have the same feelings for Michele as Alex had for Alice. He desired a love like that; he just hadn't found it yet.

Sean was always comparing other young women to Alice. He told Alex, "If I had a girl like Alice, I would never let her go!"

Alex would always reply, "Stop comparing other girls to Alice. God has a woman for you. Don't be so caught up on what you think she should look like."

Sean sighed a long sigh and said, "I know you're talking about Michele. I just don't feel that way toward her. I wish I did because I think she's cute, smart, witty, and spunky, and I like that. There's just no spark. I already put up with a lot for being a mixed kid. You and Alice are going to get a lot of flak. My dad and mom went through hell as a mixed couple. What in the world do you think will happen if Michele and I get mixed up? She is as white as they come with fiery red hair, and I'm as tanned as they come, and everyone knows I'm mixed. I'm praying God will not let me miss out on a blessing like Michele if she is the one for me."

Alex was just saying goodbye to Alice when his dad walked in the room. He looked at Sean with disgust. He knew they were up to something. He just didn't know what it was, and he wanted to know. He was a man that prided himself in being in control of all aspects of his life and the lives of those around him, especially his children.

The problem that he had forgotten was that Alex was eighteen years old and was not a child. He only had so much control.

"Who were you talking with?" he asked.

"A friend," was Alex's reply and nothing more.

His dad knew by the tone he should back off. He then geared his questions toward Sean. "The staff tells me that you are up here every evening at eight o'clock sharp. Is there a reason for that? You do know visiting hours are over at seven p.m.," he said with a tone of agitation.

Sean responded cleverly, "Yes, I know what time visiting hours are over; however, Alex has asked me to come up and help him with a project when I get off work, and since I don't get off work until seven thirty, I can't get here any sooner. We cleared it with Doctor Pearson. You know, my uncle just happens to be the head of the orthopedic department here, and he said as long as Alex is feeling up to it, I can continue to come."

"It sounds like you gentlemen have it all figured out, don't you?" Alex's dad said.

Alex said, "We are working on it."

Alex was aware that his dad was trying to get him transferred home to continue his therapy. In his dad's mind this was the way he could control who came in and out of his house. He might not be able to control who came in and out of the hospital, but he could in his home.

Dr. Davis turned to Sean and said, "Do you mind if I have a private conversation with my son?"

Sean said, "Not at all Dr. Davis. I was just leaving." He and Alex did their special hand shake and off Sean went.

"Son, how are you feeling? It has been a week since the accident, and I know you must be getting tired of this hospital food and being cramped up in this room. I'm trying to make arrangements for you to finish your therapy at home," he said.

Alex took a long breath before he spoke. "I'm not ready to come home yet. I spoke with Dr. Pearson today, and he shared your idea with me. I explained to him I'd like to walk out of this hospital on my own two feet, not be wheeled out of here like an invalid. Besides dad, they have a phenomenal rehab facility across the street, and in a few weeks, I'll be transferred over there. I won't be coming home as of yet," Alex said to his father.

This infuriated Dr. Davis. First, he couldn't understand why Dr. Pearson would have that conversation with Alex without him being there. Alex was a mere boy. Yes, he was eighteen, but he was still not responsible enough to make this kind of decision. He had been a physician for well over twenty years and he knew what was best for his son. What he wanted was for him to come home so he could watch him and make sure he didn't make any life altering decisions.

When he spoke, he spoke with authority, "I guess you've settled it. How is Alice?" he asked attempting to throw Alex off to see if he could get more information.

"I guess she's fine since you made it clear she can't come see me because she's not family," Alex said with anger in his voice.

His dad quickly tried to fix it by saying, "Your mother and I didn't know if you were going to live, die, or ever walk again. I wasn't trying to be rude to Alice. I was just trying to make sure you could concentrate on getting well and graduating with your class. I also believe Alice has feelings for you more than just for a friend, and you know that can't happen. You're going to be a physician one day, and while things have changed, you still need to be with your own kind."

His statement made Alex sick to his stomach, but he knew he needed to remain calm or he would give it away. He looked at his dad and said, "I never would have thought you were a racist, dad. We attend one of the largest multiracial, multicultural churches in Lyonsville, GA. You happen to be on many boards to further education, health, and school opportunities for minorities, and all the while you think for some reason there is a difference because of the color of someone's skin."

His dad said "I'm not a racist," with venom. "I'm not prejudiced. I know what people would say if you were dating Alice. I know that your future career as a doctor would be jeopardized. I'm just giving you food for thought, young man. You don't have all the answers you think you do." His dad didn't give Alex any time for a rebuttal. He turned on his heel and left.

Alex was hurt, sad, and angry. He loved Alice, and no one was going to tell him that their love was wrong except for God. He'd prayed ever since he was a sophomore in high school. He had begged God to remove his feelings for Alice if it was wrong and not God's desire. Instead God took him to Songs of Solomon where he read of the black girl and Solomon. Then, God showed him what happened to Moses's sister Merriam and Aaron when they had complaints about him being married to an Ethiopian/Cush woman. It was with these scriptures, much prayer, and talking with his uncle that he found peace in his love for Alice. They both prayed, sought God and wise counsel on their relationship, and came to the conclusion that they were not in sin and that God had chosen them to be husband and wife someday. Alex was confident that this was the path he was to follow as well as being a pastor. God had clearly called him into the ministry, and he'd known it for a very long time.

Alex knew he was only eighteen, but he was wise beyond his years. He was always seeking out wise, unbiased Godly counsel to make sure he was on the right track. He also believed in fasting and praying, which he did often. He and Alice had set a time each week that they'd both fast and pray for themselves and others. These were things that their parents were not aware of, but they understood that once God called him to a life with someone, it was between the two of them. They were building a solid foundation with God.

Alex drifted off to sleep in prayer, knowing in his heart that God would have to work things out with his dad. He asked God to show his dad and open the door for someone to share what real love was to his father.

The nurse woke him up by simply calling his name. "Alex," she said, "It's time for your pain medication and for you to eat something. You didn't rest well at all last night. You tossed and turned groaning most of the night. Why didn't you ask for something for pain?"

Alex replied, "I just thought if I could get through the pain, I'd be okay."

The nurse replied "Tolerating pain doesn't make you a man and it isn't a testament to being a man. God created doctors, nurses, and medication for us to use wisely when in need. I've brought you some breakfast. I want you to eat, and I'll be back in a few with an injection for pain. Do you understand me?"

Alex smiled that huge smile of his and said, "Yes ma'am, I do understand." With that said, she was gone.

Alex reached for his Bible and began reading and praying. He didn't want to miss any time with the Lord. He knew this was a crucial time in his life, and he wanted to make sure that he was on the same page as God in all that he did. As he finished reading, the phone rang.

"Hello," he said. A voice on the other end of the phone said, "Hi sugar, how are you doing this morning?"

It was his mom. She knew Alex's secret and she had been so worried about him. Alice's mother had called and confided in her. They had been friends for years, and both women agreed not to share what they knew with their husbands. They also knew that if God had ordained this relationship, they had better get on their knees and pray for their children and their husbands.

"I'm fine, mom. How are you doing this morning?" he asked.

"I'm fine. I was in your room, and wanted to know if you want me to bring you anything from your room," she said.

"Would you please bring me my book bag, and if you'd stop by the donut shop and get me one of those huge cinnamon rolls, I'd be so grateful. Also, if you would bring me my yearbook, I'd appreciate it," he said.

His mom was more than willing to accommodate her one and only son. He was the baby, and she'd almost died delivering Alex, but God made all things new including her relationship with the Lord. She always said, "You never know where you are in your walk with the Lord until you almost meet him."

She was a changed woman, and she knew it. God had changed her life on that delivery table, and she was better for it. She sent kisses through the phone to her son and hurried to shower and visit with him. She knew she couldn't reveal what she knew about him and Alice without giving up Dianne. They had decided to continue to pray for their children and husbands and be there when they needed them.

Alex finished his breakfast, and the nurse helped him clean up and gave him his injection for his pain. He had drifted off to sleep when his mother came in. She sat by his side and watched him sleep, and then all of a sudden, he started talking. "Alice, I love you more than life itself. I know God wants us together. I'm sure of it. Don't cry, my sweet Alice. Everything is going to be all right." He continued to talk in his sleep for a few more minutes; then, he settled down again. She just rubbed his hand. She had no idea her husband was standing in the door way and had heard his son sleep talk.

He entered the room with anger and disgust on his face. He started, "Did I just hear Alex say he loved Alice?"

Joan responded, "Did you?"

"Yes, Joan, and you heard it as well. You and I both know that's bad news and he will have to just forget about little Ms. Alice Taylor. I told him last night that he needs to be with someone his kind."

Joan looked at her husband and said with all the wisdom she could muster up, "Alex is dreaming. They just gave him a lot of medication for his pain. Apparently, your little conversation last night upset him so much he was in pain and refused to call for pain medication."

As they were talking, Alex woke up but kept his eyes closed. He wanted to hear how this conversation was going to go.

"Charles, I love you, God knows I do, but if you don't leave Alex alone, you're going to lose him. You don't know if Alex's medication is making him say this stuff or if your halfwit conversation last night about being with your own kind made him dream this," she said.

Alex had spoken with his mom over the phone before she came to visit him and shared with his mom what his dad has said about Alice the night before. She was so hoping that her little spiel would get him off the trail of Alice and Alex.

It must have worked because Dr. Davis said, "Do you really think he was just dreaming from the medication and that when I spoke with him last night it just sent him into an unconscious dream?"

Joan looked at him and said, "You're a doctor. You know this pain medication can make you dream all sorts of things. Don't you remember when I gave birth to one of the girls I didn't even think we were married and was so afraid that my daddy was going to kill you because I had gone and gotten pregnant out of wedlock?"

Dr. Davis did remember that, and it settled his thoughts and he smiled at his wife. "Don't be angry at me. I just want the best for Alex. He's my only son, too, you know. I like Alice; she is a nice young woman. Did you hear she's going to medical school on a full scholarship? She's really smart."

Joan knew well that her husband did not care for people marrying out of their race. He didn't think he was wrong, but she thought he'd get over it since their pastor was a black man and many of their close friends were black. Then, she remembered all of their friends were well-to-do black people, and he really didn't have friends who weren't what she would call influential people. What she did know was that she would have to keep him off of these kids' trail if it killed her.

Alex pretended to be waking up when the conversation ended. He yawned a sleepy yawn. "Hi mom," he said.

His mother looked into his eyes and said, "Are you still in pain?"

"No, I'm feeling a little better. I am just groggy." He still hadn't acknowledged his dad because of their heated conversation last night.

His dad said, "Son, you were sleep talking and were saying silly things like I love you, Alice."

Mrs. Davis gave her husband a look of let it go, but he wouldn't. "So, is there any truth to your feelings for Alice or was it just a dream?"

Alex so wanted to tell his father the truth, but he said, "I don't know. Maybe it was just a dream, dad. Who knows? Only time will tell."

His dad became infuriated all over again because he wanted to hear his son say no, I don't love Alice, but he didn't say that. He was getting ready to start on the subject of interracial relationships when Dr. Pearson came in.

"So, how is the patient doing?" he said looking at Alex.

"I don't know because I can't feel anything."

Dr. Pearson said, "Let me examine you." He pulled the cover from Alex's legs, and both were swollen more than they had been.

He said, "I need to run some more tests, but right now I'm going to start you on a round of antibiotics. I believe you may have some infection brewing."

He called the nurse in and gave her orders. Dr. Davis said, "Paul, can I speak to you in private?"

Alex stopped all of that by saying, "Dr. Pearson, I'm eighteen years old, and I can make my own medical decisions, isn't that right?"

Dr. Pearson said, "Yes, by law you can."

Alex said, "I don't want my dad having conversations about me or my care without him talking in front of me is that clear?"

Dr. Pearson said, "Okay Alex. You're the patient and you're in charge."

Dr. Davis was so infuriated he said, "If you're so damn grown, then pay for your own hospital bill, because I'm taking you off of my insurance."

Mrs. Davis spoke up and said, "You'll do no such thing, Charles. You will not take him off of your insurance. He'll stay on the policy until he finishes college!"

Dr. Davis looked at his wife and knew she meant business. He also knew she had her own money, and she'd just get Alex his own medical insurance policy. He really didn't want to make her mad. Her dad had been the former mayor of the city, and she had connections beyond what he could even imagine.

Just then all the bells and whistles started going off on the machines attached to Alex, and he was convulsing. Dr. Pearson called stat to the nurses. Alex was having a seizure, and he didn't know why. Since Dr. Pearson was calling the shots, he called for a specialist, a black woman, Mrs. Doris Jackson. She was the top neurologist in her field and she would be able to see what was going on if anything. They gave Alex something to stop the seizure and he settled down, but more tests needed to be completed.

Sean came at his normal time, but Alex was asleep. The nurse told Sean everything that had happened earlier that day. Sean wept at his friend's bedside. He then picked up the Bible and read it to his friend. He knew that would be what he would want done.

He called Alice and informed her of Alex's condition. She was crying, and Sean said, "If anyone can reach him, you can. I'm going to put the phone to his ear, and you talk to him, okay?"

Alice said okay, and Sean placed the phone to his friend's ear. He knew he would have to be quick because Dr. Davis wasn't far away.

"Hey you," Alice said, "Wake up sleepy head, I'm over here worrying about you, and there you go and have a seizure. You're always trying to get attention. I love you, Alex Davis, and you better not die on me." She started crying, and Sean removed the phone as he heard Dr. Davis talking to the nurses.

"Hey, I've got to hang up. Dr. Davis is coming."

Sean hung up just before Dr. Davis walked in the room.

"Sean, you can go home. As you can see, my son is in no condition to work on a project with you or anyone else."

Sean said "Alex is my friend and my best friend at that. I would think you'd want as many people around Alex as possible, especially those people who love him. I don't think I'll be going anywhere tonight. I will stay as long as I like and unless my uncle or his doctors ask me to leave, I'm staying."

Their voices had gotten loud, and Dr. Jackson and Dr. Pearson came in the room and just looked at both of them.

Dr. Jackson spoke first. "I'm not sure what this is about, but this certainly is not the time to have a heated conversation in your son's room. I'm trying very hard to find out what is happening to him, so if you don't want me to ask you to leave, please keep it down."

Dr. Davis didn't like being spoken to like that by a woman and especially not a black woman. However, he knew she was the best, and she was in charge of his son's care.

Dr. Pearson said, "Alex is your best friend, and I know I told you that you could visit as long as there were no problems, but now I'm going to ask you to do me a favor and go home. I'll keep you posted on Alex's condition, I promise. He's in a medically-induced coma, and I want you to be at your best when you see him."

Sean had great respect for his uncle, so he left the hospital and headed to the youth group at church since it was Wednesday night. When he got there, Alice hadn't arrived yet, so he told Michele about Alex's condition. Before he could get all of it out, he began to sob. She let him cry on her shoulder. He was her friend, too.

She prayed for Alex, Alice, Sean, Alex's parents, and all involved, including all who were caring for Alex. Alice entered the room as she was praying, and the three of them locked arms, wept, and prayed silently.

CHAPTER FIVE

The Cure!

It had been a week and Alex was still in a medically-induced coma His doctors had found out that he had an infection, but they still didn't know what type of infection. They were running test after test after test. The neurologist had good news that there wasn't anything neurologically wrong with Alex, so they had called in a doctor that specialized in immune/infections. He was working day and night to find out what type of infection Alex had. Right now, they were treating him with antibiotics.

Alex's parents were beside themselves but not talking at this time. His mother was in some ways blaming his dad for upsetting him to the point that he had a seizure. She knew it truly wasn't his fault, but she needed someone to blame, and she wasn't going to blame God. Her husband was upset with Alice and Sean, saying that Alice was pressuring his son into having a relationship with her although he truly had no proof of the relationship between the two of them. He had gotten a court order that neither Sean nor Alice could visit the hospital to see Alex.

Alice prayed, fasted, cried, and wrote encouraging notes to Alex. She placed each one every day in a box that she had covered with pictures of Alex in the church choir, church picnics, and school functions, any pictures that she had from childhood until now were on the outside of the box with scriptures and prayers that God had laid on her heart to pray for Alex. One night as she lay in bed praying for Alex, God spoke to Alice and said go to the hospital. She thought it was odd because it was eight o'clock, and she knew visiting hours were over and no one would let her see Alex because of the court order. She lay there a little longer and tried to go to sleep, but God said, "Go to the hospital, Alice, now."

Alice knew her parents would protest as they had all had words with one another on the topic. Her father as the pastor had told her she had to honor Alex's parents' wishes and not disrespect them by going to the hospital.

Alice had tried to tell her dad that she and Alex were friends, but her dad wouldn't listen, saying to her, "I knew there was something more and you lied to me. I don't want to hear it. You have no business dating or wanting to be in a relationship with Alex Davis. His dad doesn't want it, and I don't want it either. There are lots of eligible, successful black young men that you could date. Instead, you went behind my back and started seeing Alex. No, you will not go to the hospital"

Alice knew that if God wanted her to go to the hospital, he'd have to make it clear. Just then her dad called to her.

"Alice!"

She answered, "Yes, what is it?"

"Your mom and I have to go meet with a couple at the church. There seems to be some sort of an emergency. If you need us, you can call the church. I don't expect we will be back here before 10:00," her dad said.

Alice looked up at the ceiling, clapped her hands silently, and said, "Okay, Lord, this is on you if I get in trouble."

As soon as her parents had been gone for a few minutes, Alice got into her car and drove straight to the hospital. Once she was there, she was led to the chapel. She sat on the front row and prayed, "Lord, I'm here, now what?" It was then that she heard, "Be still and know that I am God."

Alice continued to sit there, and a hand touched her shoulder. It was Dr. Pearson. "Hi, Alice. What are you doing here at this time of night? Visiting hours are over, and you know I can't take you upstairs to see Alex," he said.

She responded, "I know, Dr. Pearson. I didn't come to see him. I really don't know why I'm here other than I felt as though God asked me to come."

Just then the infectious disease doctor came in. He was talking about Alex's condition and how he just couldn't get a handle on what was going on.

Dr. Pearson introduced Dr. Gabriel Lord to Alice. He was the top infectious disease doctor in the country. He said, "It's so nice to meet you, Alice."

He went on to say that Alex's condition reminded him of a condition of someone who had been bitten by an insect, but he hadn't found any of the signs like a rash. He also noted that Alex had not complained about being tired, having leg cramps, or even having a headache before the accident as far as he knew.

Alice spoke up immediately. "Dr. Lord, I don't know if this means anything or not, but the day before the accident, I noticed a rash on the back of Alex's neck, and he said he thought it was from the soap he'd been using. I didn't say anything because he said his mom had given him some type of ointment for it and it should clear up in a few days."

Dr. Lord said, "Thank you. This is exactly the information I was looking for. I spoke to his parents but neither of them remembered Alex complaining of a rash."

Alice went on to say, "I also know he'd been talking about a headache and a fever but thought it was because he was trying to lose weight and working out more and picking up more hours at the youth center that his brother-in-law and sister run across town.

Dr. Lord looked at Dr. Pearson and they both nodded as if they were on the same page. They thanked Alice for the information and left her in the chapel.

Alice knew she needed to leave the hospital as quickly as possible. It was 9:15, and she needed to be home before her parents made it back to the house. As she was leaving the hospital and walking to her car, she saw the Davis's car. Hoping they didn't see her, she hurried to her car and drove straight home. As soon as she got into her bed, she heard her mom and dad come into the house. She thanked God and went to sleep.

Alex was resting when both Dr. Pearson and Dr. Lord entered into his room. Dr. Pearson spoke first. "Let's see if there is a rash on his neck." The doctors turned Alex over slightly and sure enough, there was a huge red rash on his neck. It looked as though it had spread from his neck moving downward toward his spine. They also examined his hands. There were rashes on both hands.

Dr. Pearson said, "These rashes weren't evident when they brought Alex in last week from the accident."

Dr. Lord spoke, "I'm sure they were there, but you all were concentrating on his injuries. The rash looks to be from Lyme disease. Let's test him and if it is, we can use a different antibiotic, and it will clear up pretty quickly."

All the tests were ordered, and as they suspected, Alex had Lyme disease on top of his injuries from the accident. The next morning, they begin the process of bringing him out of the coma. The swelling in his brain had started to go down as soon as they started the antibiotics.

Dr. and Mrs. Davis arrived at the hospital and were met by both Dr. Pearson and Dr. Lord. Dr. Lord spoke first, "I want you all to know that Alex should be awake in an hour are so. We've started the process of bringing him out of the coma. The swelling from his brain has gone down significantly from last night. As soon as we found out what the infection was and where it came from, it gave us the knowledge we needed to treat Alex's condition appropriately with the right antibiotics."

Dr. Pearson spoke up, "Alex has Lyme disease. He must have gotten bitten by a tick somewhere in the last few weeks and just ignored the symptoms. They can be so vague sometimes and then hit all of a sudden. I believe that the trauma from the accident made the disease speed up its effect. However, we are on it and he should make a full recovery."

Dr. Davis was the first of the couple to speak, "I don't understand how you all found out it was Lyme disease? What would make you think that? He had so many different symptoms."

Dr. Pearson spoke with hesitation because of the sensitive situation. "Well, Charles, it was Alice. She was here at the hospital last night, and she shared with us that Alex had a rash on the back of his neck and had been complaining about a headache among other things. She saved his life actually."

Dr. Davis was infuriated. "What?" he said with venom. "I specifically told this hospital staff that Alice Thomas was not supposed to visit with my son. She is part of the reason he's in the shape he's in. I have a court order that she and your nephew Sean are not to be in contact with my son at all," Dr. Davis Spewed out.

Dr. Pearson spoke with authority, "First of all, Alice didn't visit with Alex. She was in the hospital chapel praying when I came in. Dr. Lord joined us, and we both thought a little prayer for Alex wouldn't hurt since we all were at an impasse and had no idea what this infection was that was invading your son's body. Certainly, you had no idea of what was going on. Alice simply gave us information that saved his life, and she left the hospital after the conversation. She never saw Alex nor did she ask to see Alex."

It was Mrs. Davis who spoke next. She looked at her husband and said, "You are an ungrateful man. God has blessed us with our son's life, and all you can do is spill venom out about a young woman who has been nothing but kind, respectful, thoughtful, and caring for our family. Her father is our pastor for Pete's sake, Charles. What in the world is wrong with you?"

At that point Mrs. Davis asked, "Is it okay if I visit with my son now?" She couldn't stand to look at her husband. She was so very disappointed in him and the entire situation regarding Alice and Alex. Although she knew they were in love with one another, her husband really had no proof other than his speculations. She was quite thrilled to hear that her son would be fine and be healthy and happy other than possibly walking with a slight limp from his ankle injury. Before she went to her son's room, she stopped by the hospital chapel and prayed. She thanked God for her son's life and for Alice. She asked God to forgive her husband's ignorance and to open his eyes to what is important. She wept hard from anger and happiness all at the same time, angry at her husband because of all the ill feelings he had caused and happy because God was giving them all a second chance in this now what moment in life. She understood everyone will encounter now what moments, but it's what you do with those moments when God has intervened that will no doubt change the course of your life.

CHAPTER SIX

Mothers Know!

lex was awake and back to his old self. He was eating, laughing, and talking. He visited with his mom often. He was now in the Rehab Center across the street from the hospital. He wasn't talking with his father after finding out that his dad had gone to a judge to declare that Alice and Sean could not visit. He had told his dad until he dropped the court order he would not be coming home.

Joan and Dianne decided to meet at the hospital and talk with Alex candidly about what they knew about his and Alice's relationship. First, they met for coffee at the hospital coffee shop.

"Good morning, love" said Dianne Davis.

"Good morning, sweetie" Joan began. "I'm looking forward to Alex knowing that we know about him and Alice, and it's okay with us. Does Alice know you know, Dianne?" Joan asked.

"No, she doesn't since all this drama with Charles having a court order and Tom is not happy about Alice's feelings toward Alex either. You know he's always liked one of his fraternity brother's sons who is an attorney and four or five years older than Alice. He's had in his head for years that Alice would fall in love with this young man. To be honest with you, Alice has only met him once, and she wasn't interested. I don't know that the young man was that interested in our daughter either," Dianne said.

The women looked at each other and both at the same time said, "Stubborn." However, they both knew it was more than stubbornness. They knew it was sin on both sides. Both husbands were wrong, and they understood that both men thought they were protecting their children, but they were doing more harm than they could know. These wise women, without insulting or making their husbands look bad in any way, more than anything wanted God to be glorified in their own lives and their children's lives. If God wanted these young people together, who were they to step in the way. They only wanted the men to move out of the way and let God have his way.

When they entered Alex's room, he was reading his Bible. He set it down and smiled when he saw his mother come in the room.

"I have a visitor with me," she announced. Alex immediately had a huge grin on his face. He thought it was Alice, and when Dianne came in the room, his grin faded to a smile.

Dianne knew he was disappointed, and she understood and didn't take it personally at all.

"Good morning, Alex, how are you feeling this morning?" she asked.

"I'm good, Mrs. Taylor, how are you doing?" he asked. "How's Alice doing? Is she okay? Does she know that I don't blame her, and no one should she didn't upset me and that is not why I had a seizure."

He was rambling so that Mrs. Taylor had to put her hand up so he'd stop talking and she could get a word in.

"Alice is fine, and she understands the situation, Alex. That is why your mom and I decided to visit with you this morning. Your mom and I know that you and Alice are in love. We know that you both feel that God has called you two to be together, and we want you to know you have our support," she said.

Alex's mom grabbed his hand and said, "We've known for a while, but your dads are totally against this. We are praying that God opens their eyes. You and Alice both have to understand that as their wives, we can't change their minds or interfere in this. That it would show disrespect toward them. However, we want you and Alice to know we support you."

Alex had a huge sigh of relief and said, "How did you find out? We've been very careful not to share it with anyone but our two best friends and made sure that we were always in a group type of environment as not to bring attention to ourselves. To be honest, we've known since we were in junior high school, but we both thought it was wrong to date or marry outside of our race. Being born in the South, we've heard stories and didn't want to bring any type of hardship on our families. Consequently, we both tried to just be friends and ignore our feelings. However, we began to search scripture, pray, and fast, and asked God for direction. Finally, through scripture and counsel from Uncle James, we found out that it was okay to marry outside of your race. He's been counseling us since our junior year of high school."

Dumbfounded that these two young people were so in tuned to God's direction for their lives, both women smiled.

Mrs. Taylor spoke first. "I won't pretend that your life with a black woman is going to be easy, but I will tell you that this now what moment in your life will change the rest of your life. I do have a question for you. Do you love Alice with all of your heart and why do you love Alice?"

Alex exhaled and said, "Alice and I are best friends first. We sought God together and separately. Alice has a faith that carries her through tough and turbulent times. When I'm at my worst, she can tell without me saying a word. She sees the best in a situation, not the worst. Even if we couldn't be together, Alice would find a way to find joy in Christ. I love her because she loves God above all else. Regardless of whether God allows us to marry or not, she will still do the right thing and serve God with her whole heart. Yes, I love Alice with everything I am and I will protect, provide, support, and pray for her for the rest of my life." He continued, "We didn't want to be disrespectful to our parents, so we decided to wait until after high school when we were adults to announce how we felt. We were never going to infringe what we knew God wanted us to do. Mrs. Taylor, I love your daughter and I have since I was a kid. I know you all still look at us as kids and we are to some extent, but we are each eighteen and are considered adults according to the state of Georgia."

Mrs. Taylor said, "I appreciate your honesty, Alex. Your mother and I are going to meet with Alice this afternoon for lunch and have the same conversation with her as we've had with you. Understand Alice will not come to visit you long as there is a court order that says she can't. She will not break the law."

Alex grimaced and said, "I know, and I don't expect her to. I have a plan. I've called for Judge Brooks to come see me today, and I'm going to ask him to drop the court order. While I was unconscious, I couldn't speak for myself, but because the state considers me an adult, I can request it be dropped."

His mother smiled at Alex and said, "I'm so very proud of you, but remember to respect your father in all of this. Respecting him doesn't mean you don't have a difference of opinion. It just means you respect him in your tone of voice and your actions as best you can."

Alex nodded his head. Both women hugged and prayed for Alex. Then, they left to meet Alice for lunch.

The conversation was much like their conversation with Alex. The women told Alice that they knew about the secret relationship. Alice cried, saying she wasn't trying to be deceitful but wanted to obey God and follow her heart regarding what she felt God's calling was in her life. She explained that neither she nor Alex would have made a move about their relationship until they had graduated from high school, trying their best to respect their parents. Alice went on to tell the women that it didn't matter anyway since she couldn't even visit with Alex and that she never wanted to come between him and his dad.

Mrs. Davis spoke first, "Alice, I love you. I always have. I admire how smart, witty, and funny you are. Most of all I love the respect you have for your parents. It's not easy being a PK,' she said. "I know because although my dad was mayor, he was also a pastor, and people have such high standards for us PK's, don't they?"

Alice smiled and nodded her head yes. It was late, and the women departed and went their separate ways. Alice felt better knowing that her mom knew and that possibly her dad would change his mind about her and Alex. However, it was all in God's hands and she'd wait on him. She decided to go shopping for her dress for graduation. They only had a few weeks, and she knew just the dress she wanted. As she walked through the mall, she saw a beautiful necklace with an ivory stone and the words, "now what, God?" She knew she had to have this necklace. She went in the store and inquired about the necklace. It wasn't as pricey as she thought it would be, so she purchased four of them, one for her, Alex, Michele, and Sean. This would be her graduation gift to them. She was so thrilled that God had placed these little gems in her hand. She reached her favorite store called Classy Women and walked in. The ladies knew her well. This was her place.

"Hi, Alice," came the voice of Rose, the store owner and manager.

"Hi, Rose, did my dress come in today?" Alice asked with a huge grin on her face.

"Yes, it did, and it has a wrap that matches that came with it. Do you want to try it on to make sure it fits?" Rose asked enthusiastically.

Rose knew Alice had been waiting for this dress to come in for a few months. She'd been looking through her catalogs for the right dress for her graduation, and she found it a beautiful white chiffon dress, with layers from top to the bottom. It hit her right below her knee and with matching shoes that wrapped around the ankle she knew she'd look like a million bucks. She was happy she already had her shoes and purse and knew how she wanted to wear her beautiful long sandy brown hair. She would have her mom make a French roll in the back and bangs in the front. She had already talked with Michele about doing her makeup. She was ready for graduation, but would she get to see Alex at all? She'd been praying that God would work it all out.

While Alice was shopping, Alex was meeting with Judge Brooks. Judge Brooks was a fair man. He wasn't very tall, but he demanded authority wherever he went. It was not because he was mean or forceful, it was just the opposite. He was kind, thoughtful, and listened to every word a person had to say, even in a courtroom. Everyone really got a fair shake in his courtroom.

When he met with Alex, he said, "What can I do for you, son?"

"Judge Brooks, my dad had you sign an order that my two friends Alice Taylor and Sean Matthews can't come see me in the hospital. I have been reading, and I'm eighteen years old and I'd like those orders dropped. What do I have to do in order to have the order dropped?" Alex asked.

Judge Brooks said, "You can't have the order dropped. Your dad has to request it. Yes, you are eighteen, but this is his case. You can file a case in court, and I'll hear both sides. Then, I can make a decision, but I can't just drop the case. When your Dad filed the case, you were in a coma and couldn't speak for yourself, but now that you are awake, I'll have to have your doctors testify that you are of sound mind and body and then I can hear both sides. Does that sound like a fair deal, Alex?" the judge asked.

Alex said, "Yes, how do I go about getting this done?"

The judge explained the process and Alex got right on it.

Alex was released from the hospital, and as he said, he decided not to go home. Instead he moved in with his older sister and her husband. They were also furious with Dr. Davis regarding this court ordeal. Alex was resting when he heard his dad downstairs arguing with his sister Cynthia. He was questioning her. "Did you know your brother is taking me to court? How could he do this? I'm a respected man in this community."

Cynthia was strong. She could handle her dad.

"You're wrong. Why would you do that? Why would you get a court order saying Alex couldn't see two of his best friends? It's wrong, and you know it. Alex is eighteen. If you don't drop the court order, he's taking you to court and Judge Brooks will decide for himself what is right according to the law and the word of God. You know Judge Brooks loves God, and he's not going to go for any mess in his court room."

Dr. Davis said, "I want to talk to Alex right now."

Alex had entered the room without him knowing it. "Yes, dad what do you need?" he said with the most humble and respectful attitude.

"I want you to drop this court nonsense and move back home with your mother and me where you belong," Dr. Davis said.

Alex responded, "Drop the court order and allow me to see my friends, and I will consider it. If you don't, I'll stay here with Cynthia and Jackson until I graduate from high school which is in a couple of weeks, and I'll see you in court. I'm not doing this to hurt you, dad. I'm not, but these are people who are important to me, and I love and care about both of them."

Dr. Davis hated to hear the words love and Alice's name in the same sentence. He knew that there was way more to the relationship than they were telling, and he wanted to keep them apart as long as he possibly could before Alex ruined his life.

Dr. Davis said, "I'm doing this for your own good. You may not understand it but I am. I don't think you are thinking clearly. You're only eighteen. Heck, when I was eighteen, I made a lot of mistakes, and I wish someone had intervened for me. I would have done a lot of things differently, but no one did. I won't drop the order. If you see

Alice Taylor or Sean Matthew, they will have broken the law and will suffer the consequences. I know you don't want that."

Alex looked at his dad with tears in his eyes and said, "I'm so sorry you feel that way. I guess I'll see you in court next week."

Dr. Davis stormed out the door. He was so upset he didn't see the mail truck coming and it almost hit him. He stopped in his tracks, and said, "I won't give my son over to a black woman. I won't let her ruin his life."

Dr. Davis had nothing personal against Alice. It was just the way he was raised. Everyone has his place, and everyone needed to be in his place, and as far as he was concerned, there was no place in his son's life for Alice.

CHAPTER SEVEN

The Plan

Alice woke early hoping to get a good run in before church began. She heard a gentle knock on her door. "Come in," she said. "Good morning mom, you sure look pretty. What's wrong? You have something to tell me?" Alice asked with a questionable look in her eyes.

"I do have something to tell you, but I don't want you to jump to any conclusions. The Davis's have left our church, and because there is a court order for you and Alex not to see one another, your father has asked Alex not to attend our church for now. He's just trying to protect you," her mother said.

Alice was hurt, furious, and calm all at the same time, "Thanks for telling me. I appreciate it more than you know," Alice said. She looked down at her fingers and began to hum Amazing Grace. Then, she said, "Now what? Lord, you have a plan. Show it to me, give me an answer, show me the way, I want to love you and I want to obey."

Her mother knew that Alice was the type of young woman that would need time to process all of what was going on and it would be a few days before she'd talk about it all. Alice came downstairs to the kitchen for Sunday morning breakfast. Pastor Taylor was sitting in his usual chair, sipping his coffee. "Good morning. Princess," he said.

"Good morning, Pastor Taylor," Alice said with a trace of anger.

"Oh, so I'm not daddy anymore, I'm Pastor Taylor," Her dad replied.

"Aren't you the one who is supposed to bring people to Jesus unless they want to date your daughter or they happen to have the wrong color skin?" Alice replied.

Her dad stood up and walked over to stand right in her face. With clinched teeth he said, "Let me tell you something, Alice Elizabeth Taylor, you may be eighteen in years and the state may say you're a grown woman, but you're in my house and you will not disrespect me because of some little silly romance that you think is more important than family. You will continue to call me dad, daddy or father, but you'd better never call me Pastor Taylor as if I'm some stranger because you can't have life the way you want it. I have a church to run, and I didn't ask the Davis's to leave. They chose to leave, and because there is a court order, young lady, that says you can't be seen near Alex, I had to ask him not to come to the church to protect you." He was angry because he didn't know why she was blaming him when he was just trying to protect her.

Alice looked at her dad and said, "I'm sorry," and walked away. Her mother was ready to talk with her husband but thought better. She went into her bedroom, closed the door, and prayed.

Alice had decided not to attend their church. Instead she went to another church across town that she had visited several times. As she was leaving the service, she saw, Michele, Sean, and Alex all walking toward her. They hurried, grabbed her, and in the car they went.

They drove without so much as a word for quite some time before someone said, "Where are we going?"

Sean was driving. He said, "Somewhere we can talk candidly."

He made a right onto a gravel road, and there, high on a hill, was a large white brick building with a house sitting adjacent. He pulled around back and got out. He opened the door, and Alex climbed out. He was walking with a cane but doing quite well. Sean took a key out and opened the back door to the house. No one said a word. They just followed him.

Once they were inside, Alex said, "Sean, where are we?"

Sean said, "This is my grandparents' place. I'm sure you didn't notice when we left the city limits of Lyonsville My grandparents live here in Easterville, Georgia, which is about an hour and half outside of Lyonsville. They are out of town for the rest of this week. They'll be back next week for graduation. We all needed to get out of our town, and I knew my grandparents weren't here. I thought this was the best place to come up with a plan so that we could talk candidly and not be interrupted or caught."

He continued by asking, "Alex, do you love Alice? Alice, do you love Alex?"

They both said, "Yes," at the same time. Alice and Alex stared at each other. They hadn't seen each other for what seemed like an eternity.

Sean said, "I know that there is a court order that we are not to see each other, but if you all got married, the court order would be null and void."

Alice said, "Who told you that Sean?"

My uncle is an attorney, and he said because you are eighteen, you can legally get married. You don't need your parents' consent. Court is Tuesday. You can get a marriage license tomorrow. My cousin is the county clerk in a little town called Solid Rock, GA. It's another hour and a half outside of Easterville, which will place us far enough from Lyonsville that nobody will know us. You can get a blood test and marriage license all in one day. It costs about $50.00, and you'll need two witnesses which you have with me and Michele. When you go to court, you'll be married."

Alex walked over and took Alice's hands in his and said, "I'll marry you right now. What do you want to do?"

Alice said, "Yes, let's do it. We were going to marry in a month or two, but let's do it now."

Monday morning Alice woke up with a huge smile on her face. She needed her driver's license and birth certificate, and she had them both, Michele was going to pick her up as though they were going to school together. They would all meet at Sean's grandparents' house again and then head to Solid Rock, GA, which was a little over two hours from Lyonsville. The plan was set.

Alice whispered, "Now what, Lord? Please stop me if I'm making a mistake. If this is your will, let it go like clockwork."

Alex was still living at his sister Cynthia's house. Sean was picking him up. He decided to place his navy suit in a dress bag and hang it by the door and just pick it up as he left as though he was going to take it to the cleaners. He made sure he'd read his Bible that morning and prayed, "Now what, Lord? Please, if this is your will, let this work like clockwork, but if it is not, stop us in our tracks. We want to be in your will."

The doorbell rang, and it was Sean. He was dressed already but didn't have on his suit jacket. Alex answered the door, handed Sean his suit, and said, "I'm gone," to his sister Cynthia, who was in the kitchen. She said, "Okay, see you later, Alex," and he closed the door. Once in the car, they drove straight to the house and waited for Michele and Alice. Alex was nervous. He didn't know if Alice's' dad or mom would catch her and stop the entire plan, but he had prayed.

Alice and Michele knew they'd have to be more secretive than the boys, so Michele came over Sunday night after the afternoon conversation and took Alice's dress with her. It was a light blue and white linen suit with shoes and purse to match. She had purchased it for her Easter Sunday outfit and thought it was perfect.

As Alice was leaving, her mom met her at the door and said, "You aren't driving today?"

Alice replied, "No ma'am, I'm riding with Michele today. Is that okay?"

Her mom said, "Sure, I'll see you later. I love you, Alice."

"I love you, too, mom! Have a great day." She was out the door in Michele's car and they were off. They drove the hour drive to Ron's grandparents' place where Sean and Alex were waiting for them.

Once they were all together, Sean blindfolded Alex so he wouldn't see Alice until they got to the county clerk's office. Once they were all there, his cousin took their paper work and asked for the $50.00 fee for the marriage license and blood test. Alex pulled out his wallet and paid the lady.

She smiled and said, "Are you nervous?"

Alex said, "Just a little bit."

Then, she saw Alice. She smiled. She knew the entire situation because Sean had explained everything. Sean's uncle was the judge, and he had no qualms about marrying them. Once they were in his chambers, he said, "Before I marry you two, I want to talk with you."

"Are you absolutely sure this is what you want to do?" he asked them, looking them both in the eyes. Alex said, "Yes sir, I have no doubt in my mind I love Alice and I want to spend the rest of my life with her no matter what the cost."

Alice had a slight smile on her face. She cleared her throat and said, "I've never been more certain of anything in my life other than my salvation to Jesus Christ. This is the man God wants me to marry, and I will follow him, love him, honor him, respect, and obey him for the rest of my life."

The judge looked at them both and said, "You know when you two walked in my chambers, at first I had my doubts, but I have none now." He opened up his chamber door and called Sean and Michele in. They were the witnesses at the marriage. The judge told each one what to do and what to say. They repeated after the judge, and when it was time for the rings, Sean had the ring for Alice and Michele had the ring for Alex. They were simple bands that read on the inside of each ring I love you Alex and I love you Alice. They exchanged rings, and the judge said, "I now pronounce you husband and wife. What God has joined together, let no man put asunder."

It was done. The judge, Sean, and Michele left Mr. and Mrs. Alex Davis in the judge's chambers for some time alone. They held each other for a long time. With a gentle kiss, Alex said, "No one will ever be able to separate us again, Mrs. Davis."

Alice smiled and said, "Now what?" Our parents are going to be so angry with us, but I'm okay with it as long as we are together."

The four of them left the little town of Solid Rock, GA, and traveled back the hour drive to Sean's grandparents' place. They laughed, sang, and stopped at a little diner and ate. They changed their clothes, and all was well, or so they thought. They had all ditched school and never thought to call the office to say they wouldn't be there. Once back at Sean's grandparents' house, they separated. No honeymoon night for the newlyweds. They each had to go back to their respective home until they could announce what they'd done.

Alice's mom was furious with her when she walked in the door. "Alice Elizabeth Taylor, where have you been all day?"

Alice knew she was busted. She looked at her mom and said, "I just didn't feel like school today, so I just didn't go, mom. Can we talk about this later? Besides, I'm considered a graduate already. There's nothing really going on at school, I needed to clear my head."

Her mom knew there was more to the story, but since things for her daughter had been rough the last few weeks, she thought she'd go easy on her and let it be.

She said, "It's okay, sweetie, what are you getting ready to do?"

Alice said, "I think I'm going to work on my graduation speech for Saturday. It's my big day. I get to speak as the valedictorian of my class. I'm excited."

Alice had removed her wedding band and placed it in her coin purse. She knew not to wear a ring on her third finger on her left hand. That would cause a war. When she got upstairs to her room, she prayed this time silently because that is how her mom found out about her relationship with Alex, listening at the door, so this time she just prayed in her spirit.

She was right because her mom was standing at the door hoping to find out something, but nothing was said, just silence. Her mom went into her own room and prayed, too.

Alex wasn't so lucky. As he entered his sister's house, Cynthia said, "Where have you been? The school called and said you didn't go to school today."

Alex looked at his sister and said, "I took the day off. I just didn't feel like it today."

Cynthia was sharp and grabbed his left hand. "Why are you wearing a wedding band?"

Alex looked at her, and his face told it all. He had a twinkle in his eye and a little smirk on his face.

Cynthia pulled him into her bedroom and asked straight out, "Did you and Alice get married today?"

Alex said "Yes, we went to a town called Solid Rock, Ga., with Sean and Michele and got married. When we go to court in the morning, we'll be Mr. and Mrs. Alex Davis."

Cynthia said, "Oh God help us. Now what? Alex where are you all going to live? What money will you live off of? Dad is not going to give you your inheritance because he's not going to support the marriage."

Alex said, "I was hoping you'd let Alice and me live in that little apartment over your garage. It's a one bedroom with a little kitchen, a sitting area, and a bathroom. That's all we really need right now until we leave to go to school. We can get married housing when we leave in the summer."

Cynthia said, "Let me talk to Jackson. We were in similar place when we got married except we had a wedding, and dad walked me down the aisle. Yes, he was reluctant, but he did."

Alex said, "Yes my dear sister, dad did walk you down the aisle, but it was because you faked a pregnancy, and he didn't want to be embarrassed. When he found out that you weren't pregnant, he didn't speak to you for six months."

Cynthia responded, "I know, but I married the man of my dreams, and I haven't looked back. Let me talk with Jackson and see what he has to say."

Just then Jackson came in the room. "Ask me what?" he said.

"Your brother in law married Alice Taylor today," Cynthia announced.

Jackson fell across the bed laughing. He said, "Who else knows this news?"

Cynthia said "You, me, Sean, Michele, and the bride and groom. Alex wants to know if he and Alice can live in the apartment over the garage until they leave for college this summer. If you say yes, we can use that as part of Alex's payment for helping with the youth organization this summer. We are strapped for funds and didn't know how to pay him anyway."

Jackson said, "You don't have to convince me. The apartment is yours, little brother. Wow, this is something else! What in the world are your parents going to say? What are Alice's parents going to say when they find out?"

Tuesday morning couldn't come quick enough. They all filed into the courtroom and the honorable Judge Joshua Brooks came into the court room and took his place. Alex came in with his sister and brother in law. Alice arrived with her parents, and Sean and Michele came in together. Alex's dad and mom arrived, and then Dr. Pearson and Dr.

Lord came into the courtroom. The hearing started, and Alex asked if he could approach the bench. Judge Brooks allowed it. Alex whispered something to the judge and handed him a piece of paper. The judge looked at him and called Alice up to the bench. He then said, "I need to see these two young people in my chambers."

They followed him into his chambers. He looked at both of them and said, "This is a marriage license. Are you two telling me you're married?"

They both responded with a smile and said, "Yes." The judge said, "This changes everything now."

Alex said, "Judge Brooks our parents don't know yet, and we'd like for you to announce it for us."

Judge Brooks said, "Alex this makes my ruling easier, but I'm still going to ask some questions. You two just go sit back where you were. Once I'm finished, I will ask you two to join me in the front of the courtroom."

Alex and Alice agreed. The judge then looked at the signature of the witnesses. He saw Sean Mitchell Brooks and Michele Ann Graham. The judge looked at Alex and asked, "Did my son take part in this," knowing the answer but wanting to hear it from Alex.

"Yes sir, he did," Alex replied.

The judge said, "I'll talk with him later. I'm glad I didn't know because I would have to throw this out and give it to another judge. Since I didn't know, I will have to bring my son up to be a witness that he told me nothing of this so your father won't try to bring a case against me."

They left the judge's chambers and took their perspective places in the courtroom. The judge came out, and the deputy sheriff said, "All rise! The Honorable Judge Joshua Brooks." Judge Brooks took his place and slammed the gavel, stating, "Court is now in session."

CHAPTER EIGHT

The Annoucement!

Judge Brooks called Dr. Davis to the stand. He swore to tell the truth and the whole truth, so help him God. Judge Brooks asked him if he still held fast to his court order that Sean and Alice were not to see Alex although Alex was out of the hospital and doing well.

Dr. Davis said, "Yes, Judge Brooks, I love my son and I just want the best for him. Although he's eighteen, I know he believes that he knows what is best for him, but I believe that Sean and Alice, although their intentions may be what they believe is right, are very young. I believe a little time apart will give Alex the time he needs to grow up and make better decisions, so I won't drop my court order." He continued, "As far as Sean is concerned," he paused and remembered that Sean was the judge's son. He would need to choose his words carefully. "I understand and appreciate that Sean's quick thinking may have saved my son's life. I know Sean is your son, judge, but you and I both know Sean is very immature and headstrong among other things, and I don't believe he holds my son's best interest at heart. I believe a lot of bad decisions that Alex makes are because of his association with Sean; therefore, I won't drop the order for him either."

Judge Brooks was steaming, but he didn't let on he knew the doctor's kind, and he simply said, "Dr. Davis, you may step down."

He then called Dr. Pearson to the stand. Judge Brooks and Dr. Pearson were brothers in law. Dr. Pearson's sister was Judge Brooks' wife. It truly was a family affair. Dr. Pearson was sworn in by the bailiff.

Dr. Pearson began to explain, "Alex had a really bad injury, and he was unconscious when he arrived at the hospital but gained consciousness soon after arriving. We performed a lot of tests to make sure there was no brain damage, and there was none. We also placed him in a medically-induced coma, and he had some brain swelling because of an infection that was going through his blood stream, but again after several rounds of antibiotics, there is no brain damage. Alex is aware, he's very intelligent, and he can make good sound decisions."

Judge Brooks thanked Dr. Pearson and was getting ready to let him take his seat, when the doctor requested to make a statement on behalf of his nephew, Sean.

The Judge allowed it. Dr. Pearson stared straight at Dr. Davis and said, "Charles, you've made some pretty awful accusations against my nephew, and I take them personally. I want you to understand that Sean is a respectable young man. He's honest and has been a loyal friend to Alex since they were in kindergarten. You've never liked Sean because his dad is a white man and his mom is black woman. She happens to be my sister and the judge's wife. You seem to have an issue with the color of people's skin, Charles. You can't name one incident where Sean has led Alex astray. In fact, it was Sean who introduced Alex to Christ. It was my nephew Sean who helped Alex pass his math class in sixth grade. It was Sean who started the blood drive when Alex was in that car accident and needed a blood transfusion their freshman year of high school. Sean has proven over and over again that he is a great friend to Alex. Oh, and by the way, if it hadn't been for Alice, we may never have found out that your son had Lyme disease on top of his injuries, so Charles, if anyone shouldn't have contact with Alex, I believe it's you with your hatred and venomous words."

Dr. Pearson looked at Judge Brooks, and said, "Thank you, Judge, for allowing me to have that time. I truly appreciate it." He then stepped down without taking his angry gaze from Alex's father.

Judge Brooks then called Dr. Lord and asked him the same line of questioning and received the same answers.

"Alex Davis has made a complete recovery, has no brain injury, and can make well- informed decisions," he testified, "and, Judge Brooks, I'd just like to add that it was Alice Taylor that provided us with the information we needed to provide the right treatment and antibiotics to Alex. I truly believe he may have not made it had it not been for her. Although she wasn't supposed to come to the hospital, she came anyway. She didn't ask to see Alex. In fact, she didn't even attempt to see him. She was just in the chapel praying. Since Dr. Pearson and I couldn't for the life of us come up with a clear diagnosis, we went to the chapel to pray, and that is where we saw Alice, just sitting there praying. I just wanted to keep the record straight, too."

Judge Brooks said, "Thank you, doctor, you may take your seat."

The doctor stepped down and returned to his seat. This time it was Dr. Davis who glared at him with contempt.

Judge Brooks left his bench and walked to the front of the court room. He called Alex, Alice, Sean and Michele to join him. Judge Brooks started by saying, "I've known both of these families for over twenty-five years, and it breaks my heart that this is going on. I love these families, and I've watched these four young people grow up in this community. Of course Sean here is my beloved son I'm well pleased with and proud of. He has worked in my courtroom for the last four summers as a junior intern as he prepares for college and law school."

"Michele has always been a sweet smart young lady and has also worked in the court for the last few summers under another judge but will be working for me this summer. Alice is in the top of her class and going to medical school on a full college scholarship, and Alex has a full college scholarship as well. These are faithful, loving, kind, obedient, caring young Christian people. I've never seen these young people in my courtroom for disobeying the law, and that says a lot in this day and age people."

Dr. Davis got ready to interject something, but Judge Brooks said, "You've had your time. Now it's my turn. Please sit down."

Dr. Davis knew that he'd need to obey the law, especially in Judge Brooks' courtroom.

Judge Brooks continued with his speech, saying, "I know you believe you made the best decision for Alex, and while he was in a coma and healing, I felt you were doing the right thing as well. That is why I agreed to the court order in the first place. However, things have changed more than you know. As a result, I'm dropping your court order."

The judge then looked at Alex and said, "Alex, you are free to be friends with whomever you feel God would want you to be friends with. I would caution you to be wise in making friends and use your Bible as guidance in life decisions. Based on the three people standing next to you, I see you've made some great friends."

Judge Brooks took a huge breath before he continued, "I know you all are wondering why Alex and Alice were in my chambers, but before I make my announcement, I must bring my beloved son to the stand. Sean, would you please honor me with your presence on the stand?"

Sean saw the look in his dad's eyes, and he knew his dad was not happy with being placed in the middle let alone placing his character and career on the line. Sean took the stand, and the bailiff swore him in. Judge Brooks looked at Sean and said, "Sean you are well aware of the announcement I'm about to make. Am I right?"

"Yes sir," was Sean's reply.

The judge cleared his throat before continuing with his questioning. "Sean, did you share the information that I'm about to announce with me or your mother before this hearing took place?"

"No sir, I did not," was Sean's reply.

"You may step down. I would now like for Michele to take the stand," the judge ordered. His gaze was not as cold as it was with Sean but a little disappointed. Michele was sworn in as well.

The judge asked Michele the same questions that he had asked Sean, and her reply was, "No sir, Judge, this information was not shared with you or your wife. No one except Sean, Alice, Alex and I were privy to this information."

"You may step down now."

Michele left the stand and took her seat next to Sean. She was shaking, and Sean took her hand in his. That is when a spark hit them both, but neither of them made eye contact or acknowledged this feeling.

The judge came back down from his bench and said, "The other reason I dropped the order is that you can't very well have an order against your wife can you? It seems that Alex and Alice were married yesterday."

It was then that Pastor Taylor looked at Alice with anger, disappointment, and betrayal. He immediately left the courtroom with Alice's mother.

Dr. Davis was so enraged he forgot he was in the courtroom and yelled, "Alex, you just ruined your life. No one is going to hire you as a doctor, and you'll never see your inheritance. I won't support your marriage, so consider yourself cut off."

Judge Brooks asked Dr. Davis to compose himself or he would be held in contempt of court. At that moment he left the courtroom with his wife. There was no one left in the courtroom but Alex's sister, her husband Jackson, Sean, Michele, Alex, Alice and Judge Brook. It was then that Judge Brooks said, "We need to pray. You all have a huge road ahead of you, but with God, all things are possible. It's no secret that my wife is a black woman and while we've had our share of challenges, God has proven himself over and over again to be faithful to us. I can tell you that when God has called you together, there won't be any obstacle you can't overcome."

CHAPTER NINE

New Beginnings!

A lice drove straight to her house to talk with her parents. When she arrived, her mother met her in the driveway and raised the garage. All of her belongings were packed and in boxes--everything from wall hangings to her bedroom furnishings.

Her mother spoke first, "Alice, I love you so much, but how am I supposed to support you when you sneak off like you did and get married? You deprived your dad and me of being part of one of the most important days of your life. Your dad will never get to walk his only daughter down the aisle and give you his fatherly advice. You robbed him of that. I won't get to fluff the veil of your wedding gown, assist you in planning your wedding, and place the announcement in the paper. You've made supporting you and Alex difficult, especially when you lied to my face yesterday. While I know why you and Alex felt you had to do it, this way it was wrong."

Just as she finished her speech, a large moving truck turned into the driveway. Alice's mom said, "I will always love you. That is why I hired the moving truck to help you take your things to your new home. Your dad won't see you or talk with you at this time. He feels betrayed, hurt, humiliated, and angry."

Alice looked at her mom with tears rolling down her eyes as she tried to speak. "Mom, I'm so sorry. The last thing I ever wanted to do was to hurt you and dad. I knew I'd have consequences, but I didn't think it would look like this. I know I have no recourse but to accept them. I pray that one day you and dad will forgive me for taking away your opportunity to give me a proper wedding. It was never my intentions to hurt either of you."

Her mom knew her daughter's apology was heartfelt and she meant every word of it, but she also knew it would take time for all of them to heal. The movers loaded the truck. Alice got in her car, and they followed her to Alex's sister's house. Alex had had a similar conversation with his mother, except she said that she would try to help them as much as possible. She also said she'd try to talk with Dianne before their high school graduation next week to see if Alice's parents would at least attend that in support of their daughter. As she finished her conversation, Alice arrived with the moving truck.

Alex went to her side immediately. When she got out of the car, she broke down in tears saying, "I've lost both my parents. They wouldn't even allow me in the house. They packed all of my stuff. My entire life is in this truck, Alex."

He held her in his arms and said, "I'm so sorry, Alice. I never thought this would happen. I just thought they'd see how much we love each other and work it out with us, but now it's us and the Lord. Let's get this stuff moved into the apartment and get as settled as possible. We have a long road ahead of us.

Alice's queen sized bedroom things fit nicely in the apartment. Alex had purchased a small living room set from a local consignment shop that he and Alice had been in a few months back. She had fallen in love with it, and he'd purchased it the next week and hid it in his sister and brother in law's garage. Their place was small, but it was theirs. They had everything they needed. They were exhausted after moving all of Alex's clothes and personal belongings as well as Alice's things from the truck. His sister and brother in law along with Michele and Sean helped them get everything organized, and they ordered pizza for dinner. They'd been married two days and their young lives were turned upside down.

Cynthia and Jackson led them in prayer. It was Jackson who prayed the sweetest prayer. "Lord, we thank you for this marriage between Alex and Alice. We know that their parents are angry, hurt, disappointed, and maybe even feel betrayed. If Alice and Alex were wrong in getting married this way please forgive them, but I pray for restoration of the families. I pray for forgiveness and healing, Lord. I pray that Alice knows we are her family and we love her, and she need not feel as though she has no one because she has us, and we are proud and grateful to have another sister in our family. Lord, we pray that Alex will be the husband you've called him to be and that he'll remember his vows to cherish, love, protect, and honor his wife. I pray that Alice will remember to allow Alex to lead although this is a difficult time. Maybe it wasn't done the way we all would have wanted, but they still will need you to continue to lead and guide them through this marriage, high school graduation, college, and the rest of their lives. Lord, bless their marriage as only you can do in, Jesus' name I pray," and they all said amen through sobs from everyone.

Everyone left, and it was just Alex and Alice in their little garage apartment. It was cozy and cute. Truly God had provided everything they needed. Alice had brought her queen size bedroom furniture which included dresser and chest of drawers and two-night stands. Alex had purchased the living room set which came with couch, love seat, and coffee and end tables. Alex's mom had given them several sets of bath towels and sheets and a brand-new comforter set that she had purchased for one of her extra bedrooms but decided she didn't want.

When Alice went through her things, there was a card from her mom that read, "I may not agree with the way you've done things, but I love you and you'll always be my daughter. I hope this will help you and Alex get started with your new beginnings. Enclosed is a check for $5000.00. This is your graduation money. Please use it wisely."

Alex's mom had done a similar thing and gave him a check for $10,000. They had a nice little nest egg to get started. They sat on the couch at the same time and said, "Now what?" They turned the living room lights out and headed to the bedroom. They were exhausted emotionally and physically.

Alice and Alex both realized it was really officially their honeymoon night. They looked at each other and smiled. She spoke first, "I'm going to take a shower, okay?"

He said, "Okay."

When she finished showering and went into the bedroom Alex was on his knees praying but had fallen asleep. Alice touched his shoulder, and he looked up and smiled at her. She said, "I'm finished. You can have the shower now."

He got up from the floor and showered. When he came back to the bedroom, Alice was asleep. He smiled, touched her sandy brown hair, and said, "I love you, Mrs. Alice Davis." He slid in beside her and fell fast asleep.

The birds chirping woke Alice up. Alex was already up and getting ready for school. It was their last week. Saturday was graduation, and they had a lot of prepping to do before that day.

Alice joined him in their living room. "Good morning, Alex," she said.

He came over to her and wrapped her in his arms, "Good morning, Mrs. Davis, my love. How are you feeling about things this morning?" he asked.

Alice looked him in his eyes and saw all the love she could ever need. Although she would miss her mom and dad, she knew they had made the right decision for them. She knew that God had ordained their marriage. She smiled at Alex and said, "I feel great. I'm sad about my parents, but I'm happy I'm married to you today. I know we have a lot of hurdles to get through but with God all things are possible."

She said, "I don't want to change my name to Davis until after graduation. Is that okay with you?"

He agreed that was best that when she walked across the stage, she would be Alice Elizabeth Taylor for the last time, but that was showing respect to her parents. They left for school and said they'd meet up after school. They needed a small kitchen table and they had seen one at the consignment store where Alex had purchased their living room set.

The day seemed long before Alice and Alex found their way to the consignment store. She was browsing when he walked in.

"I'm sorry I'm late. I had to meet my mom at the bank and transfer my money from her account into my own account. I also opened up a savings account for us, too. I put $8,000 dollars in the savings from the check my mom gave me plus I have money in my checking account. Once we graduate we can go to the bank and put your name on the account too and we can both save together," he said.

Alice knew that Alex had a sound financial head on his shoulders. She also had money in her savings account and her checking account from working at the hospital as a unit clerk on the ob-gyn ward.

They browsed the store for a kitchen table set, and it seemed they weren't going to find anything until they turned the corner and there it sat--a small oak table with four chairs. It had a leaf so they could let the leaf down and two chairs could sit at the table until they needed the other two chairs. They purchased the table and chairs but realized it wouldn't fit in either of their cars.

The sales lady said, "We can deliver it to you tomorrow for $50.00 if you'd like?" Alice looked at Alex for direction, and he said, "Yeah, that'll be fine." They left the store and headed for home.

Once home they realized they hadn't gone to the grocery story, so they had no food at all, not even a bottle of milk.

Alice said, "Do you want to go to the grocery store with me or do you want me to go by myself?"

Alex always wanted to be with Alice, so he said, "I'll go. This will be our first time as a married couple grocery shopping."

They entered the store and began their shopping spree. All of a sudden, Alice froze. Her dad was in the store. As soon as he saw her, he turned his back on her and walked in the other direction. He had noticed them before they saw him. He saw she was happy, which made him happy, but he was still hurt because she had denied him his fatherly right to walk her down the aisle. He also felt as though Alex had disrespected him by not asking for his daughter's hand in marriage. This was appropriate, especially in the South.

Alice wanted to run to her dad and beg his forgiveness, but he left the store without even purchasing anything. He left his basket half full. Alice felt the need to put every item back where it belonged for her dad. She let Alex finish the shopping for them. They arrived home with bags and bags of grocery and personal items. They hadn't realized how much you need when you are starting out. Once everything was put away, Alice asked Alex how much they had spent, and he said just under $200.00.

Alice said, "Wow, we're going to have to be careful with our spending, Alex"

He said, "I know but listen don't start getting worried just yet. We have enough. I still have my job working at the youth center although they aren't paying me. We get the apartment for free, so we don't have any rent. We agreed to pay part of the utilities here to help out so that will save us money. Also, Chapel Hill church has asked me to come on as their assistant youth director until we leave to go to college. They are going to pay me $12.00 an hour, and I can work about thirty hours a week. You are still working at the hospital part time, right?"

"Yes," she answered, "so we'll be okay."

"Everything we purchased we needed. We didn't splurge at all," he said.

They put all their things away and realized they hadn't eaten anything. They were tired and weren't very hungry, so Alice made them ham and cheese sandwiches for dinner, and they were satisfied. She was sitting on the love seat reading when Alex slid next to her and kissed her neck. Their lips met ever so gently, and she said "Alex, I love you."

He looked at her and said, "I love you more."

This was truly their new beginning. They'd been married three days and had yet to consummate their marriage. As they made their way into their bedroom, they knew this was the beginning of no return. Without taking their eyes off of each other, they made their way into each other's arms for their first experience of sweet love, a love ordained by God. They were newlyweds and as they found the love God had planned for a husband and wife, their desires were fulfilled and satisfied. They knew they'd done it the right way, knowing that marriage and the bed are honorable.

As they lay in each other's arms, Alex asked, "Are you okay, Alice?"

She smiled as the moon light shone on her face. "Yes, I'm more than fine. I'm complete." She smiled, and he wrapped his wife in his arms and said, "Now what?"

Alice looked at him, smiled, and said, "Let's go to sleep." They slept well, knowing that their new beginning had just begun with love that no one could ever take it away.

Saturday came so quickly. As they woke up, they both smiled and said together, "Graduation day!"

Alice had invited Sean and Michele over for a graduation breakfast. They hadn't seen much of their friends since they'd helped them move into their new home. Alice got up first and showered. She dressed quickly and headed to the kitchen. Alex made the bed and headed to the shower, hoping to be dressed before their friends arrived. He barely made it.

There was a knock at the door. Alex answered the door and there stood their friends and confidants. Smiling, they both said, "It's here! Graduation day!"

The four of them had a hearty breakfast of eggs, bacon, toast, fried potatoes and onions, orange juice, and coffee. Graduation was at 3:00. They had to go to the Centerstage Hall and decorate before graduation. As they were decorating, Alice wondered what she would do if her parents didn't attend her graduation. She knew that Alex's dad wouldn't be there, but she knew his mom and sisters and their husbands would be. They had kept their marriage a secret, and since the courtroom procedure was closed, no one knew they were married except those in their immediate family. They weren't saying anything until after the graduation out of respect for Alice's family. She understood her dad was still the pastor of a very large congregation, and she didn't want anyone to look down on him because of her actions.

Alice's mom was getting dressed to go to the graduation. Pastor Taylor came into the bedroom.

"Dianne, how can you attend the graduation after Alice betrayed us?"

"Tom," she began, "she is still our daughter. I don't agree with what she did, but this is her graduation, and I'm going. I wish you'd change your mind."

He was a stubborn man, and he couldn't stand to hear them call her Alice Davis instead of Alice Taylor. He had worked hard for her to graduate. He wanted her to graduate with her birth name, and he just couldn't stand to hear his legacy ignored.

Dianne spoke, "Two wrongs don't make a right. Yes, she was wrong. She has asked for forgiveness and as her father, you should forgive her. I know your heart is broken, but she is just following her heart and trying to obey the plan she believes God has for her."

He looked at his wife and said, "Do you believe that God told my daughter to sneak off and marry Alex? I don't. What happened to doing things decently and in order, huh?" he asked.

His wife said, "I love you, but I'm not going to miss my daughter's graduation. You can if you want to, but I'm not going to."

He knew his wife was right and said, "Then wait on me, but I'm going to sit in the very back, and I'm not going to talk with her or Alex. Understand?" She agreed.

The hall was decorated with purple and gold, their school colors. Alex was nervous because he knew as the president of the class, he had to give a speech and introduce Alice. He wanted to make sure he didn't mess up and call her Alice Davis instead of Alice Taylor. He saw them first--her mom and dad walking across the parking lot. He smiled and thanked God. He knew this would make Alice's night for sure.

He made his way to her and said, "Your mom and dad are here. God is working in their hearts."

Alice asked, "Is your dad here?"

He dropped his head and said, "No, just my mom and sisters and their husbands."

She hugged him extra tight and said, "I'm here."

They took their places in line. He was in the front and she was in the back because of their alphabetical position. The young men were in the yellow cap and gowns and the ladies were in the purple cap and gowns. They marched into the auditorium to the traditional Pomp and Circumstance. Alice's eyes met her dads' eyes and she mouthed, "I love you, daddy."

He turned away, not wanting her to see his tears. She was hurt because he didn't mouth it back. A single tear fell down her face.

The program continued. Alex had finished his speech. He made sure he said, "I now would like to introduce to you our valedictorian, Ms. Alice Taylor."

Alice reached the stage and gave him thumbs up for a job well done. They each were trying so hard to respect her dad and his family by not flaunting their marriage. They knew God would honor their actions. As she took the podium, she started by saying, "I'd like to first thank the Lord Jesus Christ but I'd also like to thank my parents, Pastor and Mrs. Thomas Taylor IV. Without my mom and dad's guidance over the years, I wouldn't be standing here today. We all need to remember that our parents played a huge role in getting us to this day, a day of gratefulness, reaching a goal that many of us may have never reached. This day is a day of new beginnings. Some of us will stay in Lyonsville and take our rightful place in our community while others will leave our homes and venture out to the unknown, carrying with us the knowledge our school staff, community, and families have provided with us. Wherever you end up, my prayer is that you look back on these days of friendship, classmates, basketball, football, rallies, cafeteria food fights, bonfires, and church retreats and say a little prayer of thanks because it could have been worse. Most of all I pray that you'll have the confidence that the life you are seeking and living was led and guided by God above. I wish you all the happiness in the world."

Her speech had ended and she took her seat. It was time to call the names of the graduates. They went through the alphabet, and Alice was approaching and the administrator said, "Alice Elizabeth Taylor." She walked proudly across the stage and received her diploma. Knowing she had respected her dad and mom, she made eye contact with her mom, and she winked at her and blew her a kiss. Her dad smiled slightly and waved. Alice felt like for now this was all she could expect, and she was happy that God gave her that. She whispered, "now what?"

CHAPTER TEN

Challenged Love!

It was June 21st, the first day of summer. Alice was now working full time as a unit clerk at the hospital. She saw Dr. Davis often, and he'd always look away as if she didn't exist. It was hurtful to Alice, but she knew her new father in law didn't think she was an asset to his son's life. If he needed to ask her a question, he'd simply say, "Ms. Alice, would you please assist me with this or that?" He never smiled, and he never said thank you after she assisted him. He'd just walk away.

Alex was still working at the youth community center as a summer coach. He also was the youth director at Chapel Hill Church where he taught life skills to youth as well as assisted the youth pastor any way he could. His enthusiasm encouraged and confirmed to the youth pastor that Alex had a calling of being a pastor one day. He considered it an honor to be part of Alex's growth and journey of being the man God had called him to be. He'd always tell Alex that "many are called but few are chosen," quoting a popular scripture. Alex had his doubts sometimes, but each time he had doubt, God would once more confirm the direction that he wanted Alex to go.

It had been a long week. Alex and Alice looked forward to seeing each other. While Alex worked days unfortunately, due to his dad, Alice was placed on the night shift, so they rarely saw each other during the week. This was done by his father in hopes that it would cause an issue and Alex would come to his senses and have the marriage annulled. However, little did he know this only made their love stronger. Friday's were their favorite because Alice worked the day shift every Friday. This was their night to study God's word together, cuddle, and spend time with family and friends. Alice hadn't seen her dad since their graduation June 1st. She'd spoken with her Mom a few times, but things were still strained. However, Alex's mother had joined forces with them and spent as much time with her son and new daughter in law as she could. Her husband had told her he no longer considered Alex his son and he certainly wasn't going to call Alice his daughter or daughter in law, stating he would give the marriage a year and Alex would tire of her. He was a boy just playing house. These statements were made often, and Mrs. Davis had learned to ignore her husband and stayed in prayer often.

Alex had prepared their favorite grilled steak, corn on the cob and asparagus for dinner. He grilled on the patio with his sister and brother in law.

"Hey Alex," came a voice behind him. He knew it was his sister Cynthia. Her red shinning hair reminded him of a firefly.

His reply was always, "How are you doing, Red?"

Cynthia smiled. "I'm fine. What are you grilling? It smells delightful."

Alex was always in a good mood. He turned to his sister and said, "I'm making Alice's favorite, grilled steak, corn on the cob, and asparagus. Would you and Jackson like to join us? I made plenty."

Cynthia said, "I can add to the dinner. I made Mom's homemade potato salad last night for a women's meeting at church that was cancelled, so I have a huge bowl, and I have homemade German chocolate cake."

Alex smiled and said, "Sounds like a feast for family and friends. Do you mind if I invite Sean and Michelle?"

Cynthia said, "Of course not. I haven't seen those two for a few weeks. What's going on with them?"

Alex said, "I'm not sure but I think they've been secretly seeing each other. They don't want to jinx it, so they're just not saying anything. Alice and I were talking about it, and she thinks the same thing."

Cynthia laughed and said, "You know they are smart not to let anyone in until they know for sure that this is God's will for their life. Many people get together because everyone says they should, but really we all need to wait on the Lord for marriage and companionship. Even just the simplest of friendships should be prayed over."

Alex replied with a smile, "I totally agree. I know many of our friends couldn't believe that Alice and I were married. I'm glad we kept it a secret until after our graduation. We just didn't want all the speculations that she was pregnant and that is why we got married, and we didn't want to disrespect her dad any more than he already felt we had."

Just as they ended their conversation, Alice drove up and smelled the aroma of steak grilling. She smiled as she approached her husband and new sister in law.

"Hi, Al," she said as she placed a gentle kiss on his lips.

He accepted the kiss with another kiss and another kiss wrapping his wife in a full embrace. She started to giggle like she always did when he would perform in such a manner. He let her go, and she was finally able to acknowledge her sister in law.

"Hi Cynthia, how was your day?"

Cynthia replied, "It was great, but I have to ask. Does my brother greet you like this all the time?"

Alice smiled and said, "No, most of the time he's asleep since I'm working the afternoon shift. I don't get home until 10:00 most nights, and he's already sleep, so the most I get out of him is, 'Hi babe, I love you babe, see you in the morning babe.'"

Cynthia smiled and said, "I have a praise report. The youth center received a donation of $500,000 today from an anonymous donor. We can purchase our building and fix a few things."

Alice grinned and said, "Praise the Lord! I'm so happy for you and Jackson. You've put a lot of hard work into the youth center."

Jackson joined them on the patio as they were talking about the youth center. He had a huge grin as he interjected, "We serve a mighty God, and I'm excited to give you this," and he handed Alex and Alice a check for $1000.

Alice and Alex both looked in surprise as Alex spoke first. "What is this for?"

"It's your wedding gift/pay check for working at the youth center," Jackson replied.

Alex handed him the check back and said, "You agreed my payment would be your letting Alice and I live in the garage apartment. You know you all could very well be renting that place and making a good $500.00 a month for it, but you let us stay for free. So no, we can't take this," and he attempted to hand it back. However, his sister spoke up and said, "We knew you two stubborn people wouldn't take it, so that is why we said wedding gift. That way you have to take it."

Alice began to sob. It was Cynthia who reached her sister in law first and embraced her saying, "What's wrong? Please don't cry."

Alice managed to say between sobs how blessed and loved she has felt these past few weeks. Not being able to spend time with her mom and dad she reminded them that she was an only child and that she didn't have cousins because both her parents were only children as well. That is why Michele and she were so close, because they'd known each other since kindergarten and lived across the street from each other. She was as close to a sister as Alice had, until she married Alex. Alex had made his way over to his wife and was now holding her securely in his arms. To watch the two of them you would think they were so much older than eighteen. They had wisdom beyond their years.

Alice was the love of Alex's life and he was hers as well.

The food was ready, and they were just waiting on Sean and Michele to arrive. They were both working for Judge Brooks as junior interns since they both were seeking careers in law. They arrived together and were laughing when they realized all eyes were on them. They both stopped talking and looked at their audience, and said in unison, "Now what?"

Alice was the first to speak. "You two tell us now what," she smiled.

Sean and Michele decided to continue with their secret and said, "We have no idea what you all are talking about."

Alex said, "Michele, how did you get here tonight?"

She replied, "I rode with Sean, but before you make something out of nothing, my car is in the shop. Since we both work for Judge Brooks, Sean has been nice enough to pick me up for work. Since you called and invited both of us to dinner, he was kind enough to let me ride with him over here. I don't see the problem with that."

Alex saw Alice's face telling him to leave it alone, and he could read his wife pretty well, so he dropped it. They had a great evening laughing, eating, and joking with one another. .

Alice made her way to the apartment first.

Alex followed and said, "Hey Alie, are you angry with me? Did I do something wrong?"

"No Alex, I need to talk with you about something, and it's pretty serious."

"Okay sweetie, what's wrong?"

"I know we both decided to go to school away, but I was contacted by a private college today. They want me to enroll and do not only my prerequisites but also my entire medical program there. They will accept my scholarship, and as long as I keep my grades up, we can stay here in town close to our family, and we can stay in the garage apartment."

Alex sighed long and said, "That is great, but my scholarship is not to this school. It's in Oklahoma, which is where I thought we'd plan to go. It would be so much easier on both of us. Allie, you see how we are treated around here. I don't like it, and I just need a break. I hope you didn't give them an answer because I don't want to stay here. I want out and the sooner the better."

Alice understood what Alex was talking about. They had been asked to leave several local restaurants that didn't agree with the interracial relationships. It broke their hearts.

Alice dropped her head and said, "I understand. I know." She looked at Alex and said, "No I didn't give them an answer. I thought I'd talk with you first and then give them an answer."

Alex reached his hands out for hers. She stepped in front of him as they held hands. He looked her in her beautiful hazel eyes and said, "Allie, I'm so sorry because I gave you an answer based on my emotions, and we haven't prayed and asked God for his direction. Of course if He tells us something else we'll obey Him."

Saturday morning called for thunderstorms, and the thunder woke them both up. Alex reached for his wife, but she was gone. He leaped from his bed thinking something was wrong but found her sitting with their little patio doors open to the small balcony watching it rain. The air was dry and it was warm outside, so having the doors open brought in fresh aroma of rain.

Alice was quiet, and he could see she'd been crying.

"What's wrong?"

"Nothing," she said "I'm just thinking about family and how when it would storm when I was small I'd run and jump in my parents' bed, and they'd just laugh and say, 'Did that storm scare you?'" She smiled and said, "It was always family time when it rained, and now I'm not even welcome in their home. Alex, what have I done?"

He sat next to her and said, "I can't tell you how to feel. We went into this with our eyes wide open. We knew it wouldn't be easy, but it's worth it, don't you think? Or do you regret getting married? I don't want you to be unhappy, Allie, I really don't, but I believed we were following the Lord. Are you having second thoughts? Let me know so I know how to pray for you and me."

Alice took a minute to get her words right "I don't regret marrying you. I don't. I just wish we had waited until we received our parents' blessings. Somehow, I think we may have jumped the gun, so to speak. Don't you think your father would have come around?"

Before Alex could answer, a knock came at the door. It was a certified letter to Alex from a law firm.

He opened the envelope. It was a letter written to him with a copy of his dad's will, which had been changed to leave Alex $1.00. His dad had done just what he said he would do, disinherit him.

He gave Alice the letter and said, "Read this and tell me what you think."

Alice read the letter and said, "Oh Alex, I'm so very sorry. It's all my fault. If I had just said no to my feelings for you instead of giving in, you'd be a wealthy man."

Alex looked at Alice and said, "Do you think any amount of money would be enough to keep me from loving you? It is not. My dad is a controlling man with forgiveness issues. If I let him choose who I marry, next he will tell me how many children I can have, and then where to live, what church to attend, and it would never stop. Alice, I may be young, but I'm still a grown man. I may not have all the experience of others, but I'm growing every day. I know God told me to marry you, and I don't regret it. I'm just sorry you are having second thoughts." And he walked out of the room.

Alice knew she had hurt Alex's feelings in allowing him to believe she was having second thoughts. She just missed her parents so much. Maybe his dad wasn't going to come around, but certainly her dad would have, had she presented it to him in the right time and right way. She didn't regret marrying Alex, she just wished it was done differently.

Just as she was getting ready to talk to Alex, the phone rang. She answered, "Hello?"

"May I speak with Alice?" the voice on the other end of the phone said. "This is she," Alice replied.

This is the central office at the hospital. We are short staffed this morning because of the flood, and we'd like to see if you can come in."

Alice agreed, hung the phone up, showered, got dressed, and left. She didn't even say goodbye to Alex. He knew she must be going to work because she had on her scrubs. He was hurt and didn't know what to do. He sat in the living room watching the storm and thinking to himself, now what?

CHAPTER ELEVEN

College Calls!

I t was late when Alice came home. Alex had already gone to bed. He'd tried to stay up and wait for her, but sleep just wouldn't let him. Besides the day had been a rainy one, and not just outside. He had cried and prayed, asking God for direction for him and his wife.

There was a note on the coffee table with her name on it. She opened the note, and it read, "Dear Allie, I know we are young, and I know that our marriage is not acceptable to many, but it is to God. We've made a covenant with God to love each other through sickness and in health and any other issues. I've prayed for both of us, I know your scholarship takes you anywhere in the country but mine is to the Christian college in Oklahoma. My desire to be a pastor and work in Ministry is as strong as yours is to be a doctor. Please know that I only want the very best for us so that we can do as God has instructed. Please let's keep our communications open and not allow the tricks of the enemy to destroy us before we get started. The best thing about being married to you is that I married my very best friend in this world. I love you. Alex."

She sat with tears streaming down her face. She knew Alex was right. She could go to any college in the United States. Why did they offer this to her now, at this particular time? She believed it was a trick from the enemy too, and she began to pray, "Lord please teach me to love Alex the way a wife is supposed to. Keep me focused on our marriage first and not my career and desire to be a doctor. Lead Alex and me both. Keep us grounded and true to your word. Above all, Lord, show me how to show Alex that I love him and I'm sorry for making him second guess my decision to marry him. I love him with my whole heart, Lord. Thank you for your son Jesus dying on the cross for our sins, and Lord I love you. Amen."

Alice showered and slid into bed next to her husband and fell fast asleep.

The aroma of bacon woke her up. It was Sunday morning, and she knew Alex was preparing for church. Alex saw that Alice had read his letter. He smiled and said, "Now what, Lord? It's in your hands."

As Alice came into the kitchen, Alex smiled and said, "Good morning, Mrs. Davis, and how did you sleep last night?"

Alice walked over and wrapped her arms around his waist and said, "Like a dream. Alex, I read your letter and I want to say I love you. Wherever you want to go to school, we can go. I don't care as long as we are together and on the same page. We can't allow the enemy to come between us. I hadn't thought of it that way until I read your letter. I thought why did they offer this opportunity now? I interviewed with them when I was interning at the hospital last year, and they had no room for me. Now all of a sudden they have room. I believe we need to stick with our original plan and move to Oklahoma as planned."

Alex pulled his beautiful wife closer to him and smiled. He wanted her to know he wasn't trying to change her mind. He just wanted them to be of one accord. They just stared into each other's eyes before Alex spoke.

"I love you, and if I thought staying here was the best thing for us, I'd find a college to attend, but I truly believe this is what God has for us. Chapel Bible fellowship owns the college in Oklahoma. I didn't know that until Pastor Carl shared this information with me about a week ago.

It is a university, and you can go to their medical college if you'd like. They've offered me married housing if I'd head up their youth center there in Oklahoma. We can go down next week and visit if you'd like and get the layout of the town and see what it's all about."

Alice smiled and said, "I think that is a great idea. I just need to decide pretty quickly where I'm going to go to school for the next four years and see if someone will pick me up as an intern."

Alex prayed over their breakfast, and they ate in silence, knowing God had once again answered their prayers. He was protecting them, two eighteen-year-olds taking on the world.

Michele and Sean were waiting on them in the church lobby when they arrived. They were now members of Chapel Hills Bible Fellowship. All four had decided that since Alice and Alex couldn't go to the church they grew up in, they'd all just go where Alex was on staff.

Church was great, and they all knew they'd been fed well scripturally.

Sean was the first to say, "Let's go out to eat today, my treat!"

Everyone agreed. Michele rode with Sean, and they met at a quiet little Italian restaurant outside of town. The waiter came to their table and greeted them with a smile. "Have you all decided what you want to eat yet?"

"No," they all replied, laughing.

"Then may I take your drink orders and tell you what our Sunday specials are?"

The waiter went over the menu, and they all decided what they were going to eat. During lunch Michele started the conversation by saying she had been accepted to one of the small universities right outside of Oklahoma and she would be moving into a small cottage as a nanny for couple of attorneys that Judge Brooks had mentored several years ago. She was so excited to finally have her school and living quarters nailed down. She was a law major just as Sean was.

Alice looked at Sean and said, "Well, Sean, what are your plans?"

He smiled and said, "I'm also going to the same college with Michele, but I have to live in the dorm. That is not my idea of a fun time."

Alex said, "God has a plan my friend, but I have a question for you and Michele. Are you two a couple or what?"

Sean looked at his best friend and said, "We are praying to see what God wants for us. We know we enjoy spending time together, but we don't want people to think we are together because of you and Alice, and we don't want to feel that way either. We want what you and Alice have, but we want to be as sure about how we feel about each other as you two do. Consequently, we are praying and asking God for direction at this time. We know that we are great friends, but past that, we don't know yet."

Alex looked at both and said, "Then please don't let others rush you two into giving your relationship a title before God gives you a title."

They all agreed and ate, talking about everything, anything and nothing. Lunch ended and they all said they were sleepy. Alice suggested that they all come back to their little place and take nap. Before they could say anything, she said, "Michele and I will take the bedroom, and you and Alex can nap in the living room. By the time we wake up it will be time to go back to church anyway." They all agreed and went back to Alex and Alice's place.

Once the ladies were alone, Michele said, "Well?" with a huge smile on her face.

Alice knew her best friend well. She had questions about the wedding night. Alice said, "Michele you have no shame, do you?"

Michele said, "I've never been with a man and I don't know anyone else I can ask these types of questions, so I'm asking you, not for details but how did you feel inside doing it God's way? You know so many of the girls we went to school with did it the wrong way. I want to know how it is to do it God's way?"

Alice smiled and said, "Wait on God. It is gentle, loving, and altogether beautiful, and you don't wake up with regrets. You just wake up feeling like a married woman with joy, knowing that you did it God's way."

Michele said, "I knew it. You have a glow about you. That is how I knew you had consummated your marriage because one day you looked like a girl and the next time I saw you, you looked like a married woman. Not that that's bad, but you were different. There was a maturity about you, and I knew."

Alice looked at her best friend and said, "Do you love Sean or is it infatuation?"

Michele said "I don't know about being in love with Sean, but I do like him a lot. I love spending time with him. He's super fun and protective. He's so much like Judge Brooks, caring, understanding, and Godly. I believe I like that the most. His relationship with God is so amazing. I'm not sure if he shouldn't be a pastor because he has such a passion for people, especially the elderly. I'm just asking God to make it so plain to both of us."

Alice said, "Do you want to pray?"

Michele said sure, not knowing that the guys were having the same conversation and were praying for the same thing in the living room.

They slept so well that they missed church. It was well after 7 p.m. when they woke up. The phone rang, it was Pastor Carl, asking if everything was okay. Alex answered the phone and apologized for missing church service. He explained they had eaten at the little Italian restaurant outside of town and were so full that they had to bring food home.

Pastor Carl said, "I know that place. It puts me to sleep too. Don't worry about it. I took your class. It happens to the best of us, I'll see you tomorrow bright and early okay?"

Alex agreed. The four of them decided to warm up the Italian leftovers, watch television, and call it a night. They'd had a great time with their friends. They knew in a couple of weeks they'd all be going off to college and another part of their journey would begin.

CHAPTER TWELVE

The Move!

A lex was packing up the last of the U-Haul as they prepared to move to their new home in Romans, Oklahoma. It is a small little town on the outskirts of Tulsa, Oklahoma. Alex's mom, sister Cynthia, and her husband Jackson were the only ones there to see them off. Alice had tears in her eyes as Mrs. Davis spoke with her.

"I talked with your mom, and I'm not sure if she'll come and see you off, but I know she and your dad both love you very much. This has just been a little difficult for them to swallow. You understand, don't you sweetheart?"

Tears were streaming down Alice's eyes when she saw her mom's car swerve into the driveway. She leaped out of the car, ran over to Alice, and threw her arms around her only daughter, her only child.

"Oh, sweetie I'm so sorry it took me so long to get here. I was talking with your dad, trying to convince him to come say goodbye to you, but he is just so darn stubborn. Now Alice, you know I would never let you leave and not say goodbye. I love you so much. I want you to be happy. I know Alex is the husband you are supposed to have. God has given me confirmation a long time ago. We just wanted to provide you with a proper wedding. I hear you have been accepted into the medical school. I'm so proud of you."

Alice began, "You know I never meant to hurt you or daddy. Alex and I felt like we had no choice. His dad wasn't going to ever let me see him again. He had plans to make Alex go to medical school in Texas. He has disowned Alex and disinherited him. Alex received a letter saying his dad is leaving him $1.00 when he dies."

Just as she finished her statement, Alex walked up and joined the women. He placed his arms around Alice.

"Mrs. Davis, I'm so happy you came to see Alice off. It means the world to both of us that we have the support of our mothers in this situation. So many people already do not approve of our relationship. We really do need your prayers, love and support. I love your daughter with all my heart and I'd never do anything to hurt or harm her, you have my word. I will protect and provide for her as best I can with God's help."

Alice's mother hugged Alex and said, "I know you love Alice, and I'm really okay having a Godly son in law who loves Jesus first and then my daughter. I'm blessed to know that you'll be taking care of her. Please, Alex, make her take her allergy medication. She hates taking it!"

Alex said, "I stay on her all the time about her allergies. Don't worry. I'll take good care of her and her allergies."

They were soon joined by the entire gang, Cynthia, Alex's sister, Jackson, Cynthia's husband, Mrs. Davis, Mrs. Taylor, Sean, and Michele.

Jackson was the first to speak. "Let's lay hands on them and pray for save travel. Lord," he began, "please protect Alex and Alice as they travel to their new home in Oklahoma. Provide all of their needs according to your riches in glory. Give Alex the wisdom, knowledge, and understanding in his classes as you've given him in your Word. I pray that you'll provide miraculously for them spiritually, financially, emotionally, romantically, and in every area of their lives. Lord, provide for Alice the wisdom to be the wife that you've called her to be with the same zeal you've given her to be a great doctor. Give her your wisdom, and knowledge as well, bind their hearts ever to yours and to one another. Give them safe travels to their new home, provide for them new friends that will become family to them. Provide a great pastor and shepherd in their life, give them spiritual food overflowing in their life. In Jesus' name I pray," and they all said, "amen," with tear filled eyes.

Alice and Alex climbed into the U-Haul truck towing Alice's car behind. They would fly back in a couple of weeks and pick up Alex's jeep and take it back then. They held hands as they drove away, waving until they couldn't see anyone.

Alice sighed long before she spoke. "I'm happy sad. I know this is the course that God has laid out for us, but the unknown has always frightened me."

Alex glanced over at his beautiful wife and said, "Most of your new beginnings you've had to start alone, going to school, entering new journeys, but this journey you are not alone. You have a best friend with you, a husband, a protector. He then quoted a familiar scripture, "and a threefold cord is not easily broken."

Alice smiled a huge grin and said, "Mr. Davis, you always know how to make me feel safe, loved, and complete."

Alex looked at Alice and said "I love you, and I always will. I know we've given up everything to follow our dreams, to follow the plan we believe God has for our lives. We can't allow anyone, including our loved ones, to interfere in our relationship with God or one another. Please, right now let's make a clear, conscious decision and promise to keep our eyes, our hearts, our communication with each other and with Christ open no matter what. Promise me we won't keep secrets, no matter how bad they are, and we know it can get bad, because we are in a spiritual battle."

He knew things could get ugly. He'd been in the church all of his life. He had seen the good, the bad, and the incredibly ugly in people.

Alex had seen marriages destroyed over lies. He'd seen pastors fall over infidelity and families torn apart by supposedly Christian people, so he knew anything was possible. He was young but, in many ways, he was not an amateur. He knew Alice was very naive in so many ways, and he knew he needed to protect her from the evil one. He was suddenly silent.

When Alice touched his hand, as if she'd read his mind, she said, "I promise, I do I love you more than you'll ever know. I know this is a scary time, but I also know that God honors obedience, and I don't think we are being disobedient. I believe with my whole heart we are right where we are supposed to be. I'm actually certain of this very thing. "If God is for us, who can be against us?"

Alex smiled, but all of a sudden, he had a huge knot in his stomach and his heart started to flutter as if it was missing a few beats, with a fear that something very bad was about to happen. He'd only felt this feeling of doom in his life once, and the end of that resulted in the death of some very special people in his life.

He began to pray silently, not wanting Alice to be scared. "Lord, I know this warning sign. You've given it to me before. Protect me and Alice from the evil one, give me strategy, direction, purpose, and show me your perfect plan for our lives. Please, help me!"

The nervous stomach and feeling of gloom and doom was lifted. Alex didn't know if God had changed the course of this evil plan that was coming their way or if God just provided him the peace that passeth all understanding. Whatever it was, that "now what" moment of fear and destruction was gone! He thanked God silently and kept driving.

CHAPTER THIRTEEN

A Home with a Name!

Alex and Alice arrive in the small town of Romans, Oklahoma. They were exhausted from their day and a half drive. They had arrived at the campus of Chapel Hill University in Romans sweaty and tired. Alex drove to the dean of married students' housing. He had a key and directions to their little apartment. He found the dean's house. Being very protective, he asked Alice to stay in the truck until he was sure he was at the right house.

Alex rang the doorbell of the huge Victorian style house. He felt small next to the huge structure. A thin tall man came to the door. "Hello, may I help you?" the man asked.

"I'm Alex Davis. Is Dean Johnson here?" Alex asked.

The man said, "I'm Dean Johnson. Nice to meet you, Alex. Would you like to come in? Where is your wife Alice?" he asked.

"She's in the truck. We are wiped out. We've been driving for a day and a half and we were just trying to get the keys from you and find out where the married housing is so we can get moved in. I know classes don't start for another week, but we still need to register and purchase groceries and things like that," Alex replied.

Shaking his head in agreement, Dean Johnson said "Let me get my keys and you can follow me to the apartment house. It's only about a block and a half from my house."

They drove the few minutes to these huge houses that had been converted to apartments. Each house had six apartments in it. They weren't anything fancy, but they were nice. As they drove up a group of young men were standing around waiting. It was the men who were part of the ministry team. They all greeted Alex, and when Alice got out of the truck, silence fell. They didn't realize Alice was a black woman. She immediately addressed them by saying, "Hi gentlemen. I'm Mrs. Alice Davis. I'm hoping that Alex and I aren't going to have the same issues we had in Georgia. You know it is not a crime or sin to be married to someone of another ethnic race. Moses in the Bible was a Jew and married an Ethiopian woman, and besides that, gentlemen, interracial marriages have been legal since 1967, I believe."

Mr. Johnson was the first to speak. "It is so nice to meet you, Alice, and no, you and Alex shouldn't have any issues here at Chapel Hill University. This is God's university, and if he is okay with you all being married, we are too. Right, guys?"

They all said, "Right," in unison.

The first guy that they met from the group was David. He was a young black man, tall built, clean-shaved, with a smile big as the world. He said, "Hi, Ms. Alice, my name is David Brown. My major is music. I believe God has called me to be a minister of music somewhere on this planet," he said with a huge grin.

Alice said, "Nice to meet you. My major is medicine. I believe God wants me to help people heal physically and spiritually. Alex and I truly appreciate your helping us. Do you live in married housing, too?"

"Yes ma'am, my wife and I have been here two years. We are the marriage counselors of the apartment house in which you and Alex will be staying. Each apartment house has married counselors and each house has a name. The name of the apartment house you and Alex will be living in is the House of Prayer."

Alice smiled and said, "That is so fitting for Alex and me, and I'm sure we will need all the prayers we can get."

Just then a tall, thin black woman with a long ponytail and bangs came over and grabbed Alice in a hug. "Hi, my name is Rhonda Brown. I see you've met my husband David."

Alice said, "Hi Rhonda! It's nice to meet you. Who are these other ladies you have with you?"

Rhonda began to name the ladies and tell her who their husbands were and what apartment house they lived in. "This is Tracy Sanders. She's married to Tom Sanders, that tall lanky red-headed guy over there. They live in the apartment house catty corner over there. It's called the House of God. This is Mrs. Clara Johnson. She is married to Dean Johnson, and she lives a block or so down the street. You met Dean Johnson, right?"

Alice nodded yes. "This is Robin Gray. She's married to Derrick over there, the guy with the red cap on backwards, and they live in the apartment house across the street which is called the House of Refuge. Finally, this is Marissa King, and she's married to Brady King, the young man with the plaid shirt on over there. They live in the apartment house behind yours, and it is called the House of Mercy.

The ladies had met, and they had instructed the men to start unloading the truck while they helped Alice put order to the apartment. It wasn't as small as Alice thought it would be. In fact, the apartment had a rather large bedroom with an attached bath, a small second bed room where they could put a day bed and desk, a living room with a bay window which Alice loved, and a nice sized eat-in kitchen. As soon as the men would bring a box in, it was unpacked and things were put away. By the time the last item was brought in, the apartment was well put together.

Dean Johnson was the first to speak, "Alice and Alex, it looks like you are all set. Is there anything else any of us can do for you all?"

Alex spoke, "Yes, could someone please show us where the nearest grocery store is? We didn't bring food with us. We just figured it would be best to shop once we got here."

Rhonda Brown was the one to speak up, "We've already taken care of that. Please go to the refrigerator, and you'll find it has been fully stocked along with your cupboards. The ministry provides food as a welcome gift to the new couples that move in. I hope the things we purchased are things you all like," she said.

It was Alice's turn to speak. With tears in her eyes they could all hear her heart felt thank you as she began. "Thank you all so very much first for being here and available to help us move in and for your encouraging words during this time. The food is just another way God is showing Alex and me that he's chosen the right school for us to continue our education to honor him in our life. It is overwhelming to see such love from people who we've just met. I know none of you are blind and see that I'm a black woman, even with my freckles, and Alex is white. We've had our share of frowns and nasty comments as well as threats because of our marriage. Some of the great folks in Georgia still don't approve of interracial marriage, and they don't have any problem voicing it." The tears were flowing freely. Alex came to her side and took over the conversation.

He started, "Alice and I are eighteen years old, but we are quite mature for our age. We've known there was something between us since we were in middle school, but we knew our parents as well as others in our small community may not approve since Alice's dad and my dad are both prominent men in our community and they are on several boards together as well. We didn't want to bring any burden or embarrassment to them; however. I had an accident a few months back. That is why sometimes you'll see me walking with a limp. I also contracted Lyme disease and had to be placed in an induced coma. It was at that time that my dad had a court order placed that Alice and my best friend Sean couldn't come near me. When I got better, he still wouldn't allow them to see me, so Alice and I secretly got married. When we went to court for me to have the injunction removed, they had no other choice but to remove it."

Dean Johnson's wife, a very wise woman, said, "Let us all pray for Alex and Alice. We may not have the same challenges as they do, but we all have our own tests, trials, and temporary assignments from God. I believe God has brought us all here together for such a time as this. When Dean Johnson and I got married, our families weren't happy either. He comes from a very rich family and mine was poor as they come, but I had received a full scholarship to this school, and we met in our psychology class. However, many years later our families have grown to be very close. That comes in time, my dears, and only God can change a heart."

Dean Johnson took the helm, so to speak, praying a heartfelt prayer starting with, "Dear Lord, I praise you for my wife Clara. She's been a blessing to me since I first laid eyes on her. Her sweet spirit and love for you have carried me through many trials. Lord, these couples that you've laid in our lives to lead, guide, and take care of for the next four years or until they leave us are so important to us. Give us the wisdom to speak your words into their lives and teach us how to love them and to provide for their every need. Lord, we can't do any of this without you, but we believe and know you'll give us what we need to fulfill our journey. We thank you for Alex and Alice joining our little community in Romans and this university. We know you handpicked them for their educational and marital journey to begin right here. Lord, let them feel your love, your peace, and your protection. Lord, get in front of this interracial injustice and show people that you made us all. Oh Lord, we call on your name and your Son Jesus to walk before each of us and teach us your love, your mercy, and your grace, and it's in Jesus' name we pray. AMEN."

Not a dry eye was in the room when they all got off their knees. The knot Alex had in his stomach was gone. He knew they'd chosen the right college, and so did Alice. Everyone bid them good night and promised to meet the next day for Bible study at the dean's house.

Alex walked next to Alice, embraced her in his arms, and said, "Welcome home, Mrs. Davis. I love you more today than I did the day we married."

Alice smiled, and their lips met in a kiss of all kisses. Alex held his wife for a long time, and then said, "I'm hungry. Let's look at all the goodies in the fridge."

They couldn't believe their eyes. They couldn't have nor did they need to purchase anything. It was all there and everything was perfect. Alice said, "There is some turkey and swiss cheese, and look your favorite chips. Would you settle for a turkey and cheese sandwich tonight and in the morning, I promise to make you your favorite breakfast?"

Alex laughed and said, "That is fine, sweetie. We're both tired. I'll take a shower now and if you'll fix our sandwiches, we can eat in bed and watch television.

Alice said, "That is fine."

By the time Alex finished his shower, Alice had prepared their meal and was ready to jump in the shower. Alex waited for her to get out, so they could eat their first meal in their new home together. They prayed and sat in bed, watching a funny romance movie eating and laughing. It was past midnight before either one of them remembered they hadn't contacted either set of parents to say they'd made it to Oklahoma safely. They then decided they'll call them in the morning.

CHAPTER FOURTEEN

Caring Friends

The morning started as Alice had promised. She met her husband with a huge breakfast of eggs, bacon, fried potatoes and onions, biscuits, sausage gravy, ham, and sweet rice. Alice had gotten up before daylight to spend time with the Lord, praying and reading her Bible. Their little apartment had a balcony off the kitchen, she pulled a chair from the kitchen closet to sit, read, and mediate on the word of God. She remembered the verse in Proverbs 31 that says, "She riseth also while it is yet night, and giveth meat to her household, and a portion to her maidens."

The rising up early she knew was so important to get her time in with God. She began cooking and humming a song. She was happy. Although they'd been through a lot in the past few months, this was a time to meet new people, forge friendships, and use this space and time for forgiveness to take place in the hearts of Alex's father and hers. Their moms had already made peace with things, but now maybe their fathers would.

Just then the Holy Spirit said, "Write your dad a letter."

Her thoughts were interrupted by huge arms around her waist as she turned the bacon and ham over in the skillet. "Alex Davis, is that you hugging me?"

Alex stepped back with a grin and frown at the same time and said, "Who else would be hugging on my wife like this? No other man better ever put his hands on you. I would do some serious harm to him."

This time his voice was very serious. He'd heard of men taking advantage of women in violent ways, and he was prepared to defend Alice. Even though they were in Oklahoma, he still knew there were people that didn't agree with the choice he and Alice had made regarding being an interracial couple. He had just read before moving to Oklahoma how a white man had violently raped and killed a young interracial couple just because he didn't agree with their choice of marriage partners. The man claimed to be a warrior from God cleaning up messes that people create. Alex was sickened when he read the story. Then, another story came to mind that he had read where several black men beat and killed a white man for being married to a black woman. They, too, claimed to be doing God's work. So Alex knew that he may not be in the south per se, but he knew hatred was everywhere and that all Satan needed to do was fan the flames and sparks would go everywhere. He was concerned for his and Alice's safety all the time, and he stayed in prayer. The scripture that came to his mind was 1st Peter 5:8. "Be sober, be vigilant; because your adversary the devil, as a roaring lion, walketh about, seeking whom he may devour."

He would not be a victim, and neither would he allow Alice to be a victim and prey for the Devil.

Just then Alice lightened the mood by shoving some bacon in his mouth. "Hush, Alex. God will protect me, and you. Let's not talk about the what if's or could be's in life. We've had enough of them." They certainly had.

Alex devoured the huge breakfast Alice had prepared for them and was just about to call his mom when his cell phone rang. "Hello," he said.

A voice of concern and frustration came over the phone. "Alex Davis, did you and Alice make it to the university? I've been waiting for a call and so has Alice's mom. We expected a phone call from one of you saying you are safe."

Alex apologized profusely to his mom saying, "By the time we realized we hadn't called, it was after midnight, and we were going to call you both this morning. We just finished our breakfast. Really mom, I'm so sorry."

While he was apologizing to his mom, Alice was on her cell phone apologizing to her mom as well. Both ladies had a sigh of relief and planned to visit them as soon as possible.

They both hung up from their moms with smiles on their faces, and at the same times said, "Aren't we glad that's over!" and laughed.

It was Sunday, and they knew everything on campus was closed, but they also knew they had a chapel where church services were being held, so they got dressed and walked to the chapel. They didn't want any grass to grow under their feet. They knew they needed the continued guidance of the Lord. The chapel was not far from their apartment house. They entered the church and were met by a nice man named Bruce. He was one of the pastors at the church and taught the young married couples' class. He introduced himself to them and took them to his class. When they entered, all of the couples they had met were in the class, and they felt right at home.

Church ended with prayer and praise, and as promised, they all went to Dean and Mrs. Johnson's for a hearty spaghetti lunch with all the trimmings, including several different types of desserts. It was August and warm. They sat on the veranda and ate. They became further acquainted with their new friends.

It was almost evening before Alice and Alex made it back to their apartment. They loved their new home. Alice was wondering how Michele and Sean were doing. She said a small prayer for them and took an early shower. Monday would be hectic with enrolling in school and looking for supplies as well as books. She also needed to meet the cable man to install their cable, one in the kitchen, bedroom, and living room. Alex had a meeting at the church. He had volunteered to work in the youth ministry as well as to counsel at risk youth in town. They had their life pretty much planned out for the next four years.

Alice prayed before lying down. She thought of two special women that she'd met, Rhonda and Ms. Johnson, the dean's wife. She knew these women would somehow play an important role in her life. She was thankful for them. They both brought wisdom, honesty and kindness that she'd seen in her mom. When new people would join their church or move in to the community, it was her mom who would take them under her wing and personally befriend them. She remembered a particular time when a single mom joined their church and moved a few doors down from them. Many people in the church had started a rumor that the woman was a former prostitute and had twin daughters out of wedlock. These few busy bodies, as her mom called them, wanted nothing to do with the woman or her children, and their rumor spread fast and caused a lot of damage until Alice's mother became involved and shut it all down.

Mrs. Taylor personally made it her business to befriend the woman and her children. The truth was this lady was married, and when her children were 3 years old, her husband was killed coming home from his military base by a drunk driver. He was only a block from home. The lady, Veronica Marshall, was a very smart woman. She was a pharmacist and was getting ready to take a new position at the hospital. She was trying to line up before and after school care for her children before starting her new job. It was Mrs. Taylor who started the before and after care ministry at their church to help Mrs. Marshall out, which after that became a huge ministry not just for single moms but for all families.

It was at that point that Mrs. Davis asked her husband to call an emergency meeting in the church to stop the gossip about this woman. Pastor Davis was going to speak, but instead since his wife was spearheading this situation, he allowed her to speak. Alice remembered that Sunday evening service like it was yesterday. Her mom took the stage and began by saying, "You know I love you and would do anything in my power to help you grow in every area of your life. That is why this evening is so difficult for me. I can't for the life of me understand why anyone in our church would start a vicious rumor about a new member in our church that you know nothing about. It was at that time that she brought Mrs. Marshall to the podium with her and said, "Let me introduce to you my new friend, Mrs. Veronica Marshall. Mrs. Marshall moved to our small community of Lyonsville about three months ago, and in that small amount of time, a rumor of infidelity, prostitution, child abuse, and drug addiction has been spread about this woman behind her back. None of you know her, yet I've watched with my own eyes as you've avoided eye contact, you've avoided shaking hands, hugging, or even talking to her."

"Some of you have even gossiped to me about her, not knowing I already had a friendship with her. You all know who you are." Mrs. Davis went on to say, "To be honest with you, I wasn't even sure I wanted to do this, but I knew her reputation needed to be cleared up, and as my grandmother used to say, charity starts and home and spreads abroad. This rumor started right here in our church. Let me give you some facts, the truth about Mrs. Marshall." Alice remembered her mother placing her arm around Veronica's shoulder as tears streamed down her face.

"The fact is Mrs. Marshall is a single mom not because she was a prostitute as someone shared with me. She is a single mom because her husband, who was in the military, was killed a block from home by a drunk driver. You've seen her at the pharmacy so many times because she is the new pharmacist at one of the local hospitals in town, and several of them were interviewing her to see which hospital she'd fit at best. Her daughters were crying not because of child abuse but because they were playing on my steps, and their mom had asked them to stop horse playing on the steps or they'd certainly get hurt. Because they are six years old and six-year old don't always behave themselves. They took a tumble and scraped up their little legs and arms. The infidelity rumor? I have no idea where that came from other than someone just wanted to make this young lady's life just a little more difficult."

"You should be ashamed of yourselves. If you were little children or even baby Christian, I could understand. If you had not been taught the word of God, I could probably give you a pass on this matter, but the fact is you all are mature, well taught people, and this type of behavior will not be tolerated. For the people who personally came to me with rumors about Ms. Veronica, I will be having a private conversation with each of you, and when I find out who started these vicious, ugly, nasty and mean rumors, I'm sure Pastor Taylor will have some words for you as well."

It was at this point that Alice remembers her father taking the mic from Mrs. Taylor's hand and saying, "Folks, First Lady Taylor is upset, first because Veronica Marshall is new in our midst, and secondly because what you did was truly mean and hurtful. It truly is because of Veronica that the "Serving the needs day care Center" was created, to help parents whether single or married with before and after school program. You should be thanking her because she's the one that talked with my wife about how she ran one in her other church to help out parents."

Alice's dad ended the evening with prayer and asked everyone to come up and personally apologize to Veronica. Whether they talked about her or not, he said, "If you listened, you were part of it because you didn't stop it!"

Alice was brought back to reality when a knock came at the door. Alice looked through the peep hole. It was Rhonda, and she looked frantic.

Alice opened the door, "Rhonda, what's wrong?" she asked.

"It's David. He has been in a car accident. We only have one car, and I need a ride to the hospital. Could you or Alex take me?" She had tears running down her face.

Alice ran to the bedroom, woke Alex up, and they were on their way. The hospital was about fifteen minutes away from the school. Alice wrapped her arms around Rhonda saying, "God has a plan. We're praying for the best. Let's just stay positive until we know something."

Rhonda said, "All they said was are you Mrs. David Brown? When I said yes, they told me my husband has been in a car accident and asked if I could come to the Romans Community Hospital."

Alice said, "I've worked at the hospital in our home town since I was in junior high, and that is really all they can say to you. We'll know more when we get there."

When they arrived, a heavy-set man with a white coat wearing a mohawk was at the front desk. He said, "May I help you?" with a kind and caring voice.

He could see that Rhonda was upset. She said, "My name is Rhonda Brown. Someone called me and said my husband had been in an accident."

"Mrs. Brown, your husband is okay. He has some lacerations to his head and arms, but he is fine. He's in room 227 just down the hall. You can see him in a bit, but first the doctor wants to have a few words with you if that is okay with you?" the man asked.

Rhonda was so relieved that her husband was okay, all she could do was nod her head yes.

The doctor told Rhonda that David has some head lacerations and some cuts and bruises and needed to rest for the next couple of days. He also said that David needs to remember to wear his seat belt or next time it could be his life. When the doctor was finished, he gave them permission to see David. Rhonda ran down the corridor like a track star. She saw David and began to cry uncontrollably. David held her in his arms although it hurt.

"Don't cry, Ronie," he said, with tears rolling down his face. "I'm fine. A little banged up, but I'm fine. God is not going to let anything happen to me, to us."

Rhonda said, "Why weren't you wearing your seatbelt? I've told you over and over again you need to wear your seat belt. When will you listen to me? If something were to happen to you, I'd die."

He said, "No, you wouldn't because you understand God is in control. You may be a little upset."

She hit him in his good arm. "Ok, ok a lot upset, but I'm here right here, my love," he said.

David then noticed Alex and Alice standing in the door way, He motioned for them to come completely in the room. They moved closer to the bed. "Hey, thank you all for bringing Rhonda down here. My car is totaled, so I'm not sure what we're going to do about a car now."

Alex spoke, "Don't worry about that. We can always give you a lift or feel free to borrow our car when you need to." he said.

David replied, "Thanks man, but I can't do that. You only have one car between the two of you and now you are willing to share it with us?"

Alice said, "Yes, and we don't want to hear anything else about it!" in a motherly but loving tone, remembering she just met him a few hours ago.

David was finally released from the hospital with pain medications, creams for the lacerations, and orders to rest. They made it home in the early morning hours of Monday. They were all tired and knew Monday was the beginning of registration. Alice also remembered the cable man was coming to install their cable. They said their sleepy good mornings and goodnights and entered their separate apartments.

CHAPTER FIFTEEN

Managing Monday!

The banging on the door woke them both up with a jolt. They had overslept. Alice looked at the clock--10:00 a.m. She and Alex both leaped from the bed. Alex went to the door. Alex opened the door to an irritated phone cable company technician.

"Is this the Davis place?" the representative said with an angry tone.

"Yes" Alex said, with a tone of I'm not in the mood man. Alex instructed the cable rep with hand movement.

Alice then came into the room "Good morning sir. I'm Mrs. Davis, Alice. I'm so sorry we didn't hear you when you first knocked. We were at the hospital until the wee hours with a friend."

The technician mumbled a few words that Alice didn't understand. "Miss, in what rooms are you wanting cable to be installed?"

"Could you also make the cord long enough that it could reach into that little study room, please?"

The technician, still a little salty, said, "That's an extra $75.00."

At this point, Alex was now irritated at the way the man is responding to Alice. He came in the room, and looking at the man's tag and said, "Mr. Dobson, my wife and I are tired. As she stated, we were at the Romans Regional Community hospital until early this morning. I do understand it was a little irritating to have to wait to get in to install our cable, but my wife is being as kind to you as possible. I'd like for you to be kind as well."

The technician saw the fire in Alex's face, and his tone changed quickly.

"I'm sorry, Mr. Davis. I'm running a little behind, and I do apologize, Mrs. Davis, for my attitude."

Alice was quick to say, "It's fine. Who do I write the $75.00 check out to for the extra cable."

"Never mind the charge, Mrs. Davis. I'll just do it since you all seemed to have had a rough night and morning. Are you folks just moving into the marriage housing here at the university? I used to go here myself. It has changed a lot since I graduated a decade ago."

Alice was impressed and was getting ready to enter into a conversation when Alex entered the room; and said, "The shower is running for you Ali," She saw the look in Alex's eyes. He was still a little upset with the way the man had spoken to Alice. She exited the room to shower.

While Alex sat on the couch looking through college registration material, the technician attempted several times to engage Alex in a conversation, but Alex only responded with one-word answers. The guy looked at Alex and said, "Where you folks from?"

Alex said "Georgia"

"I didn't think the southern folks cared too much for this kind of thing."

Alex got that knot in his stomach as the guy spoke. He looked in his eye and he saw it, an evil spirit that gave him chills to the very core of his soul. This man was pure evil. He wasn't speaking evil, but he bought a spirit in that said I'm not who you think I am.

Alex responded with, "Exactly what are you talking about, 'this kind of thing'?" The guy said, "You know, the mixing of races; I know it's the nineties, but folks still believe in separation and keeping things nice and clean. You know what I mean."

Alex looked the man straight in the face, and said, "Let me tell you something. I don't know you, and you don't know me, and you don't want to know me. I'm a born again, Bible believing, God-loving man. God has made it clear in the scripture that the only people that shouldn't be married are the lost to the born again. So if you or anyone else has a problem with me and my wife and the color of her skin or mine, why don't you take it up with the Lord Jesus Christ, because sir, believe me, he'll be more forgiving than I will!"

It was then that Alice came in the room. Alex had the man in the corner, in his face nose to nose.

Alice grabbed Alex and said, "Whoa Al, what's going on here?"

Alex said, "Nothing. I was just explaining to Mr. Dobson here how it is legal and spiritually permitted for a black woman and white man to be married in today's society!"

Alice interjected but was much softer spoken than Alex was. "Mr. Dobson, I don't know if you know the Lord Jesus or not, but I believe his word is clear on interracial marriage. I also believe that as long as we judge people based on the color of their skin, their social status, or any other thing other than their true heart intentions, we miss out on knowing people. Alex and I have known each other since we were in kindergarten. We played together, my mom and his mom both would take us to get ice-cream together, and it was never a problem until we showed an interest in one another. Alex and I knew we had feelings for each other in junior high school, but we didn't act on them. Instead we stayed as far away from one another as possible. It wasn't until God made himself crystal clear that we acted on what we both knew was God's will. I'm so very sorry if you feel as though our marriage isn't right. We certainly didn't get married to hurt people. We just want to be in God's perfect will. I hope you understand."

The man looked at Alice, but it wasn't a soft look, or a mean look. He was trying to figure out how to respond to her without revealing his plan. He just said, "To each his own," and left the room.

Alex said "There is something evil about that man. I don't care for him at all. Do you hear me? Stay as far away from him as possible. I was actually going to go to register for classes and let you catch up with me later, but then he made the statement. When I looked into his eyes, I saw evil."

Alice said "I don't think he's evil. He's set in his ways, just like some of the old folks we know back home. That doesn't make him evil, Al. You can't go around calling people evil just because they don't agree with our marriage."

Alex said "It's more than that, and I'm not leaving until this creep is out of our apartment, do you hear?"

Still, Alice wasn't convinced the man was evil. She just thought he was set in his ways.

Mr. Dobson finished his job, and said, "I'm all done. I hope you folks will forgive my bad attitude earlier. I just need some more sleep too and I'm running late. Again, there's no charge for the extra cable.."

Alex walked him to the door, and when Mr. Dobson reached to shake Alex's hand, Alex hesitated but shook his hand because he wanted him to know how very strong he was.

Mr. Dobson said, "That's some hand shake you have. You're as strong as a bull."

Alex smiled and said, "Yeah, you know us southern boys. We work on farms and things like that. I'm pretty strong. I don't know why I just am. I guess it's one of those supernatural gifts from God." Mr. Dobson's expression had changed to a question of whether he would want to challenge Alex in the future or not.

Alex and Alice said nothing more of the experience with the technician. Instead, they gathered all of their things to go to registration. When they arrived, there was a line. Classes started next Monday, and it seemed everyone was trying to register on Madness Monday. Alex was registering for ministry studies and she was registering for pre-med. What a team they would be some day.

It took the rest of the day to complete registration for their classes. They shared one class together, a psychology class which was the first class of the day. Alice was happy because she knew she'd be able to get Alex to class on time and he would not be late for the rest of his classes. She also knew she'd be able to fix him a healthy breakfast every day.

When they returned to the apartment, it was almost six o'clock in the evening. They hadn't even eaten anything. Since the cable man took so long and they had slept in, they had totally forgotten to eat.

Alice suggested that they stop across the hall to see how David and Ronie were doing and see if they needed anything. They gently knocked on their door, not wanting to disturb them if they were resting.

Rhonda opened the door. "Hey, you two! How are you doing?" she asked.

"We are fine. We are checking on you and David," Alex said. "Do you all need anything?" he asked.

"We were just getting ready to have a bite to eat. You all want to join us? Rhonda made pork chops, green beans, cornbread, and some chocolate cupcakes. You are more than welcome, and we have plenty," he said.

Alex said, "If we are not imposing, we'd love to have dinner with you. We haven't had anything to eat all day. The cable man came at 10:00 and didn't leave until almost 1:30. We were late getting to registration, and we just left completing that, so yes, we'd love to break bread with you."

They laughed and talked for a while. Alex took David aside to ask about Mr. Dobson.

David said, "He's not a very nice man, in my opinion. I can tell you that is just my speculation. The man has never done anything to me except speak, but I can tell he doesn't care for me. There have been some rumors about him harassing the ladies on campus, but nothing has ever been proven. I always tell Rhonda not to let him in when I'm not home. He's never attempted to come, so I've just chalked it up to me being a protective alpha man."

Alex knew he was on to something. He thought he'd keep this information to himself, but he would be on the lookout.

They had a wonderful time with the Browns. It was almost 10:00 when they left their apartment and went across the hall to their own. Alex told Alice that he would come to bed later. He wanted to study his Bible and pray. She understood and went straight to bed. She was so tired and a meal like what Rhonda had made only made her sleepier.

Alex went into the little spare room to study. He fell on his knees praying and calling out to God for protection for Alice. He knew he would be fine, but he wanted protection for Alice from the evil one. His heart was heavy because he knew there was unseen danger lurking about

Alex fell asleep praying. The next morning, Alice was up as usual fixing him a hearty breakfast. They needed to get some shopping done today for books, supplies, and other things. Alice thought a nice center rug for the kitchen and living room would be good. She also wanted a couple of bookcases for her and Alex's books.

Alex was eating with a frown on his face. "Is it that bad?" she asked.

"Is what that bad?" he said with a puzzled look.

"My food. Is it that bad? You're frowning."

"Oh no, sweetie. I have a headache, and my neck is stiff from sleeping in the study."

Alice smiled and hugged her husband and said, "I love you, Alex Davis. We have so much to do today. We have an adventure today. While we are shopping, we can also explore the city of Roman if you're up to it.

We need so much, and because we didn't have the traditional wedding where people give you gifts, we have to purchase everything. We don't even have a wedding photo. " Her voice trailed off. Alex knew there were sacrifices made because of their quick marriage, but he intended to make all of that up to Alice.

Alice arrived home with more bags than she expected. First, they stopped at the university book store and picked up all of the books for both their classes. Since they both had full ride scholarships, they didn't have to pay for books, which was a blessing. Then, they were on the adventure of a lifetime. Alice had no idea that her last statement of not having any wedding pictures stung Alex's heart. He was very sensitive when it came to her, and he thought he'd make it up by allowing her to splurge today.

He knew exactly how much money they had in savings and in their checking accounts. They would be fine as long as they spent responsibly, but Alice was right. They had no new pots, pans, dishes, eating utensils, and all the other wonderful things you normally get when you have a wedding. If only they hadn't had to run away and get married. He thought since it was totally his father's fault, he would spend daddy's money on whatever Alice wanted. His mom had given him an extra credit card and told him not to worry about using it, that she'd make sure his dad paid the bill every month. He didn't want to take the card because he

didn't want anything from him, but his mom explained that since his dad had cut him out of the will, she had decided that he was going to support Alex and Alice with or without knowing. Consequently, she provided him with a credit card that was in her name, but Alex was a secure user on the card.

They went to the local Save and Mart. They had everything from pots and pans to clothing. Alex pulled Alice close to him and said, "I love you, and I want you to be happy, so this is take care of your wife Tuesday. Whatever you want, you can purchase today and today only."

Alice looked at Alex and said, ""Are you sure we can afford this?"

He smiled and drew her closer and said, "I'm sure, sweetie, go for it!"

Alice was overwhelmed. She still had that responsible Taylor blood, so she looked for all the sale items, but she knew they needed pots, pans, dishes, dish towels, curtains for every room in their apartment, bath towels, laundry detergent, dish washing liquid, shampoo, and the list just went on and on and on. She shopped so much that they needed two baskets, and Alex never blinked once. If she said they needed it, he purchased it. He was thrilled that he could spoil her. He knew this wouldn't happen again for a very long time, so he allowed her to pretty up the apartment, so she would be proud when people came over.

Alice even found a china pattern that was on sale that she had seen in a catalog back home and said if given the chance, that would be the pattern she wanted. It was on sale, so Alex purchased it. When they were done, the grand total was $2,500.00. Alice looked at Alex with fear in her eyes. She was getting ready to say something, and Alex put his finger to her lips and whipped out his American Express card and paid the bill right in front of her. Her eyes were huge, and she said, "Alex, where did you get an American Express card? I thought we discussed credit cards and the possibility of going into debt."

Alex raised an eye and said, "We'll discuss this issue when we get in the car, so please, dear, grab a basket. This is a lot of stuff." He smiled and wheeled his basket out of the store.

CHAPTER FIFTEEN

Together Again

When Alex and Alice arrived home, they were tired, but Alice was beaming. She had everything her heart desired. She had the center rugs for the living room and kitchen she had wanted. She placed the china pattern in the built-in cabinets in the kitchen. She had new curtains for every room. Alex had purchased everything she asked for. She truly enjoyed taking care of your wife Tuesday. She had to talk about the credit card she knew nothing about, but first she wanted to put everything away.

Noticing that the answering machine was blinking, she pressed the button to listen.

"Hey, Alice and Alex, this is Michele."

Alice knew the voice before she heard the name. She pressed pause on the machine and yelled for Alex. He came rushing in the room.

"What's wrong?" he asked.

"Nothing. We have a message, and I want you to listen to it with me."

She pressed play, and Alex listened with a smile. Sean and Michele had made it to their destination, roughly 45 minutes away in the little town of Harmony, Oklahoma, where they were attending Midwest University School of Law.

Michele left the message with Sean interjecting words here and there as well. They had made it and couldn't wait to make a trip to Roman to see them. They would call later and make plans.

Alice and Alex were excited that their two best friends had made it, and they were going to see them soon. Alice continued to put away all the things they had purchased. Hearing Michele's voice seemed to make her have little more pep in her step. Alex had lay down to take a nap as Alice was busy putting her new items away. She wondered if Sean and Michele had turned the corner, so to speak, regarding their relationship. Had they decided to date or just be friends? She couldn't wait to have a heart-to-heart with her best friend on this side of Heaven.

She finished putting everything away and managed to make dinner. It was dark when Alex woke up from his nap. Alice had fallen asleep on the sofa. Only a small lamp in the corner shone on her as she rested. Alex didn't want to wake her up. He looked around the tiny apartment, and it was beautiful. Alice had decorated it in such a way that it looked as though they had lived there forever. Alice had acquired her mother's decorating skills and could make a small dorm apartment look as though it should be on the cover of a home and gardens magazine.

Alex also noticed that his wife had made dinner for them and set the table. He was sure she wanted to talk about the credit card issue, but she was resting, and he wasn't going to wake her up. Besides, from the look of their apartment, she had been working really hard.

The week flew by and soon the old gang would be back together again. Alice and Michele had spoken several times during the week, planning for her and Sean's arrival. They were going to spend the weekend with them and leave on Sunday afternoon. School for Alice and Alex started on Monday, but Sean and Michele had another week before their classes would start. Alice had cleaned and rearranged the apartment several times. They decided that Michele would sleep in the spare room where they had a cute day bed and desk. Sean could sleep on the sofa sleeper in the living room. They had even purchased extra food for their guests. They wanted them to have a great time. They missed each other so much, and Alice knew it was going to be like a family reunion.

A knock on the door made Alice smile. She knew it was Michele and Sean. Without looking through the peep hole, she opened the door, and to her surprised their stood Mr. Dobson, the cable man, except this time he had on street clothes and smelled of liquor.

"Hello, little lady," he said. His voice didn't sound the same. Something wasn't right. Alice tried to shut the door, but Mr. Dobson put his foot in the door, and she couldn't close it fast enough.

"Mr. Dobson, what are you doing here? It's Saturday, and I didn't call for service, and neither did Alex," Alice said with a tremble in her voice.

"I know, I just thought I'd come by and see if your service was working, and if you'd had any issue with anything," he said.

Alice's heart was racing, and she was trying her best to keep him in the hall. He hadn't yet forced his way in, but he was attempting, inch by inch.

"Everything is fine, and we'll call the cable company should something come up and we need your assistance," she said.

"Aren't you going to invite me in? I made a special trip to come and check on you personally," he said.

Alice replied, No, I'm not going to invite you in. Alex is in the shower, and he'll be angry if he finds you here and you weren't invited."

Mr. Dobson said, "Your husband isn't home. I saw your car go down the street and I wanted to have a talk with you by myself, just me and the pretty black lady." He had seen Alice's car go down the street but it wasn't Alex in the car, it was David. He had borrowed the car. Mr. Dobson had been drinking, so he didn't pay close attention to who was driving.

Alex had gotten out of the shower and heard Alice saying, "Mr. Dobson, please remove your foot from the door."

Alex came rushing into the living room and walked right up behind Alice, and said, "Mr. Dobson, why are you at my home, and why the hell is your foot in the door so that my wife can't shut the door?"

He then moved Alice strategically behind him, so that he and Mr. Dobson were now standing face to face. "I'm going to ask you again what you are doing here. We didn't call for the cable company to send anyone to our home, and based on the way you are dressed, this looks like personal visit of some sort. Since we are not friends, why are you here?" Alex asked.

Mr. Dobson was still surprised that Alex was home. He knew he saw their car drive away. He started to stammer, "I just thought I'd check in on you since I was in the neighborhood. I know sometimes equipment can be faulty. That's all, and I just wanted to make sure you folks were doing okay being new and all," he said.

Alex knew that wasn't the truth and he also knew that had he not been home, things may have gotten out of hand.

Standing right behind Mr. Dobson were Sean and Michele. Mr. Dobson had no idea they were standing there. Sean had positioned Michele behind him and was now standing directly behind Mr. Dobson. Alex saw them when they turned the corner and started down the hallway. Sean saw the look on Alex's face and knew there was a problem. He and Alex had been friends for so long their body language had been on point for years. As Mr. Dobson continued to try to explain his presence, Alex made one statement, "Mr. Dobson, turn around," and when he did, Sean was standing right there. Mr. Dobson was totally thrown off by Sean's presence and his size. Although he wasn't huge in height, he was in muscle mass. He just stared at Mr. Dobson as if to say, "If I were you, I'd leave."

Mr. Dobson attempted to move, but Sean wouldn't let him. Alex started to speak. "Mr. Dobson I don't know what your plan was today, but let me set the record straight. You are not welcome in my home, and I will be calling the cable company and reporting this incident. I'm also going to report it to the campus police. Let me make myself perfectly clear. Don't you ever show up at my home again. Whatever evil plan you are scheming, you'd better get that right out of your mind."

"I don't know what you're talking about. I said I came by to make sure all of your equipment was working. Okay, yes, I have on my street clothes. That should tell you I care because I came on my own time," he said.

Alex wasn't buying it, and he knew Sean wasn't buying it either. Alex said, "Mr. Dobson, nothing is wrong with our equipment, and again don't you ever show up here again. And Mr. Dobson, if anything ever happens to my wife, I will kill you with my bare hands. Do I make myself perfectly clear?"

Mr. Dobson didn't like the tone of Alex's voice and he certainly didn't like being threatened, but he saw the something in Alex's eyes that made him shudder. He said, "I'm sorry for disturbing you folks. My mistake. I thought I was being neighborly like."

They were now in the hallway and Michele had walked around them and entered the apartment and shut the door. Sean spoke up, "Mr. Dobson, I don't know you, and you don't know me, and we are going to leave it that way. Alex has told you not to come back to his home. No other conversation needs to be had. I strongly suggest you get out of here and don't ever return. I need you to understand something. My dad is a judge, and he knows judges all over the world. If something happens to my friends and you had anything to do with it, I will make sure my dad has you thrown so far under the jail you'll be eating with the snails. Do I make myself clear?"

Mr. Dobson had now moved around Sean so that Alex and Sean were facing him as he was backing down the hallway. "I don't like threats," he said.

Alex came back with, "This is not a threat; it's a promise."

Mr. Dobson left angry, humiliated, and frustrated. He had made plans to have his way with Alice that day. He had discussed it with his so-called pure club members, and they had agreed that he should go for it. They would support him and make sure he didn't go to jail. They had done this before. His brother-in-law was on the police force and one of the judges was his cousin, so several times things had been swept under the rug and evidence had come up missing when they had gone to court. However, he didn't realize he was messing with real Christian people, and he didn't know that Alice's father was a very prominent man in the South and that Alex's dad was, too. They may not be talking with their kids right now, but if their children were in danger, all bets were off, and both men would come to their aid. This was something Alice and Alex knew for sure, and it didn't hurt that Sean's dad was a judge as well.

Once that fiasco was over, Sean and Alex entered the apartment. The hugs started, and the tears started to flow.

"Who the heck was that guy?" Sean asked.

"He works for the cable company and installed our cable last week. I told Alice I saw something evil in him, and I was right. I just didn't think he'd show his true colors so quickly," Alex said.

Alice was crying, and Michele was holding her and telling her everything was going to be okay. Alex came over, and Michele moved to the love seat and sat next to Sean.

"Look at me." Alice raised her head, so Alex could see her beautiful hazel eyes. "I love you with every fiber of my being, and I will die protecting you. Do you understand that? No one is going to harm you on my watch. God has made me personally responsible for you, and I take my job seriously as your husband. But also, Alice you are my best friend and my sister in Christ, and even if we weren't married, nothing would change. I'd still protect you because it is the right thing to do." Alex exclaimed.

Sean was angry, too. He said "I should have just decked him, but the Holy Spirit wouldn't let me. He kept saying live as peacefully as possible with all men. I knew the Holy Spirit was leading and wanted to be in God's will."

Michele looked and Sean and said, "I'm so proud of you. I know you could have decked him, but God gave you both the courage to face the danger and at the same time use your words to let the enemy know that you're not afraid of him. I don't think Mr. Dobson will ever come back here again, but you should still report it to the appropriate authorities."

They all agreed that first thing Monday morning Alice and Alex would go to the campus police and report the incident. They also asked Michele and Sean to write letters validating their stories.

Alex was the first to start the conversation, "When did you all get in town, what is your campus like, and where are you staying? Spill the beans," he said.

Sean said, "We got in town on Tuesday, the day we called you. We hitched a U-Haul to my 4 runner, and Michele followed me in her car. Her mom and dad shipped a lot of things to her cottage. She isn't staying on campus. Her great aunt owns a cottage in Harmony, and she lives in Florida in the winter time. She usually rents it out from September to April or May, but when she found out that Michele was going to the college she couldn't be happier to let her stay there for free."

"Wow, what a great deal!" Alice said. "So, Sean, where are you staying?"

"I do stay on campus, but I live in one of the row house apartments," he said.

Alice said, "Row house apartment?"

"Yes, you know like you see in New York. This campus has about fifteen of them, but you have to pay out of pocket. My parents allowed me to use my college fund money and part of my savings to secure my spot for the next four years, and after that we'll discuss where I will live," Sean said.

Michele said, "Sean and I have something to tell you all, but we don't want you all to get excited. We just want you all to keep us in prayer," Alice said.

"You know we will."

Michele held out her left hand to display a beautiful gold diamond engagement ring on her ring finger. Alice gasped and yelled, "Oh my, that is beautiful! Does this mean you two are a couple?" She then answered her own question, "I guess it does. But when, where, how?"

Sean said, "I've always liked Michele. I just didn't want us to try and emulate what you and Alex had. If we were going to be a couple, it had to be what God wanted, and it had to be right. So, with prayer, and counsel from Michele's parents, my parents, and your dad, we thought it was right for us," Sean said.

Michele said, "I didn't even know that Sean had spoken with my dad about asking me to marry him. He had never said I love you, and I certainly wasn't going to be the first one to say it and make things awkward for us. I'd rather have him as a friend than not have him in my life. "

She continued. "Sean and his father met with my father and asked my dad's permission. He talked about the interracial situation, and my dad said, 'We are all people. The important thing is to be equally yoked according to the word of God.' He gave Sean permission with one codicil. They don't want us to get married until after we've graduated from college, not law school, so we've agreed."

Alice's eyes were beaming she was so happy and excited for her friends. She knew Michele was the right person for Sean and so did Alex, but they knew if it was going to work, God would have to do it.

They had one more question to ask Alice and Alex. Michele said, "Alice, will you be my matron of honor?"

Alice smiled. "Of course! You didn't even have to ask."

Now it was Sean's turn. "Alex, what do you say? Will you be my best man when the time comes?"

Alex got up from the sofa and walked over to his friend reached out his hand and said, "You know I will man. You're my best friend. I want our children to grow up like family. I'm honored to be your best man."

Sean said, "Please do me favor. Would you please pray for us? When You left Lyonsville, Jackson prayed over you and Alice. Our parents and Pastor Taylor have prayed for us, but I want you and Alice to pray for us, too."

Alex said, "It would be my honor."

As they got ready to pray, a knock came on the door. Alex went to answer the door, thinking it might be Mr. Dobson again, but it was their neighbors Rhonda and David.

"We don't want to bother you. We just wanted to give you the keys to your car. We filled it up with gas, too," David said.

Alex invited the couple to come in and meet their friends, Sean and Michele.

Alex said, "Michele and Sean are engaged, and I was just getting ready to pray over them. Would you join us please?"

David said, "Of course we will."

Michele and Sean knelt down as Alice, Rhonda, David, and Alex laid hands on them. Alex began to pray, "Dear Lord, we love you so much. Thank you that you've chosen a Help Meet for my friend Sean. Thank you that you've chosen a husband for Michelle, for your word says, 'It is not good that man should be alone, I'll make him a Help Meet.' Thank you, Lord that Sean and Michele took their time to know your plan. You know the enemy is not happy about this couple dedicating not only their lives to you but dedicating their engagement, career, and every aspect of their lives. Keep them pure, for I know the enemy will tempt them. I know the enemy will set them up, but Lord you said there is not temptation that you won't give us an escape. Please let my friends always take the escape. Protect, provide, and prepare them for marriage and for a career in law. Lord, we love you and thank you for our friends.

Not many people can say they've been friends since childhood, but we can, and we thank you for that. Keep us committed to you, to ourselves, our relationships, and most of all to your word. In Jesus' name I pray." They all said amen in unison.

David said, "It was certainly nice to meet you both. What college are you all attending?"

"Midwest University Law School in Harmony, Oklahoma. It's only forty-five minutes from here." Sean said.

"That is the university that has the fancy row house apartments that everyone wants to stay in," David said.

Sean said, "Yes, I'm one of the blessed ones to live in one. Maybe you and Alex can drive down one weekend, and we can have a boys' weekend. What do you say?"

David said, "That sounds like a lot of fun! I'm in. Just let Alex know when, and I'm there."

Michele said, "Rhonda would you and Alice like to join me at my cottage when the boys have their weekend? We can have a girls' weekend as well!"

Rhonda said, "Sounds like a plan! We had better get out of your hair so you all can catch up with your friends. I'm tired anyway, and I need a good nap." They left and went to their own apartment.

This group were becoming fast friends. Alex moved to the window and as he was looking out, he saw Mr. Dobson standing outside looking up at the apartment. He got that familiar knot in his stomach again, and he knew something evil was brewing. He said, "Now what, Lord, now what?"

The four friends spent the evening watching videos, eating, laughing, and catching up. They were so very happy. They hadn't been together in weeks, and it felt like old times.

Alice knew Michele and Sean would leave tomorrow, and classes for her and Alex would start on Monday. She hadn't written the letter to her father that God told her to write. She didn't know what to say, but she knew she wanted to obey.

Alex's mind was on the knot in his stomach. It hadn't gone away. He knew evil was near, and he knew it would be an act of God to get them out of this looming danger.

The couples retired for the evening. Alice and Michele got up early, read their Bibles, prayed, and started breakfast. Michele said, "I really like Rhonda and David. They seem to be a great couple."

Alice said, "Yes, they are. They are also the house apartment counselors. They are juniors now. David had a car accident last week and totaled his car, so I let them drive mine when they need to. Besides we are going back over Labor Day weekend to get Alex's Jeep."

Michele came up with a great idea, "Why don't you all let Sean and I drive you back in his four runner and that way you won't have to purchase plane tickets?"

Alice said, "That would be great, but will Sean want to put that kind of miles on his four runner?"

Michele said, "If he doesn't want to drive, we can take my car. It's brand new. I got it as a graduation gift from my grandparents. It was totally a surprise, but they didn't give it to me until we were preparing to move down here."

"So, what did they get you?" Alice asked.

"A Navy blue Toyota Camry. I thought it was funny. Gram and I were talking one day, and she just brought it up out of the clear blue sky, asking me if I was going to take my old car with me to college. I told her I wasn't sure because it already had well over a hundred thousand miles on it. Gram asked, "What would you want if you got another car?"

I said, "A blue Toyota Camry. They get good gas mileage and they are safe," Michele told Alice.

Alice just grinned and said, "That sounds like Gram. She can get information out of a mute."

The women were laughing when the men decided to get up and join them. They had made the southern breakfast with the trimmings. They finished eating, showered, and made their way to the campus chapel. Dean Johnson preached the sermon. He talked about unity in the body of Christ and being aware of evil around them. He told them that as this school year begins, to be wise as serpents and harmless as doves. He explained that evil was all around them, and not to think for a minute that Satan cares that they are attending a Christian college. He told them that just because they were at a Christian college to understand that there are professors as well as students who attend who don't know Christ as their Savior. His sermon was eye opening to Alice, who saw the good in everyone, but she also knew that evil existed in the world. She just didn't want to believe it.

Alex held onto her hand the whole time, and silently he was praying for her. He knew she was in danger. He also knew Sean was in danger, too. Sean was bi-racial, and he knew that men like Mr. Dobson were lurking around seeking whom they may devour. Once church was over, they were invited to Dean Johnson's home for lunch. Alex explained they had company for the weekend. Dean Johnson insisted that they bring them, too, saying the more the merrier, and he meant it. Dean Johnson was a good man, but more than that he was a godly man. He loved being over the married ministry at the college and knew it was his duty to protect them as much as he could. He had a prayer room, not closet, where on the wall he had large boards with each couple's name, date of birth, and marriage date, and he'd pray for them each morning and each night before he went to bed.

They enjoyed a huge taco lunch with banana cream pie for dessert. Mrs. Johnson was an exceptional cook. She so enjoyed the young wives helping her in the kitchen and sharing recipes with them. She took an immediate liking to Michele. They exchanged phone numbers and promised to keep in touch.

Michele and Sean packed their bags and said their goodbyes. Alice and Michele were in tears but were reminded by the men that they have telephones and that they are only forty-five minutes from each other. They could see each other whenever they wanted to. Their goodbyes were long but eventually the men had to part the ladies so they could be on their way.

Alice was sad, but she was very happy that her friends were engaged, and they would soon start planning a wedding. Tomorrow class would start, and she hoped she was prepared for her classes. She knew she was smart, but she also knew this was not high school. She sat on the sofa and looked out the window. It was getting dark. Alex joined her on the sofa and snuggled with her.

"I love you so much!" he said.

She looked in his eyes and said, "I love you more."

CHAPTER SIXTEEN

Now What!

Alice was so happy that she and Alex shared the same class in the mornings. It made it easier to get out of the house on time. She didn't have to walk to school by herself, and she didn't have to worry about Alex being constantly late to class. She knew her beloved well, and he loved to sleep. He was not a morning person. They made it to their psychology class and sat next to each other. They had no idea that the professor was the uncle of Mr. Dobson, and he had gotten the scoop on Alice and Alex. He had decided that he would cause as much a problem as possible for the couple.

First, he made up a seating chart that separated the couple. Then, he assigned project partners and would not allow them to be partners. Next, he assigned a beautiful blonde to be Alex's partner, and Alice had no partner because the class wasn't evenly numbered. Alex asked if Alice could join their study group, and the professor said no. He said that Alice was very capable of doing it on her own. "After all she did graduate as valedictorian, didn't she, or was it just given to her?"

Alex was very upset, but Alice looked at him with a look that said, "Alex I've got this."

Alice raised her hand and said, "Professor Donaldson, may I ask you a question?"

"Why yes, Ms. Davis," he said, knowing full well she was Mrs. Davis, but he didn't want to acknowledge her marital status.

Alice began "First of all, it's Mrs. Davis. Alex over there is my husband, but I'm sure you are aware of that. I have a question for you. Do you treat all of your black /African American students like you're treating me, or is it because I'm married to a white man and you don't agree with our choice of marriage partners?"

He was getting ready to interrupt her, but Alice was smart and swift. She continued, "I believe I still have the floor. You stated this was a team project. The definition of a team is two or more, and since the class is unevenly numbered, that means I can't be team alone or do a project by myself. Therefore, unless you'd like for me to speak with the diversity committee or call in the Dean of Students and the chancellor of the college, I propose that I'll be on the team with my husband Alex and the young lady over there." She pointed in Alex's direction. She then said, "Because they are sitting over there and I'm on their team, I'll be moving my seat back over next to my husband." She said this as a statement and not as a question.

Professor Donaldson was livid, to say the least. Who did this little black ink spot of a nothing little girl think she was? He would see to it that she was expelled from the school. He would destroy her. He thought to himself that he'd taken on more of her kind and won in more years than she was old. This was war in his mind, and it was war in Alice's mind as well! She knew who he was, and she knew who she was, but more than that, she knew whom she belonged to. She looked at him as if to say, "Bring it on! I'm waiting! Give it your best shot, you evil, demonic, prejudiced jerk!"

After class, Mr. Donaldson said, "Mrs. Davis, may I have a word with you please?"

"Why sure," was her response.

Alex was about to stay behind, but Professor Donaldson said, "I'd like to speak to your wife alone, Mr. Davis."

Alex was getting ready to respond, but Alice said "Alex, I'm fine. I'll see you at lunch." Alex left the room.

Once everyone was gone, Professor Donaldson let his full rage out on Alice. He told her he could make it very difficult for her. He explained he knew she wanted to be a doctor, and he could make sure she never passed his class. He also said because he had very close friends on campus that didn't like people like her or Alex, he could make it hard for both of them. He told her never to take him on like that in front of his class and that she'd tried to humiliate him. He talked so much, he inadvertently told her that he and Mr. Dobson were relatives.

The cat was out of the bag. Alice knew now what was going on. She looked at Professor Donaldson and told him she didn't like being treated like she was less than, she didn't appreciate his trying to make an example out of her, and that she hadn't done anything for him to attack her intelligence. She informed him she didn't deal well with threats, but whatever it was he thought he had the power to do, to go for it, because she was prepared to battle for what was right according to the word of God. She reminded him that they were in a Christian college. She also informed him that she was aware of who he was and called him by his name, Beelzebub.

The professor was so angry he stormed out of his own class room. Alice stayed there for a minute and prayed. She knew this was a spiritual warfare, but unlike Alex, she was not afraid for some reason. She felt God's protection, peace, guidance, and love. It was then that as soon as she got home, she wrote the letter to her Dad.

Dear Daddy, I miss you so much. I miss you laying hands on me and praying over me. I miss your guidance, protection, and your love. I'm so very sorry that marrying Alex caused you so much pain. That was never my or Alex's intention. I would like to ask you to forgive me. Even though I didn't mean to hurt you, I did, and I'm so sorry for that. I'd never do anything to hurt you. You are the strongest, kindest, smartest, most brilliant, Godly man I've ever met in my life. Alex is my husband, but he is not my dad. I still need my dad in my life.

Today was the first day of class, and I came up against the most evil man I've ever encountered. Daddy, people still don't like interracial marriages, or they just don't like it because I'm black/African American and Alex is white. They don't really pay attention when someone is Chinese and white or any other ethnic group. If it hadn't been for how you raised me to know God and see the devil for who he is, I would have been so intimidated by Professor Donaldson, but I took him on, and he left his own class room even though he called the meeting. I probably shouldn't have called him Beelzebub, but I did.

I love you, Daddy, and I hope you'll call me or come and visit me and Alex because I miss you. I'm still your little girl. You are an amazing, loving man, and I want you to meet Dean Johnson and his wife. They are over the married couples. I also want you to meet David and Rhonda Brown. They are a wonderful couple who live across the hall from Alex and me. They are the married counselors in our apartment house. Enclosed are the address and our home phone number. You have my cell phone number. Also, thank you for continuing to pay my cell phone bill. I went to pay it and they said it was already paid. I knew it was you. Thank you so much. I will always love you with all my heart. I'm sending you a big wet zerbert on your cheek.

Love, Your loving daughter/little girl Alice Taylor-Davis.

Alice left the house immediately to mail her letter. She didn't realize she hadn't taken her umbrella. The sky had started to get dark, but the mail box was only a half block away. She thought she would make it to the mail box and home before the rain came down. However, she was wrong. As soon as she reached the mail box and said, "now what?" she felt the first rain drop. It went from dripping to a full fledged thunderstorm. The rain was coming down so hard it was hurting her, and she felt as though her skin was being cut. She was running and slipped and fell. She hit her head and was knocked out.

When she woke up, the room was dark, and she didn't know where she was. She heard voices, but she couldn't make them out. She had no idea where she was and for the first time, she felt sheer fear!

CHAPTER SEVENTEEN

The Unexpected

Alice's heart was beating fast. She didn't know where she was. and no one was talking, She heard voices but wasn't sure whose voice it was. All of a sudden a man entered the room. Her vision was foggy, so she wasn't sure who it was.

Alice said, "Who are you, and where am I?"

The young man whom Alice had never met said, "You're safe, Ms. Alice. I'm Wes. My dad found you lying on the sidewalk. I think you had a fall and hit your head. You don't know me but I've heard a lot about you."

Alex had arrived home later than he planned. He missed Alice for lunch, so he assumed she was home. She wasn't there and that wasn't like her. He called her cell, and it started ringing. It was in their bedroom. Maybe she'd gone to the grocery story, but that didn't make sense to him because they still had plenty of food from the weekend with Sean and Michelle. The knot in his stomach told him Alice was in trouble, and he needed to start praying right now. He prayed, "Lord give me wisdom. Please help me."

He went across the hall and knocked on Rhonda and David's door.

David answered, "Hey Alex, how you are doing?"

Alex looked worried. "David, have you seen Alice? She isn't home and I can't imagine she'd be out in all this rain."

David said, "No, but I just got home myself. Let me ask Rhonda."

He called his wife in the room and asked her, and she said she hadn't seen Alice all day. She wasn't feeling well, so she'd been in bed most of the day.

It had started to get dark. Alex went back home and thought maybe she had gone back to the school and was in the library, but when he got there no one was there. He was truly worried and didn't know where to turn. He went back home and discovered that the power was out. He had no lights and the phones weren't working either. He had no choice but to wait on God, trust God. He knew this was definitely a now what moment in time. He prayed like never before, asking God to protect Alice. All this time he thought he was Alice's protector, but God was now putting Alex in his place. He could no more protect Alice than he could himself. God was Alice's protector as well as his.

It was still dark in the room, and Alice was talking with Wes.

"Wes, my head is hurting, but I need to get home. My husband will be worried about me." She tried to sit up but couldn't. A piercing pain went through her head and she almost fell out of the bed.

Wes came to her side and helped her get stabilized. "Ms. Alice, please lie still. You've been hurt, and as you can hear, we are having a pretty bad thunderstorm out there. In fact it's dark in here because most of the town has lost power. It is still raining pretty hard. The lightning has hit a few generators and power lines, and there have been a few fires. Please try to relax," he said.

Alice was no longer fearful, but she was worried about Alex. She knew he would be worried about her and he'd be anxious. He had a hot head and if he thought she was in danger for a second, he'd go to the ends of the earth to find and take care of her. Just then a scripture came to her mind. "Trust in the Lord with all thine heart; lean not unto your own understandings in all thy ways acknowledge him and he shall direct your path."

Alice knew God was comforting her, and she said a prayer, "Lord, I love you so much, and I ask you to forgive me of my sins. I shouldn't have taken on the professor in class. I just thought I needed to take up for myself, but I didn't give you the opportunity to take care of me in the way you wanted to. I missed that opportunity. I don't ever want to bring shame on your name, Lord. Also, would you please give Alex a sign that I'm all right? I don't know who Wes is, but he is a nice young man. I do feel safe. Lord, I know this wasn't the right time but you've allowed it so help me break the news to Alex, I hope he'll be happy because I am. Thank you Lord for protecting me, I know you love me.

Let my father forgive me and respond to my letter. Be with Sean and Michelle in this storm. Take care of all the students here at the University, and please don't let there be too much damage done to these wonderful people's property in this community. Lord, also help Mr. Dobson and Professor Donaldson to get over their fear of the unknown. Their prejudice is just ignorance and fear. Lord, forgive them, for as your son said, they know not what they are doing. Lord, lead them to your salvation. Amen."

Alice felt a peace that she'd never felt before when she finished praying, but immediately a sharp piercing pain went through her stomach. She had no idea what was happening. She started calling for Wes. As Wes came into the room, he knew something was terribly wrong. He said, "Ms. Alice, just hold on. I'm going to get help."

Wes returned with his mom. Alice's eyes showed her surprise. "Mrs. Johnson, what are you doing here?"

"I live here sweetie. Mr. Johnson is downstairs. I'm trying to bandage him up. I'll tell you the story later. First, what is wrong?" she asked

"I'm not sure, but I'm having a lot of cramping and sharp stomach pains. I've never felt this before," Alice said. Alice looked at Mrs. Johnson with embarrassment, and Mrs. Johnson knew they needed to talk woman to woman. She asked Wes to go care for his dad while she took care of Alice.

Wes walked toward the door and then turned to Alice and said, "Ms. Alice, I'm praying for you right now, and I know our Lord knows what is best. Please don't worry."

Alice could see the sheer concern in Wes's eyes. She said, "Thank you, Wes, for your prayers. I so appreciate it." Then another piercing pain hit her and she screamed out, "Jesus, please help me."

Once Wes was out of the room, Mrs. Johnson pulled the blanket back to help Alice go to the bathroom, and she gasped at the sight of blood. Alice saw the look on her face. She hadn't looked down, but when she did, she saw the blood, too.

"Oh, NO!" Alice cried out.

Mrs. Johnson's suspicions were confirmed. Alice was pregnant.

"How far along are you, Alice?" she asked.

"About six weeks. I haven't had a chance to tell Alex. I was going to tell him this weekend when Sean and Michele came to take us back home to get his Jeep. I can't lose this baby. This is an indication of our love, our first born. I know the timing stinks, and certainly this wasn't planned, but it happened," Alice said with tears streaming down her face.

Mrs. Johnson knew she would need to stop the bleeding or a miscarriage was imminent. She knew this situation so well, for she and Mr. Johnson had been in a similar situation when they first married. She also knew they served a mighty God, and he would take care of Alice.

The storm was still raging, and if Alice needed to go to the hospital, she didn't know how she would get her there. She prayed a silent prayer. "Lord, you know what is needed here right now. Please give me your wisdom, knowledge, and understanding. Be with Alice right now, Lord.

Help her to accept your will no matter what. Lord, please keep us safe. As you know Mr. Dobson and his friends may very well show up here tonight to hurt all of us. Provide protection, Lord, as only you can. Your word says that you are our refuge and strength in a time of trouble. We need you now, Lord. Please help us all. In Jesus' name I pray. Amen."

Mrs. Johnson looked Alice straight in the eyes with a warm and loving smile and said, "Alice, I'll need you to do everything I ask you to do, okay?"

Alice nodded her head with fear and tears still streaming down her face. She didn't want to lose this baby, but she knew it was a possibility. She had worked in the ob-gyn department of the hospital back at home for several years. She'd heard stories and seen women go through this first hand. Consequently, she wasn't totally ignorant of what was happening.

Mrs. Johnson helped her to the restroom and began to advise her to gently remove her clothes. She didn't want her standing long and was grateful they had expanded the master bathroom a few years ago. She had a small love seat in her very lavish bathroom. Many called her spoiled when they saw the massive room, but she didn't mind. She and her husband had worked hard for everything God had provided for them. However, now she saw why God gave her the vision for this master bedroom.

Alice was very hesitant to sit on the white love seat, not wanting to stain it with blood. Mrs. Johnson reached over to a nearby armoire and in one swift move, she pulled out several blankets and towels, threw them over the love seat, smiled at Alice, and said, "Please sit down, honey. I need you to stay off of your feet right now." Alice obeyed as she had calmed down a bit.

As she lay on the love seat, she thought of how much she loved God and how well he was taking care of her now in her need. She still was worried about Alex, but she knew that once electricity was restored, she'd be able to reach out to him. She knew it was very important right now to try to stay as calm as possible.

Mrs. Johnson continued to work swiftly to stop the bleeding. She got Alice cleaned up and provided her with a fresh set of clean underwear and pajamas.

Alice looked a little confused. Mrs. Johnson saw the concern in her eyes and addressed it immediately saying, "Alice the bed sheets, mattress, this love seat, the pajamas, the new underwear are all just gifts from God, and they are all replaceable. People are not. What you don't know about me since we've only been acquainted for such a short time is that I'm a retired RN. I've worked in this field for many years, so I know what I'm doing. God makes no mistakes, Alice. Please know this is my calling. My husband was called to take care of people's spiritual needs. I was called to take care of their physical needs, much like yours and Alex's journey."

Alice smiled and said, "I know God has a plan, and we are not always privy to the plan. I trust him no matter what happens, and if I can't be with my mom, I can't think of another person I'd rather be with than you and Mr. Johnson and your wonderful son Wes.

Just then a knock came at the door. It was Wes he had a concern look on his face. "Mom, it's dad. I think you need to look at him," he said.

Mrs. Johnson instructed Wes to pick Alice up and set her in the chair closest to the bed. She hadn't gotten time to clean the bed. Then, she headed downstairs to check on her husband. There had been a struggle between him and Mr. Dobson, who had been following Alice when she went to mail the letter to her dad. Mr. Dobson was watching when she fell. He quickly ran thinking this was his opportunity to get revenge on her and Alex. However, Mr. Johnson saw it as he was on his way home. He immediately, without hesitation, came to the aid of Alice.

The two men got into a struggle, and Mr. Dobson was very surprised at Mr. Johnson's ability to defend himself; however, he hit him several times in the head.

Mr. Johnson had a head wound and possibly a broken nose, but he managed to drive himself and Alice to his house in the pouring rain. He knew he couldn't get her in the house, so when he drove into the driveway, he laid on the horn, and his son came and immediately yelled to his mom for help.

Together they were able to get Alice to the master bedroom upstairs, and they took Mr. Johnson to the guest bedroom. Mrs. Johnson bandaged him up as best she could, but she knew he needed medical attention as soon as possible. She didn't, however, think Alice needed much more than to rest and have her head examined for possible concussion since she had hit it when she fell.

CHAPTER EIGHTEEN

The Rescue!

Mrs. Johnson came to the aid of her husband. It appeared he was trying to say something, but only jibberish was coming out. She knew the signs. He had had a stroke.

She immediately said to her son, "Call 911 and see if anyone can help us. It is imperative that we get him to the hospital now!" Then she prayed, "Lord, this is your servant, and you know the plans you have for him. I ask you to please heal him, that we may continue to do your will at this college. Lord, I know you have a plan, and I don't know it, but I trust you. I know that my husband trusts you, too. Give us some help. Alice needs more medical assistance than I can give her, and you are the great physician. You have said in your word you would be our help in a time of struggle, and we need your help. Lord, send us assistance, please. Amen."

She had no more than finished her prayer when a strong knock came to the door. It was Sean and Michele. Mrs. Johnson so grateful and thankful she fell into Sean's arms and said, "Thank God." Then, she said, "What in the world are you two doing in this storm? You live forty five minutes away! How did you get here?"

Michele spoke first, "We were going to surprise Alex and Alice and take them out to dinner after their first day of college classes since ours doesn't start until next week. It isn't storming in Harmony, so we didn't hit anything until we almost arrived here. We took our time, and we stopped under a couple of bridges. Then, all of a sudden, Sean and I both got the same feeling that Alice and Alex were in trouble. Their street has downed tree branches and power lines, so we couldn't get to Alex and Alice's, so we came here. I hope that is all right," Michele said

Mrs. Johnson told them the story pretty quickly, the short version, and said, "Sean did you drive your SUV?"

"Yes ma'am," was his reply.

"We need to get both our patients to the hospital. I don't want to take them to the county hospital. We have to get them to Trinity Faith Hospital. I worked there for more than thirty years. They know me, and I know and trust the staff. They all love Jesus, so I know both will be taken good care of as long as we get them there. God will do the rest."

Sean and Wes took Mr. Johnson and got him settled in the SUV while Mrs. Johnson and Michele went upstairs and prepared Alice. The men came in and both carried her downstairs to the vehicle. It had stopped storming and now was just raining.

Just as they were getting everyone in the car, Mr. Dobson showed up. He had blocked the SUV in so that no one could leave.

Sean got out and said, "Mr. Dobson, I have two very sick people in there, and I'm asking you to please move your car, so I can get them to safety. I need you to do the right thing here."

Mr. Dobson said, "I came to finish what I started, and no one is going anywhere." He pulled out a gun and pointed it at Sean.

He said, "You're a half-breed nigger, and Alice is just a plain nigger. Mr. and Mrs. Johnson are nigger lovers, and we don't have any place in this world for those kinds of people. It is my God-given duty to clean the world up from your kind."

Sean said, "My kind, and you think you're doing God a favor, right? You're doing God's work?"

Mr. Dobson was so set on taking Sean down he didn't notice that Wes had slipped out of the car and was standing right behind him. He grabbed him by the neck, and Sean grabbed the gun. It went off but didn't hit anyone. Sean was able to get the gun from him. and Wes had him in a sleeper hold. He was subdued, and then the police arrived. They had received the 911 call and were able to get to the Johnson's house.

Police Officer Beaux Thompson arrived. He was the son of the chief of police and loved Mr. and Mrs. Johnson. They were his godparents, and he stayed at their house every summer. He and Wes were best friends.

Wes gave him the quick rundown of what had been happening in the last few hours. They arrested Mr. Dobson and escorted Sean's SUV to the hospital. When they arrived at the hospital, Michele called Alex on his cell phone because the house phones were still out of order. Alex was frantic. They told him he needed to get out of the neighborhood and Sean would pick him up as close to the neighborhood as he could since there were trees and power lines down.

CHAPTER NINETEEN

Surprise!

Sean was able to pick Alex up a few blocks from the apartment house. The streets were flooded and it was dark, but Alex used his flashlights and put on his hiking boots. He didn't care if his feet got wet. Heck, he didn't care about anything except getting to Alice and seeing how she and Mr. Johnson were doing.

Once in the SUV, he began pumping Sean for information. All Sean would say is that Alice is fine, and Mr. Johnson is in critical but stable condition. Sean didn't want to say much more than that. He wanted Alice to break the news to Alex. and he wanted it to be just the two of them. He also wanted Mrs. Johnson and her son Wes to talk with Alex. They knew more of the story than he did anyway.

They arrived at the hospital, and Alex didn't wait for Sean to park. He jumped out of the moving SUV and ran into the hospital. Mrs. Johnson met him in the waiting room.

Alex had a look of fear and confusion on his face. "Where is Alice, Mrs. Johnson? Is she okay? What happened to her and to Mr. Johnson? Who hurt them? I need to know right now because I'm telling you, I'm going to hurt someone," Alex said.

Mrs. Johnson was a sweet, calm woman, and she said, "Alex, first I need you to sit down, and I'm going to give you some information. You're going to thank God that it wasn't worse, and we are going to ask God to help those who don't see his love, mercy, and grace. Then, we are going to extend that grace to those people, because 'vengeance is mine, I will repay, saith the Lord.'"

Alex knew that whatever she was going to tell him, he was not going to like it. It was going to take all he had in him to be calm and forgive and extend that love, grace, and mercy Mrs. Johnson was talking about.

Just as she finished telling him the entire story, Sean came in. She didn't, however, tell Alex about Alice being pregnant. Sean saw his face and knew immediately that he was going to break.

Alex stood up to walk and as he did, Sean caught him in his arms. Alex sobbed and through his sobs, he said, "I couldn't protect her. I should have been with her. This is on me. It is my responsibility to protect my wife, and I didn't do it."

Sean said, "Alex, you are not God. You can't be everywhere all the time. It is God's job to protect Alice. You are not her Savior, you are her husband, and when you get those roles clear in your mind, you'll be able to see what I see, a couple that loves God and continues to defy the odds."

Sean walked Alex to Alice's room where Michele was sitting by her bed. She had a bandage on her head and was resting. Michele hugged Alex and said, "She's not asleep. She has a headache, and she closed her eyes for a minute."

Alex thought they must have run out of beds. Maybe that was why Alice was in the maternity ward of the hospital. When she opened her eyes and saw her beloved Alex, Alice smiled and reached up for his embrace. He said, "I'm so sorry I wasn't here to protect you."

Alice looked at Alex and said, "It is not your job to protect me. It's your job to pray for me, lead me, and love me. God does the protecting.

You need to know that God knows what he is doing. Mr. Dobson is in jail, and he'll be there until we all have to go to court. I don't hate him. I feel sorry for him and people like him. We are going to experience this type of treatment and ignorance all of our lives. Believe me, if it's not about us being a bi-racial couple, it will be about us being Christians. The Devil is always busy, and we need to stay on our knees interceding for people like Mr. Dobson who are confused about who God is and what the work of God truly is about."

Alex said, "Are you okay?"

"Yes and no." Alice said with a faint smile.

Just then a rugged looking doctor came in. He said, "My name Dr. Elijah Proctor and I'm the ob-gyn doctor on staff."

Alex shook his hand. He had a look of confusion on his face. Michele and Sean were going to excuse themselves, but Alice asked them to stay.

"Dr. Proctor" this is my husband, Alex Davis," Alice said. She continued, "These are our best friends, Sean and Michele. We all grew up together in Georgia, and they are attending the law school in Romans You can talk to all of us," she said.

Dr. Proctor said, "Alice and Alex, we did everything we could to save the baby, but we were unsuccessful. You lost so much blood before you got here that you had already miscarried, I'm afraid." He had tears in his eyes as he gave them the news.

Alex was still stunned because he had no idea Alice was pregnant. He sat there for a minute. He looked at Alice with a bit of confusion, and she reached for his hand.

"I was going to tell you this weekend, when we all got together to go home to get the Jeep. I knew it was bad timing, and certainly we didn't mean for this to happen, but I knew this baby was conceived in love and God would make a way. Please don't be angry, Alex. I wasn't trying to keep anything from you. I just wanted to surprise you," Alice said with tears running down her cheeks.

Alex sat on the bed and hugged her. He said, "I'm not angry. I'm sad that you had to go through this by yourself. I believe that Mr. Dobson should be brought up on murder charges. Because of him, you lost our baby."

Alice said "No Alex, Mr. Dobson didn't have anything to do with it. I probably was under too much stress, and when I slipped and fell, that may have had something to do with it, too. We can have more children one day when the time is right, isn't that right, Doctor Proctor?" she said.

Dr. Proctor cleared his throat before he made his next statement. "Alice, I'm not going to lie to you. We were very surprised that you were pregnant. You have a very bad case of endometriosis, and the chances of your getting pregnant again will be a miracle. I'm so very sorry to continue to be the bearer of bad news," he said.

He turned to walk away and then turned back and said, "I know that we serve a mighty God, and if it is His will, you'll have children. If not, there are many children who need good homes, and I can tell that you and your husband one day will make great parents," he said. He hoped his words helped. He knew that so many young couples who desire to have children aren't always happy to hear that they can't have their own children. As he left the room, he prayed for them.

The room was silent and somber. No one said a word. They sat holding hands and staring at the floor. The door opened, and it was Wes. He came in and was silent for a minute. Then, he said, "Ms. Alice?"

They all looked up at him. Alex stood and said, "Hi Wes. I'm Alex, Alice's husband. I want to thank you for taking care of my wife. I'm sorry we have to meet like this."

Wes said, "It's all right. I came to tell you that my dad is talking now, and it looks like the paralysis is going to be very insignificant if any. My mom wanted you to know. He was asking about you, Ms. Alice, and I told him I'd come check on you for him."

Alice smiled and said, "Wes, please stop calling me Ms. Alice. We are all almost the same age. In fact you're actually older than all of us because you're twenty one. We should be calling you Mr. Wes."

Wes smiled and said, "You know, I like to be respectful. I was going to go to college here, but I got a full music scholarship at another college about two hours away. This is my junior year and I'm working on my music for my graduation concert. We each have to right an original piece. Whenever I get nervous, I try to come home because this is where I get most of my inspiration."

Alex said, "I'm sure God is going to give you something special. Do you think your dad is up to some visitors right now?"

Wes said, "Yes, I think he would like that, but I think what is best is if we all wait until tomorrow and let him and Ms…" He corrected himself and said, "Let him and Alice get some rest tonight. My mom said everyone could stay at our house tonight. She is on her way down to see Alice."

Mrs. Johnson came in the room and saw Alice's face. She knew that she had lost the baby way before they came to the hospital. She just didn't want to say it. She hugged Alice and Alex and told them she loved them and no matter what, God still is in control. They were both crying, and she knew their hearts ached for the baby they lost and for the ones the doctor said wouldn't come.

"Listen to me. We are all here, God is faithful, Mr. Johnson is going to be fine, and Alice is going to be fine. Soon they'll have this town jumping again. They are asking for help with the cleanup from the storm. The college has been officially closed for the next two weeks. It seems there was a water main break in one of the class rooms. Also, a tree fell on one of the main campus buildings, and they will have to do some construction. We might as well take the weeks to heal, pray, and thank God for our blessings because we are blessed. This could have been so much worse than what we experienced. Shall we pray, my beautiful babies?" she said.

They all bowed they heads and prayed. As the prayer ended they all said, "Now what?"

Alex, Sean, and Michel all stayed with Mrs. Johnson for the next few days. Alice was released on Friday. They kept her a little longer because of her head wound, and since this was her first miscarriage, they wanted to make sure of no infections. However, Alex was at the hospital every day. Mr. Johnson had to stay over the weekend, and he was none too happy about it.

The weekend came and flew. Mr. Johnson was home, and Alice and Alex had finally gone home. Classes were starting for Sean and Michele, and they need to get back but promised to return the following weekend. After all, it is only a forty-five minute drive, Sean would say.

Alice was lying in bed, and Alex kept checking on her. He would walk to their bedroom door and say, "Do you need anything?"

"No, Alex for the millionth time. Really I am fine, honey. Stop worrying about me. I'm resting like the doctor said, and we have plenty of food thanks to David and Rhonda, Mrs. Johnson, and all the rest of these wonderful people God has placed in our lives," Alice said.

She had no more than finished her sentence when a knock came at the door. Alex answered and to his surprise, there stood his mom and Alice's mom. He was stunned. No one had told him they were coming. They had called and told them about the miscarriage and all the other things that had happened, and Alice's mom had talked to her every day, praying for her over the phone as well as in private.

Alex took their bags and moved to the side as the women rushed into the bedroom. Alice's mom reached her first, swooping her daughter in her arms, crying and laughing at the same time. "Let me look at you. I love you so much, sweet Pea, are you okay?" she asked.

"Alex has taken really good care of me, and I'm doing fine," Alice said with assurance in her voice and eyes.

Then, it was Alex's mom's turn. She hugged her and said, "Alice, you know I love you, and I'm so glad you're okay sweetie. Do you need anything?"

Again, Alice had to assure them that she was fine.

Alex stood at the doorway and watched. His mom motioned for him to come in. She hugged her son and said, "I'm proud of you, Alex. I know you are here alone, but you've done well."

Alex said, "Thanks, mom, I appreciate that." He then said, "What are you two doing here?"

It was Mrs. Taylor who spoke first. "Alex, I realize that Alice is your wife, but she is still my baby. Did you think I wasn't coming? The only reason it took me this long is because I couldn't get a plane because of the flooding here, so I had to wait."

Mrs. Davis was next, stating firmly that they would never fail to be there for both of them.

Alice asked about her dad and Alex asked about his dad, too. The women looked at them and said, "We are still praying for both of them."

Alice asked her mom if her dad had received her letter.

"Yes he did. It touched him deeply. He didn't want me to know it, but he actually reads it every day. I catch him laughing at something you said to him. He wouldn't let me read it, saying it was written to him and not me. Alice, he's coming around. You have to keep reaching out to him and praying for him. He loves you."

Alex looked at his mom, hoping for a similar story, but that was not what he heard. Mrs. Davis said, "Alex, your dad is set in his own ways, and only God can change a man's heart. Don't get me wrong. I know he loves you, but he's old school and sometimes that is the worst school. He sent you a note and I promised not to read it."

She handed the envelope to Alex. He excused himself and went into the other room to read it.

"Dear Alex, as I sit here writing this letter, I hate to say I was right. I see that you are having the same struggles you hoped to get away from here. I know Alice is a great young woman, and I wish nothing but the best for her in her life. However, you belong with your own kind. I know you believe you love her, and maybe you do, but I know God will forgive you if you walk away. I understand that she lost the baby. Maybe that was for the best. I'm not trying to be mean or hurtful, but someone has to say what needs to be said. This marriage of you and Alice was a mistake. It's okay to make mistakes, but learn from them. I hate to see you suffer because you turned your back on your own kind. I'm praying you'll come to your senses and place yourself back in your rightful place as a Davis doctor and we can be partners."

Alex crumpled the letter up and didn't finish reading it. Tears were rolling down his cheeks when his mom came into the room. She sat down next to him and took the letter from his hands. She began to read the letter and saw the pain on her son's face. She wished she had not given him the letter.

"I'm so very sorry. If I had known that is what Charles wrote, I would never have given it to you. He's bitter and angry. I'm just sorry that you and Alice are on the receiving end of his wrath."

She hugged her son as he cried, and he lay in his mom's arms like he did as a little boy. He was a young man now but still in need of the love of his mother.

Alice heard him crying and was going to go to him, but her mom stopped her, saying, "Let his mom love on him right now. He needs the love of a parent."

Alice understood because she so needed the love of her mom. She hated that Alex was hurt. Whatever was in that letter that made Alex cry, Alice wished that he hadn't read it. Her heart hurt for her beloved

Alex, but she knew right now he needed his mom. She was so thankful that their moms were there with them.

As Alex's mom was comforting him, Alice's mom insisted that she get back in bed and rest. She and Mrs. Davis had made plans to treat these two like royalty for the time they were there, and it started with an old fashioned southern dinner with all the trimmings. Mrs. Taylor left Alice to rest and went into the kitchen. She began to unpack the grocery bags and prepare a meal fit for a king and queen. She hummed Amazing Grace as she cooked and talked to the Father. She knew everything would be all right one day, maybe not today but one day. God would rectify all that was done. She loved Alex because he loved her daughter and her Jesus. How could she not? She had known him all of his life.

Mrs. Davis joined her in the kitchen. As they cooked and sang hymns, they knew God was in control. She showed Dianne the letter her husband and written to Alex. Dianne Taylor took the letter and together they ripped the letter up and threw it in the trash! They were bonded for life. They would always been friends, and this had made their love and admiration for one another stronger. They looked at each other smiled and said, "Girl, now what?"

CHAPTER TWENTY

Conversations!

lex and Alice's moms stayed with them for a month, taking care of their children. While Alex and Alice were in class, their moms were getting acquainted with their neighbors. They had fallen in love with the little married community of the college. They also had become fast friends with Mr. and Mrs. Johnson. Since their children's little apartment couldn't accommodate them all, they stayed in a little bed and breakfast across the street from the Johnsons. It was perfect because all the ladies did was sleep there.. The rest of their time was spent helping Mrs. Johnson with mentoring young ladies, praying, quilting, and of course cooking.

Their departure was bittersweet. Mrs. Taylor had to get back to her duties at the church, and Mrs. Davis had many auxiliaries she was over. She had also become a board member at the hospital where her husband was one of the chiefs of staff. She no longer trusted her husband's judgment when it came to people in general, especially those of color. She knew when they were young that he had a problem, but she just thought it was the time they grew up in and the way of the South. However, he had not grown in this changing world nor had he grown in the love of Christ, and she could not allow him to spew his venom on any more innocent people.

It was mid-October when they arrrived back in Lyonsville. The women departed with a hug and a promise to stay in touch. Mrs. Taylor entered her home and noticed immediately that her husband was lying on the sofa, which was strange in the middle of the day. She knew this was not normal for him. She went to him gently kneeling down beside the sofa. "Tom, is everything all right?" she asked.

He said, "I'm fine. I'm just tired. You've been gone too long. You left me for a solid month, and you barely called me. We have not been apart that long since we've been married, and I missed you so much."

She smiled. He was sulking. She got up and sat in the chair next to him and said, "Thomas Taylor, you are a grown man and very capable of taking care of yourself. I'm not your mother, but I am Alice Elizabeth Taylor Davis's mother. While you are still sulking over this marriage, you are missing out on our daughter's life. I don't know what it will take for you and Charles Davis to come to your senses, but I'm not going to miss one minute of her life and her experiences. Tom, she lost a child. Do you know what that's like?"

Then, she thought no, he's man. He has no idea what that's like. She got up from her chair and said, "I need to unpack and fix some lunch. Do you have anything in particular you would like to eat?"

She was a little irritated at her husband, but she knew better than to push him. She said all she was going to say about this situation, and he knew she was done.

He looked up at his wife, and adjusting his position on the couch, he patted the seat next to him for her to come sit. She did, and he held her hands and their eyes met in a long gaze. He then said, "How is Alice doing? I know I've been holding onto this for a long time. You know I had so many dreams for her. I dreamt of the day I'd walk her down the aisle, and that was taken from me. I dreamt of meeting and counseling the young man who'd ask for her hand in marriage, and that was taken from me. I dreamt of the day she graduated from high school, and we'd take photos and have a huge graduation party for her right here, and that was taken from me, too. Every plan, dream, and prayer I had for Alice was stolen from me, and it's hard to get over those things."

Dianne hugged her husband and sat back on the couch. She rubbed his hand as she began to talk to him. "Tom, I love you with all my heart. I have since the first day I met you. Don't you not think I had those same dreams for Alice, a bridal shower, fluffing her veil before you walked her down the aisle, picking out her wedding dress, flowers, and all the things you do with a daughter before she gets married? However, that didn't happen, and we have as much to do with that as Alice did. We chose to turn our heads when she tried to talk about young men she might be interested in. We focused on old family traditions, marry your own kind. Where in the Bible does it say that? Moses was married to an Ethiopian woman, was he not? It is not a crime or sin to marry outside of your race, Tom. Our daughter found love, real love, and we should be so grateful for that," she said.

Mr. Taylor was getting ready to say something, but his wife interrupted him.

"Tom, you should see how Alex dotes over her. Whatever she needs, he's there. She is happy and healthy. They have a wonderful community of married young people that they live with, and they have the dean of married couples, Mr. and Mrs. Johnson. You would love them. They love our Alice and Alex. You've known Alex all his life. How you could not love and respect him? He's going into ministry, and he told me the reason was because of you. He told me how when he was a young boy he heard you talk about the love of Christ and how God was not a respecter of people and that our job was not just to talk the gospel but to live it that people would come to Jesus. He said he knew then he wanted to teach the word of God to people." She said all of this and then said,

"Tom, you tell me what's wrong with our daughter being married to a pastor? Her mother married one."

With that statement she walked out of the room and went into the kitchen to fix their lunch. She knew God was softening his heart, and she was grateful. She just wished that he'd do the same with Charles Davis. She chose not to share any information about the letter with her husband.

Mrs. Davis arrived home to a yelling husband on the phone, telling the dry cleaners they had ruined his shirts. He hung up in a huff.

Mrs. Davis said, "I see you're in a mood. You need to stop letting the little things in life upset you or one of these days you're going to be a patient at that hospital where you work."

He looked at her and said, "Did you need to stay there a month? I'm sure our son is doing fine with his new life and his chosen wife."

She looked at him with disdain and said, "Alex is doing very well. He has the respect of his wife and he has the respect of the community. He's excelling in all of his studies, and so is Alice. Although I know you don't care, Charles, let me make something crystal clear to you. I'm not going to turn my back on Alex and Alice. They've done nothing wrong but fall in love and heed God's calling. She is going to be a doctor and he's going to be a pastor, and there is nothing you can do about it. Oh, about your little nasty, hateful letter you wrote to him, I'd like to say, my dear husband, don't you ever ask me to deliver such a heinous, ugly, disrespectful, and hurtful letter to our son or anyone else. You've lost your mind, and I'm praying for you every day because I know that somewhere in that chest of yours is a heart."

He looked at his wife with venom. He hated that she had turned her back on him. They just didn't get it, and he couldn't make them understand his side of the story. In his mind he was the laughing stock of his professional friends. He couldn't bow down now even if he was wrong. His pride wouldn't let him. He knew that his wife was not going to change her mind. He also knew his daughters were not going to change their minds either. He felt alone and angry, and he blamed Alice and Alex for his hurt and shame. Actually there was no shame; he was just a very prideful man. He heard a still small voice say, "Pride cometh before the fall." He shook his head and walked away.

Dianne received a call from Alex saying that their court date was the week before Thanksgiving and wondering if Alice's mom and Mrs. Davis were going to be able to come to Oklahoma for the trial. Her mom had assured him that they would be there. Then, they could all be home together for Thanksgiving.

CHAPTER TWENTY ONE

Judgment Day!

Alex, Alice, Sean, and Michele picked up Mrs. Davis and Mrs. Taylor at the airport. They all couldn't fit in one vehicle, so Sean and Michele drove in a separate car. Although they talked to them all the time, they hadn't seen their parents since they had come to Oklahoma. They drove straight over to the Johnson's house, where Mrs. Johnson had just taken fresh cinnamon rolls and coffee cake from the oven. The ladies hugged each other, saying how much they had missed their new friend.

As the group sat at the table, they could see how nervous Alice was. Alice's mother said, "What's wrong? You seem a little upset."

"I am. I've never had to go to a trial. I really don't want to see Mr. Dobson. He's mean, and I'm just not sure I'm going to be able to face him again," Alice said.

"If it helps you at all, my dad has been talking to the judge on the case. They went to law school together," Sean interjected.

Alice looked at Sean and said, "Is that legal?"

Sean said, "Is what legal? For my Dad to talk to his friend over the phone?"

Sean looked at Alice and said, "Listen to me. That guy is pure evil, as evil as they come. From what I've heard, he has gotten off from some pretty awful things he has done in this and some other towns. He's part of this group they call the CFJ's (cleanup for Jesus group). They go around harassing people because of the color of their skin, the clothes they wear, and just because they don't like you."

Mr. Johnson came into the room. He was still using a cane, but for the most part he had recovered just fine. He had known Mr. Dobson for years. He knew God was now going to show Mr. Dobson and his kind who he was. They had removed Mr. Dobson's cousin from the bench so he wouldn't be the judge in this trial. That is why Sean's dad knew the judge, because they called one from out of town to preside over the trial beginning the next day. They decided to get a good night's sleep before they went to court. It would be a long day.

Alice and Alex made their way home, Sean and Michele stayed at the Johnson's house, and the moms stayed at the bed and breakfast across the street. Alice was sitting in the living room reading her Bible when Alex came out of the shower. "Are you okay, babe?" he asked her.

"I'm a little scared, but I know I've done nothing wrong and that, for the most part, Mr. Dobson is on trial for what he did to Mr. Johnson, for drawing a gun on Sean and Wes, and for trying to stop us from getting medical treatment. He never did anything to me. He didn't touch me because God protected me through the love of Mr. Johnson. I'm so grateful," she said.

Alex wrapped his arms around his wife and said, "I love you. I hate that people like Mr. Dobson exist in this world, but evil is present and we know that. We just have to be faithful in tearing done those barriers against those who seek to do injustices to others. That is why it is so important for people like Sean and Michele to become lawyers, because God will use them in a mighty way."

Alice knew her husband was right. He had such compassion for the underdog. He always had. Even when they were children, he would protect the kid that was picked on or invite the kid that had no friends to hang out with him. He was just that kind of guy.

He said, "Are you ready for bed? I'm tired, and you really need a good night's sleep."

She said "Yes, my love, I'm quite tired, too."

Morning came sooner than they expected. They dressed, grabbed a bowl of cereal, and were off to the court house. They all met on the courthouse steps, and Mr. Johnson led them in a prayer that God would have mercy but that justice would be served and that His name would reign supreme today.

They entered the court room and sat down. The prosecuting attorney approached and asked to speak with them before the trial began. Mr. Dobson was being charged with assault and battery and assault with a deadly weapon. He also was being charged with attempted murder.

When they entered the room, the attorney said, "We are not going to have a trial today. Mr. Dobson hung himself in his cell this morning. He's dead!"

They all gasped, and the room was silent for a while. Then, the attorney said, "We would have called you earlier, but his attorney told us in the judge's chambers just minutes before you came into the courtroom."

They left the courthouse and headed to a little diner down the street. Mrs. Johnson spoke first. "I sure hope he asked Jesus into his heart before he died. I'm not happy he's dead. That is not the outcome I was praying for. I was hoping he'd see the error of his ways, come to Christ, and make a change in his life."

Mr. Johnson was next. "Many times the Devil will have such a hold on a person's mind that he actually can't see any reality other than his own selfish desire. He probably thought since his cousin wasn't going to be presiding, he wasn't going to get off and he didn't want to go to jail. After all, he didn't really think he did anything wrong," he said.

They were seated and hungry. Alex, Wes, and Sean had the appetite of teenagers. It was still quite early, so they all ordered a hearty breakfast. The conversation was light and airy. They laughed and loved on each other and in their hearts were all sorry that Mr. Dobson had taken his own life. Death was nothing to laugh at, and none of them were laughing.

Sean and Michele needed to make their way back to school. They were headed home for the Thanksgiving Holiday which was some concern for Alice and Alex. They had no idea where they'd stay, but they knew they were going home.

Alex and Alice arrived at the apartment with their moms. They were going to fly back with them to Georgia for Thanksgiving and drive Alex's jeep back to Oklahoma. It had been a long four months since coming to Oklahoma in August. It was now November, and they couldn't believe so much had happened.

Alice's mom said, "You and Alex are welcome to stay at our house for Thanksgiving."

Alice said, "Mom, what about Daddy? What will he have to say about us staying there?"

Her mom said, "It was his suggestion. Wait until we get home. You'll see that it's fine. He may have a little problem with you and Alex sharing a bed together, but he knows you are married, so he'll get used to it."

Alex interjected, "Mrs. Taylor, Alice and I don't have to share a bed together. I can stay at my sister's house and come over for Thanksgiving dinner. In fact, I think I need to do that until I have a chance to really talk to Pastor Thomas. I owe him an apology, and I need to get that right with him before I share a bed in his house with Alice. I know she's my wife, but he's her dad and I want him to know I have all the respect in the world for him."

Alex's mom was so proud of her son. She walked over to him and kissed and hugged him. She said, "You know I'm so proud of the man you've become, and I am so grateful to God that he allowed me to be your mama."

Alex smiled at his mom and said, "I had a good upbringing and a great pastor in Pastor Taylor. He taught me a lot about being a godly man and so did my dad, so I'm grateful, too."

His mom couldn't believe that Alex said he learned about being a Godly man from his dad. She hadn't seen that man in a long time, yet she yearned to see him again. They all settled down and took a nap. Since there wasn't going to be a trial and Thanksgiving was next week, they decided to see if they could get their plane tickets changed to travel home the next day.

CHAPTER TWENTY TWO

Home Is Where The Heart Is!

The flight to Georgia from Oklahoma wasn't long. Alex rode with his mom from the airport to his sister's house. He wasn't going to face the wrath of his dad if he didn't have to. Of course they were all waiting on him with kisses and hugs. They knew the plan that Alice was going home to reunite with her dad, and they were all praying everything went well. Diane Taylor had invited them all to come for Thanksgiving next week.

Alex was home, and his mom couldn't be happier. She knew her husband would have a rough time, but he'd have to get through it because he wasn't going to destroy her enjoying the holidays because of his hatred.

Alice was nervous. They entered the home she had lived in most of her life yet hadn't been in for months. It didn't feel like home yet. Her dad came down the steps, and as soon as he saw Alice, he ran to her, kissed her, and picked her up off the floor.

"I've missed you so much. Please come and let's sit down. I need to talk to you and Alex."

He then noticed that Alex wasn't there. "Where is Alex?" he asked with a puzzled look on his face.

Alice said, "Daddy, Alex wants to talk to you man to man tomorrow before he comes here. He wants to apologize to you. He says he owes you that, and Daddy please let him. This is what he says he knows he must do according to the word of God."

She was still holding on to her dad's arm. She then looked at him and said, "I'm so very sorry I hurt you. I wasn't trying to disrespect you and mom. I just wanted to see Alex, and then his dad placed that injunction saying I couldn't. We really didn't know what else to do. If I had it to do all over again, I would wait."

Her dad said, "You wouldn't wait because you love Alex and I know that now. As I look back at you two, I should have known. You tried to talk to me that Sunday when you asked me what I thought of Alex, and my reply was he's a nice enough young man and he'd make some girl a nice husband one day."

"You did come back later and asked me if I needed to talk, and I said no. I should have confessed then, but I was scared and I just didn't know how to talk about it. I truly didn't want to cause you more problems. I knew Alex's dad would not approve. He probably would have made him leave town or caused some other problem," Alice said.

She was speaking from her heart. Somehow her dad didn't seem so scary now, and she knew it had only been a few months, but things had changed. She so wanted to just stay in his presence. Their conversation was interrupted by her mom saying, "Is anyone hungry other than me?"

They all laughed and sat down to a light lunch. They planned to go out to dinner with Alex's family so they could see Alice as well.

The phone was ringing woke Alice up. She still had a phone in her room with her own phone number. That hadn't changed. She thought it was strange, but then she knew her dad may have been angry with her, but he didn't hate her. He's always loved his little pumpkin.

"Hello," Alice said with a sleepy voice.

"Where are you guys? We've been waiting for half an hour. Is everything okay?" Alex asked.

"What time is it?" Alice asked

"It's six thirty," Alex replied.

"I'm sorry we overslept. I was so tired, and after talking to my dad, we ate and thought we'd take a short nap. We'll be there in fifteen minutes. Just let me wake my parents up," Alice said in a hurry.

She hung up the phone, ran down the hall, and banged on her parents' door. "Mom, dad, we're late! Alex just called me. It's six thirty. We have to go!" Her parents sprang into action, getting dressed quickly. Alice was waiting for them at the garage door.

They made it to the restaurant in record time. Dianne was hoping her husband would not get a speeding ticket. When they arrived, Alex, his mom, his two sisters and their husbands were at the table. They jumped up and grabbed Alice with a hug and kiss. She was excited to see them as well.

Alex stood up, walked over to Mr. Taylor, and put his hand out for a handshake. Mr. Taylor grabbed Alex in a hug. "Good to see you, Alex. We'll talk tomorrow, okay?"

Alex agreed. They sat down and had a most enjoyable meal together as a family. Alex sat next to Alice. They held hands through dinner and talked about all the things that had happened in the last few months.

No one noticed that Dr. Davis had arrived and was looking through the window at them. He wasn't going to come in because he still held a lot of bitter resentment in his heart. He knew that he was now the odd man out. Alice had stolen his entire family. He also knew deep in his heart it was pride. He'd been raised a certain way, and to change now would mean his father was wrong. His dad always told him, "You have to be the man of your house and the man of his house is never wrong. When you say you are wrong to your family, they lose respect for you."

He grew up hearing this all his life, and he just didn't know how to change. However, from where he stood, saying he was wrong or not, he'd already lost the respect of his family. He walked away for the first time feeling slightly different but had no idea how to change it without apologizing. His pride would not allow him to admit he was wrong!

CHAPTER TWENTY THREE

Forgiveness Is Freedom

A lice woke up early in the morning. The evening had been wonderful. She was grateful and thankful that God had brought her family together, and when she thought of family, she was thinking of Alex's family, too. She prayed that Alex and her dad would have more than just a father and son in law relationship. She knew Alex missed his relationship with his dad. They were once very close, and now it was as if they were strangers. Alice somehow thought she was to blame, and yet she knew that wasn't true. She went to her favorite place in the house, the attic.

She opened her bedroom door, and went straight across the hall and opened the door adjacent to her parents' room. She remembered her dad had the steps carpeted because she kept falling. Once they knew they couldn't keep her out of the attic, they had it renovated so she would have a type of study. It had a sofa bed, lounging chair, a table, lamps, and even a small refrigerator. She and Michele spent hours in the attic apartment, which is what they called it when they were girls.

They felt so grown up when they went there and spent the night on the sofa sleeper. It was as though they had their own apartment, and usually Alice's parents wouldn't bother them. They had snacks, television, music, and all the other entertainment they wanted. As they grew older, it became their prayer room, their secret telling room. When either young woman wanted to pray earnestly, she went to the attic. Alice would say God answers prayers in the attic. It's closes to Heaven.

As she ascended the stairs, she could feel the cool air from the attic fan. As she reached the top, she began to pray. She noticed it looked as though it had just been cleaned. She knew her mom had done it, knowing at some time during her stay she would make her way to the attic. She sat down and opened her Bible to Psalms. She loved the Psalms. She said the Psalms is where King David grew up. She read Psalms 55:1, "Give ear to my prayer, O God: and hide not thyself from my supplication."

This verse said it all. She needed God's ear as her husband and father met today. These were the most important men in her life, and she wanted their meeting to go well. She prayed for them and asked God to bless them and give them both wisdom to listen to one another's heart. She prayed for calmness in both men and to let them feel safe. She prayed that God would get glory out of this situation and bring families back together.

She then prayed the following. "Lord, I know my father in law is a hurting man. He has to be to do and say all the hurtful things he has said and done. Please forgive him and allow him to see the error of his ways. Give me the same courage you've given Alex in talking to my dad to go and talk to Dr. Davis. Lord, I'm scared, and I don't know what he'll say or do to me because he believes I have stolen his only son from him and turned his family against him. I don't want him to feel that way about me, but even if he does, I don't want him to feel that way about Alex. Help my father in law to find you, your love, and your forgiveness, so he can be reunited with his family. You've said nothing is impossible for you, and I trust your word. In Jesus' name I pray. Amen!"

She had not come to the attic to pray for her father in law, but it just came over her. She hadn't even thought about seeing him while she was there, especially without Alex, but apparently God wanted her to reach out to him; therefore, she would. She would have to do it after Alex came to speak with her dad.

She could smell bacon cooking. That meant her parents were up, which meant Alex would be over soon. She looked at the clock, and it said eight thirty. She didn't realize she had been in the attic for well over an hour praying and reading God's word. She felt at peace, and she knew God was working. As she was descending, the door opened and it was her dad. She smiled. "Hi, Daddy," she said with a huge grin.

He looked at Alice and realized she was not a little girl. She was a woman, a married woman. She was beautiful, respectful, kind, and gentle and had a servant's heart. What more could he want for his daughter. She was happy.

"What time is Alex coming over?" he asked.

"I think mom said for him to be here at nine a.m. sharp. That's why I'm getting in the shower, so I can greet him when he gets here," she said with a smile.

Her dad smiled and said, "We'll let you know when he gets here."

She had just gotten out of the shower when the doorbell rang. She knew it was Alex, and she had butterflies in her stomach. What if her dad saw Alex and got mad all over again? What if he threw Alex out of the house before she could get to them? What if Alex didn't have the chance to apologize? She was trying to get dressed quickly to intervene if she had to. Once dressed, she ran down the stairs, but it was too late. Alex and her dad were already in the study and the door was closed.

Her mother knew her daughter well. She said, "Come with me."

Alice followed her mom to the kitchen where she had breakfast waiting for the two men.

"Alice, Alice!" Her mother had to call her a couple of times before she answered, "Yes, mom."

"Stop worrying. Your dad is fine with Alex, and you've been praying, I've been praying, and Alex's mom has been praying. You'll have to trust God sometime and you also have to trust Alex and your dad. Actually there really is nothing you can do," her mom said with a smile and a gentle kiss on the cheek.

Pastor Taylor had answered the door when Alex arrived. He invited him in with a warm hand shake. "Good morning, Alex," Pastor Taylor said, greeting him with a smile.

"Good morning Pastor Taylor. How are you this morning?" Alex asked.

"I'm fine. I understand you'd like to have a word with me?" Pastor Taylor asked.

"Yes sir, is there somewhere we can speak privately?" Alex asked.

Pastor Taylor had known Alex most of his life, and he'd never seen him so nervous. He thought it was kind of funny, but at the same time it was very respectful. It meant that whatever Alex was going to say to him was serious and that the young man didn't take this talk lightly.

"We can talk in my study if you'd like," Pastor Taylor said.

Pastor Taylor led the way, and Alex followed nervously. He had not slept well, thinking about what he would say to Alice's father. He had prayed on and off all night and all the way over to the house. He hoped to see Alice before he met with her dad, but that didn't happen. Pastor Taylor sat in a chair near the window. Between the two chairs was a table. Pastor Taylor motioned for Alex to sit in the chair on the other side.

Alex cleared his throat. It was very obvious now he was more than nervous; he was downright scared.

Pastor Taylor started the conversation. "I'd like to apologize to you and ask you to forgive me for how I've treated you."

Alex knew he needed to say what God had laid on his heart, so he said, "Pastor Taylor, I don't mean to interrupt you sir, but you don't owe me an apology. I owe you one, and I'd like to say I'm so very sorry for eloping with Alice. It was an irrational move on my part. Alice deserved a wedding, and you deserved to have me come to you man to man and ask you for your daughter's hand in marriage. I did it all wrong, and I'm so very sorry. Please forgive me. What I did was wrong. I didn't think about how this would hurt you and Mrs. Taylor or how Alice would be affected. I honestly thought now my dad can't keep us apart. It was selfish of me. I should have trusted you as my pastor, and I didn't. I disrespected you as my pastor and as the father of the woman I love. If you can find it in your heart to forgive me, I'd be grateful. I love Alice with all of my heart, and I believed then and now more than ever she is the woman God wanted me to marry, but maybe not the way we did it."

Once Alex was done, Pastor Taylor said, "Alex, you are forgiven. It took me awhile to see what really was going on. Your dad had placed you all in a very difficult situation. I don't know what I would have done if Mrs. Taylor's dad had gotten a court order saying we couldn't see each other. I now know that you all were forced in a corner. I'm grateful that you came to me this way, and I can tell you that you are forgiven and I hold no grudge, animosity, or anger toward you or Alice. I'm happy that I have a son in law that I've known most of his life. I know that Alice is in good hands."

It was then that Alex broke down crying, saying, "But I couldn't protect her from Mr. Dobson, and there is no telling what he would have done to Alice if he had gotten to her before Mr. Johnson did. I know he wanted to hurt her, and I would have had to kill him, Pastor Taylor, really I would have. I saw the evil in his eyes the first time I met him. I even told Alice to beware of him because I didn't trust him."

Pastor Taylor left his chair and comforted Alex. "You are not God, and you can't be everywhere all the time. God protected Alice, and he protected you, too. You did the best thing you could during that time which was pray for Alice. Look how things turned out. She is fine," Pastor Taylor said.

Alex looked up at Pastor Taylor and said, "We lost our baby. It was too early to know if it was a boy or girl, but we would have loved it with all of our hearts. Now the doctors say we may never be able to have children."

Pastor Taylor said, "The doctors can only do their part. They are not God. They have no idea what God is going to do. Doctors told Mrs. Taylor and me that we couldn't have children also, but we have Alice. She is our miracle child. When she was born, I held her in my hands and looked at the doctor and said, 'Now what?' Understand, medicine can only go so far, but God has no limits. Keep loving and serving God with your whole heart and if children are in the plans, no one can stop it."

Alex had calmed down and was no longer crying. He said, "Pastor Taylor, may I ask you a question?"

"Of course," Pastor Taylor replied.

Alex began, "I wasn't there when Mr. Dobson tried to stop Sean and Wes from getting Mr. Johnson and Alice to the hospital, but they said that he told them he was doing the business of the Lord, cleaning up the mess that others create. Why would he say that?"

Pastor Taylor went to his desk and grabbed his Bible. He turned to the gospel of John 16:1-2 and read following scripture to Alex.

"These things have I spoken unto you, that ye should not be offended. They shall put you out of the synagogues: yea, the time cometh, that whosoever killeth you will think that he doeth God service."

"Just as Jesus was telling his disciples that the time would come that they'd put them out of the synagogues and kill them and think they're doing God's will, this type of evil mentality hasn't stopped. There are always going to be people who hate God's people. They'll use the fact that you and Alice are an interracial couple to ridicule you, but they are fighting against the one who lives inside of you."

Alex had left his chair and was standing in front of Pastor Taylor's desk. "Thank you for your support, forgiveness, and love. I appreciate it so much, and I want to ask you one more question sir."

"How can I help you?" Pastor Taylor said.

Alex said, "May I have your daughter's hand in marriage?"

Pastor Taylor looked at Alex with a huge smile and said, "You have my blessing, Alex."

They hugged, and Pastor Taylor said a prayer of protection over Alex. He gave him a book on spiritual warfare and several other books about ministry and being a pastor. He told Alex that while he was in school, if he ever needed information or tutoring in his classes, he was willing to help him. Alex knew the time was going to come when he would have to take him up on that.

The women were still in the kitchen waiting for them, but they had eaten. Pastor Taylor entered the kitchen first with Alex behind him. Alice looked to see if everything was okay. Alex gave her a wink, and she knew all was well.

Pastor Taylor said, "Did you ladies eat without us?"

Mrs. Taylor said, "Yes, honey, we were hungry, and you and Alex took too long. It is ten thirty. He got here at nine, and we were not going to continue to wait on you two. There is plenty of food, and I can warm it up. I don't mind."

Alex smiled. He was used to Pastor and Mrs. Taylor bantering.

Alice said, "Alex, would you like for me to fix you a plate?"

Alex looked at Mr. Taylor, who quickly said, "She's your wife. If she wants to fix your plate, let her."

They all laughed, and Alex nodded yes with a smile.

Alice could feel the freedom of walking in the forgiveness of her father, and she could see Alex had the freedom, too. Her father and Alex spent the day watching football while she and her mom went shopping for food for the Thanksgiving meal. She and Alex would spend the rest of their time at her parents' house. She thought it would be better if she and Alex shared the attic. It had a comfortable sofa bed, television, and fridge. It really was a miniature picture of the garage apartment. It even had a small shower.

Alex felt like a real man now that he had done the right thing. He knew he would never feel comfortable sharing a bed with Alice in her father's house without doing the right thing. He wished his father would accept Alice as Pastor Taylor had accepted and forgiven him. However, he knew his father was a proud man, and it would take an act of God to get him to reunite with him let alone Alice. He had embarrassed his father and hurt his pride, first by not becoming a doctor and second by marrying Alice.

CHAPTER TWENTY FOUR

Dinner and Dancing

Alice and her mother had been cooking. She went to the attic to join Alex, who was sound asleep. She lay next to him, and he felt her body move in closer. He drew her nearer to him. "You smell like sweet potato pie and other yummy food," he said.

She smiled and said, "Yes, it's just like it used to be except now dad has a son to watch the football games with. Mom and I used to watch them with him but just because we had to. Then, he invited some of his friends over and sometimes other family members would come by, but mom and I always ended up on the couch watching the football games." she said.

Alex was a little more comfortable sharing a bed with his wife in her parents' home, but he still wasn't going to touch her in the biblical way. That was too much. Alice felt the same way. It was a form of respect. They knew they were going to have a houseful of guests soon, so they had better try to get some sleep.

They heard a gentle knock on the door. "Come in," Alice said. To her surprise there stood Sean and Michele.

Alice said in a surprised voice, "What are you two doing here?"

Sean said, "I guess you two are going to sleep the day away. It is already eleven o'clock, and your mom invited us and our parents to Thanksgiving dinner. By the way, Happy Thanksgiving. Get your butts out of the bed!"

Alex said, "Hey man, we are tired, and we want to sleep in, but if you two intruders would get out, we'll get showered and come downstairs."

Their friends were happy to wake them up and happy to join the Taylors downstairs. They reported that they had accomplished the mission.

Alice's mother had told Sean and Michele that Alice went to bed about four thirty this morning, and she was just going to let them both sleep in until they were ready to get up. Sean insisted on waking them up, and as the friend he was, she knew he would with no problem. It didn't take Alice and Alex long to join them in the family room. Michele and Alice helped her mother put the finishing touches on the dinner and setting the tables.

It wasn't long before everyone was there. Alex's family were all there except his father. Pastor Taylor had called and spoken with him for quite some time and encouraged him to come have dinner with everyone. Dr. Davis insisted that he was on call at the hospital and would pick up a bite to eat there if he got hungry. He confessed that he had not had much of an appetite in a while, but he was fine. He told him to tell everyone Happy Thanksgiving and hung up.

Alex's mom spoke with Pastor Taylor alone. "What did he say, Tom?" Mrs. Davis asked.

"Well," he began, "He sounds tired. He sounds like the fight is gone, but he's holding on for dear life. He said he's on call and he'll be at the hospital and if he gets hungry he'll eat at the hospital."

Joan said, "This is the first Thanksgiving we haven't been together. I'm worried about him. I know he's still has issues with Alice and Alex, but I think it's more than that. I just wish he would see someone if he's sick."

Pastor Taylor said, "I'm praying for Charles. I know he's a prideful man and that is not good. The entire time I was upset with those kids God would not let me sleep. I could hardly preach on Sunday. It was a struggle, and that is why several Sundays out of the past few months I've had guest speaker. I know many thought I was doing something special, but actually I couldn't get a word from God. I knew I was wrong too, but my pride wouldn't let me forgive and move on. When I found out Alice had been hurt, I knew I had to get this thing handled and quickly."

Joan said, "I miss Charles, but I'm not going to let Thanksgiving be ruined. The kids will be leaving on Sunday to go back to Oklahoma, and I'm going to enjoy every second I have with them." And with that she turned and walked out of the room.

Alex's mom joined Mrs. Taylor in the kitchen. She had tears in her eyes and didn't want them to fall, but they did. Dianne reached for her friend and said, "You know it's going to be okay. God will work this out. You are married to a stubborn, proud Southern man. God sometimes has to bring you to your knees to get your attention. Then and only then will a person submit his will to God almighty."

Joan leaned on her friend's shoulder and said softly, "I know, but I don't want God to take his life."

Dianne said, "Let's just ask God to spare his life and change his heart."

It was then that God gave Joan an overwhelming peace she had not experienced in a long while. In her heart of hearts she truly thought Charles was as good as dead. She knew he had turned his back on God. Although he was in church every Sunday, his heart was not with God. She knew and Charles knew it.

The women looked at each other and said their famous words, "Now what?"

They both knew God was in control and they knew He had heard their prayers. They had a relationship with the living God of Israel, He never breaks his promises to his people and they were his people.

It wasn't long before they were bombarded by the other members of their family and Michele who they considered their daughter as well. The doorbell rang and in came Judge Brooks and his wife, Michele's parents, and, to their surprise, Mr. and Mrs. Johnson along with their son, Wes. What a surprise it was for everyone involved. Pastor Taylor asked that everyone meet in the family room. As they gathered together, Pastor Taylor smiled.

He then said, "I want to thank each and every one of you for sharing Thanksgiving with my family. This has been a very difficult time for all of us in some ways. God loves all of us and wants us to be a true family. I'm so glad God woke me up and showed me the error of my ways. I've apologized to my daughter and son in law and asked them to forgive me for my actions and attitude toward them. Alex and I had a private heart to heart talk, and all is well with all of us."

He paused and continued, "I'm a blessed man because I have a wonderful Godly wife who I know has been praying for me while I was trying to work through my feelings and emotions regarding Alice and Alex. I want to thank all of you for your prayers. Mr. and Mrs. Johnson, I thank you for taking care of our children. That includes Sean and Michele, too."

Judge Brooks interjected a hearty, "Amen and thank you."

Michele's parents nodded a thank you as well.

Pastor Taylor prayed, and they all sat down to a wonderful Thanksgiving dinner. There were laughter, tears, stories, and lots of love shown throughout the day. Dianne Taylor's spirit was full of joy and thanksgiving. She never sat down.

Then, Alice turned on the record player and started playing music. All of a sudden Pastor Taylor called for his dance partner, and Mrs.

Taylor came to his call. They danced and showed the young people how it was done. Before the night ended, everyone was dancing, laughing, and enjoying Thanksgiving as if they didn't have a care in the world.

However, standing in the kitchen looking out the window was Joan Davis. How she missed her husband, but she knew God was working things out. Alex saw her from the other room and eased away from the others.

Joan felt a strong arm around her shoulders. "Mom, are you doing okay?" Alex asked.

Joan was once again reminded that she was not alone. She couldn't speak because of the lump which had formed in her throat, so she just shook her head yes. He knew she was missing his dad, and he was truly sorry for that. He said a silent prayer for his dad and held onto his mother. She was strong and had been strong for him when he was weak. Now it was his turn to hold her up, and that is what he did.

CHAPTER TWENTY FIVE

Can You Hear Me Now!

Thanksgiving was a blast. Everyone had enjoyed their time in the Taylor's home. There was so much food that Mrs. Taylor insisted that everyone take what they wanted, saying, "Look people, it's just me and Tom here. You all aren't going to stick me with all of this food. Alex and Alice will take some home on Sunday. Alice has already packed up what they want and it's in the freezer, so please take this food," she pleaded.

Everyone took what they wanted, and there was still plenty to eat. They offered for Mr. and Mrs. Johnson and their son Wes to stay with them, but Judge Brooks and his wife had already snagged them. It was all taken care of.

Everyone slept in the day after Thanksgiving except for Alice. She got up early to pray. She was on a mission she knew she needed to do without the knowledge of Alex or anyone else. She sat in her Jeep and said, "Okay God, you've sent me on this mission of love, and I pray it goes the way you've planned it. I have no expectations because I don't know what you're up to. I'm just going to go."

She headed down the street and turned the corner going toward the hospital. She was afraid, but she knew it was her turn. Alex had talked with her dad. She turned into the hospital parking lot, and there was Dr. Davis's car. She couldn't believe he was still there. Had he gone home at all?

She reached his office and knocked on the door. He said, "Come in."

His voice was low and raspy as if he was still sleep. She entered and said, "Good morning, Dr. Davis."

The second he heard her voice, he was immediately engulfed with rage. He jumped up from the sofa he'd been sleeping on and said, "Alice, what are you doing here?"

Alice was getting ready to speak, but before she could, he was in her face.

He began, "Don't you think you've done enough? You've stolen my son from me and now my wife, daughters, and son in laws. You've taken it all because you wanted what you want. I blame you, Alice Taylor. You're not fit to carry the Davis name. I told my son he needed to marry his own kind, but no he had to go and fall in love with a black girl."

Alice thought for a moment he was going to use the N word, and she truly would have been hurt. She had backed against the wall and was crying. This did nothing but fuel the fire for Dr. Davis.

He said, "Your tears mean nothing to me. I wish my son had never laid eyes on you. I have no idea what he even sees in you. You're an experiment for Alex. He wanted to know what it was like to experience the love of a black woman, and now that he has, he'll leave you and come to his senses. I know he will." He knew everything he was saying was wrong, but he didn't care. His rage and pride were out of control.

Alice did manage to say, "Dr. Davis, I'm sorry. I never meant for any of this to happen. I came to ask you to forgive Alex. Even if you continue to hate me, forgive your son. He loves you so much."

As soon as she finished that statement, Dr. Davis looked at her straight in the eyes and said, "I'll forgive him when he divorces you!"

He was now screaming and yelling so loud that Sean's uncle Dr. Pearson came out of his office. He came into the office and saw Alice against the wall and Dr. Davis in her face yelling and screaming at her. He saw the sheer fear in her eyes.

Dr. Pearson said, "Get out of her face. Back off now!" he yelled.

Dr. Davis looked at him and said, "Sure, take her side. You know what she did. She stole my family from me. Now she's come to ask me to forgive her, and I won't do it."

It was at this point that Dr. Davis grabbed his chest and fell on to the sofa. Dr. Pearson knew exactly what was happening. Charles was having a heart attack. He was gasping for air and trying to talk at the same time.

Dr. Pearson said, "Charles, are you okay? Be still please. Don't try to talk."

Dr. Pearson advised Alice to call the operator and tell them there was a code blue on the 4th floor in Dr. Charles Davis's office 402.

Alice followed instructions, and the hospital emergency room team came ASAP! They loaded Dr. Davis onto the stretcher and took him straight to the emergency room. Dr. Pearson followed but not before saying, "Alice, please call Charles's family for me. We're going to the emergency room. They can meet me in the waiting room."

Alice was very upset. She now blamed herself for Dr. Davis's heart attack. She was crying when she called her dad.

"Alice, I can't understand you, sweetie. Calm down, please," her dad said. She finally got it all out, and her dad's soothing voice calmed her down. He assured her no one would blame her and that he would get Alex up and everyone would be notified.

Dr. Davis was taken to Pod three where he had the very best of care. The cardiologist on site was Dr. Josiah Gray. He was one of the best in his field. His wife was there as well. She was the anesthesiologist, Gladys Gray. They were a team and usually worked together at the hospital. They knew the situation.

Dr. Gray came in and said, "Dr. Davis, I need to run more tests on you, but my preliminary diagnosis is that you've had a heart attack. These tests will tell me more."

Dr. Davis was still pretty uncomfortable, so he just nodded. They provided him with medication to make him a little more comfortable.

His family arrived and were talking to Alice. She continued to cry even though everyone told her it was not her fault. Alex held her close to him to ensure she knew he didn't fault her at all.

Alex's mom asked Dr. Gray if she could see her husband.

"He is resting right now. He was a very agitated when they brought him into the emergency room. I'd like him to stay as calm as possible until I can get the rest of the tests completed," he said.

She totally understood and knew he was right. She gathered everyone and asked Pastor Taylor to pray. He immediately asked everyone to hold hands, and they prayed for Dr. Davis.

It was during their prayer that Dr. Davis woke up, and a man was sitting in a chair next to his bed. He had on a beautiful coat with many colors.

He said, "Hi, Charles Davis, how are you feeling?"

Dr. Davis said, "My chest is hurting a bit, but I'm fine. Do I know you?"

The man didn't answer the questions; he just smiled.

"If I told you that God loves you, what you would say to me?" the man asked him.

Dr. Davis said "God can't love me. I have sinned so much, and hurt so many people."

The man said, "My name is Joseph, and God sent me to tell you that he loves you so much, no matter what you've done."

Dr. Davis was weak and thought he was dreaming. However, for some reason he wasn't having any pain. The man was holding his hand, and it seemed to keep him calm.

Dr. Davis said, "You don't know the things I've done and the way I've treated my son and his new wife."

Joseph said, "God knows it all, and he sent me to tell you that all you have to do is ask him to forgive you and he will."

Dr. Davis had a faint smile on his face. "Are you sure he will forgive me?"

Joseph said, "Yes, he will. His word says so, and God is not a liar. May I ask you why you don't like your daughter in law?" Joseph asked.

Dr. Davis had to look deep in his heart. He said, "When I was a little boy, my dad always said that we shouldn't mix with others, that everyone should stay with their own kind. I always prided myself in obeying my dad. It was my way of keeping his attention and love. My dad also taught me that God said that children should obey their parents."

Joseph smiled at Dr. Davis and said, "Your dad was half right. Children should obey their parents. You must remember that your dad was a human and fallible man. I'm sure he meant well. It was never God's intention to separate people no matter what the color of their skin is. He made all people. That is why I wear the coat of many colors. It represents every race of people and every nation everywhere."

Dr. Davis smiled and said, "That makes good sense to me, but I've never seen a purple or blue person."

Joseph smiled and said, "You're right. Let me share with you what these colors mean. Purple is royalty. Blue means many things like sincerity, wisdom, confidence, and Heaven. All of the colors have a true meaning. When you get better, you should study about it."

Charles looked at Joseph and asked, "I'm not going to die?"

Joseph said, "No Charles, God has so much for you to do. I have one more question for you, if that is okay?"

Charles said, "Go ahead. I don't mind at all. In fact, I feel better."

Joseph said, "What color do you see when you look at your daughter in law?"

Dr. Davis thought long and hard before he answered. She wasn't dark complected and yet she wasn't really light skinned. She was kind of copper but yet brown in tone.

He said, "She looks more like this."

Joseph pointed to a color on his coat and said, "That is what we call amber. It's in the earth tone colors of God. That color represents the glory of God, sanctification, and purity. You can find this in the book of Ezekiel 1:27-28 where it talks about the color amber."

Dr. Davis smiled and thought of Alice. She was pure and did set herself apart. His heart was heavy, thinking of how he'd treated her and his son. Tears were now streaming down his face. His pride was broken. God placed a mirror in front of him and what he was--ugly. Although he was no longer having physical pain, he was now experiencing the pain, sorrow, and shame of his actions over the last few months. He had torn his family apart and had blamed Alex and Alice. He had especially blamed Alice. He was truly broken.

Joseph patted his hand and said, "God knows everything. Talk to him, Charles. Talk to your Heavenly Father!"

Dr. Davis said, "Please Lord God, please forgive me for being prideful, ungrateful, prejudiced, evil, mean, and hateful toward my daughter in law. (He had never called Alice his daughter in law.) Lord, I've been so wrong. Please let my family forgive me. I've run them away. Show me how to love, forgive, obey your word, and be faithful in what you've given me Show me in your precious word how to obey. Lord, forgive me please."

When he opened his eyes, Joseph was gone, and Dr. Gray was sitting in the chair holding his hand.

"Where is Joseph? " Dr. Davis asked,

"Who?" Dr. Gray said.

"The man who was sitting there in the coat of many colors. He was sitting right there, holding my hand. He was helping me pray. God sent him to me. Really, God sent him to me to give me a second chance at loving people."

Dr. Gray smiled and thought to himself it was the medication. He was very surprised that Charles had not had a heart attack. He had to be the one to tell Dr. Charles Davis that he had misdiagnosed him. He was a little fearful because it was known throughout the hospital that you didn't make mistakes when he was around. Therefore, he didn't want to be the one to be on that end of the conversation, but he had to tell him.

Dr. Gray began by saying, "Dr. Davis, it seems that you didn't have…."

However, before he could say anything else, Dr. Davis sat up and said, "It's okay. Gerd will give you the same signs of heart attack. You don't need to fear telling me that. Dr. Gray you're one of the best in your field. Now what do you recommend?"

Dr. Gray was surprised. Who was this man talking to him with a gentle smile? What in the world had happened to Dr. Davis? This man was as gentle as a lamb.

He cleared his throat and said, "Dr. Davis, I would like for you to spend the night here so I can do a few more tests and make sure it is Gerd. I'm pretty sure it is, but I want to make sure."

"Ok," Dr. Davis said, "but can I please see my family?"

"Yes, of course you can. I'll go get them right now," Dr. Gray said.

Dr. Gray entered the waiting area and everyone jumped up. They were all talking at once. He stood there with a smile, and Mrs. Davis said, "Please everyone, let Dr. Gray speak."

Everyone got quiet and Dr. Gray said, "I'm pleased to tell you all that Dr. Davis is fine. He didn't have a heart attack. He has what we call Gerd. It's a condition in which you have chronic heartburn and esophageal spasms. It can mimic a heart attack because the esophagus runs directly behind the heart within the chest. I'm going to keep him overnight to run a few more tests, and he can go home tomorrow."

They all cheered and were relieved, especially Alice. She had been so upset. She thought she was the cause of him having a heart attack or even worse if he had died.

As if he had read her mind, Alex said, "but he didn't die."

She looked up at him and said, "How did you know what I was thinking?"

Because the Bible says, "And they shall be one flesh." Alice smiled and laid her head on his shoulder.

Dr. Gray continued, "He wants to see you."

Mrs. Davis said, "Can we all go back there?"

Dr. Gray said, "Yes, you all may go back."

As they were preparing to see Dr. Davis, he was in his room, talking to God. He looked up toward Heaven and said, "Lord, I'm really sorry, and I can hear you now. You've opened my heart and my eyes are open, too. Thank you for sparing my life, and please Lord, never leave me. Keep me close." He knew in his heart he was a new man.

CHAPTER TWENTY SIX

Family

While Dr. Gray was talking with Dr. Davis's family, the staff quickly moved him to a private room. This was something done especially for hospital staff. Everyone crowded in his room except for Alice. She was still fearful he would blame her for his attack even if it wasn't a heart attack. She stayed as far in the background as she could.

However, once everyone had seen that he was doing okay, Dr. Davis quickly asked for Amber. No one knew who he was talking about. They all said, "Who is Amber?"

They thought he was talking about a nurse. He realized he was calling Alice Amber and quickly corrected himself.

"I mean Alice. Where is Alice?"

She slipped to the forefront and was trembling a little.

Dr. Davis said, "If you all don't mind, I need to talk with Alice alone."

He then looked at his son and said, "Alex if you don't mind son, please?"

Alex knew by his father's tone something was different, and he was confident that Alice would be okay. He kissed his wife's cheek and said, "You'll be okay."

They all left and wondered what in the world was going on. Alice stood at the foot of the bed.

"Dr. Davis, I'm so very sorry I upset you to the point that you had such an attack. It truly was never my intention. I'm so very sorry."

Dr. Davis patted the side of his bed for her to sit next to him.

Alice obeyed. She sat ever so gently on the side of the bed. Dr. Davis reached for her hand and said, "I want you to know from my heart to yours how very sorry I am about all of this. I'm sorry that I scared you and yelled at you. I'm so sorry that I was ugly toward you and Alex. I'll talk to him next, but I need to ask you to forgive me. I've been hateful toward you, not allowing you and Sean to visit with Alex when he was in the hospital. This entire situation is my fault, and I'm asking you to forgive me. You are a wonderful young woman, and you'll make Alex a wonderful wife. I have no problem with you and Alex being married, and if I can do anything for you while you're in medical school, you let me know. I'm so very sorry about your miscarriage, too. My grandchild is in heaven. Although they say you may not be able to have more children, don't you believe it. God is going to give you and Alex children one day."

Tears were now rolling down his cheeks, and Alice was crying, too.

"Dr. Davis, I forgive you. I love Alex so much, and all I've ever wanted was for all of us to be a family. I've been praying and asking God to help me show you how much I love your son, hoping that if you saw that, you would be okay with our marriage."

Dr. Davis then asked for Alex to come in the room. He saw that Alice had been crying and was prepared to take on his dad, but then he saw that his dad had been crying too and was touched by the scene. He knew in his heart something had happened.

"Alex, please sit with me," his dad said.

Alice was getting ready to leave the room, but Dr. Davis asked her to stay. She sat in the chair next to his bed, and Alex sat on the bed next to his dad. His dad was clearing his throat to speak, but words would not come out, only sobs, and in between them, Alex could hear, "Please forgive me, please forgive me."

Alex touched his dad's hand and gently whispered, "Dad, I forgive you. Please calm down. I don't want you to get yourself all upset."

Dr. Davis composed himself. Then, he told them the story of Joseph and the coat of many colors and how God had changed his heart. He explained about the color amber. They now understood why he was calling Alice Amber. She thought that was such a beautiful story.

Dr. Davis said, "I know it sounds crazy, but this really happened. It really did. Not everyone will believe me and that is okay, because I know God sent Joseph to talk to me about my attitude toward people that are different than me. We are all sinners and in need of a Savior."

This was truly a miracle from God. Alex and Alice knew it, and they were overwhelmed with joy. There were so many tears.

Soon Dr. Davis asked Alex to bring everyone in the room again, and he shared his testimony of God changing his life. He didn't tell them about his visitor from Heaven. That was special between him, Alex, and Alice. He would share it with his wife but not now. He knew that not everyone got visitors from Heaven, and he also realized not everyone would believe it, but God would use it one day and he would be prepared to share this life changing experience.

Pastor Taylor was standing at the foot of the bed when he said, "Charles, we serve an amazing God. While we both opposed the marriage of our children, in hindsight I believe we both knew it was coming, even maybe before they knew. We just didn't want to accept it because we had made plans for them ourselves. This is a lesson to all of you who are yet to have children. God has plans for our children, and we'd better move out of his way so that he can work those plans out or he'll move us out of the way. In Charles's and my case, we almost lost that which we love so much because we wanted our own way and not God's way." He then said, "Let us pray."

With bowed heads they all stood around Dr. Davis's bed, holding hands praying for the miracle of a changed heart and life, each knowing that their prayers had been answered in some way. God had been merciful to their family, and they knew it. When the prayer ended, they each said their goodbyes. Mrs. Davis had prepared to spend the night, but Dr. Davis insisted that she go home. He was hoping that Joseph would visit with him again. They all left, and he was there in his hospital room with the lights dim. As he rested, he knew he was not alone, for Jesus was with him.

He had his family back, and for that he was truly grateful. God had allowed him a second chance at living for him, and he was not going to blow it this time. The past was the past. He had many things in his heart to do for his family and friends. He planned to start as soon as they let him leave the hospital.

CHAPTER TWENTY SEVEN!

Double!

Alex and Alice returned to Oklahoma feeling overjoyed, blessed, and fulfilled. The school had started decorating for Christmas, and it was almost both their nineteenth birthdays. They both were born on Christmas day. They were amazed as young kids when they learned they were the same age. Alex was born in the early morning, and Alice was born in the afternoon, so he always said he was older.

They returned to their regular schedule. Christmas coming, which meant final exams for both of them. Alex was still working with at risk youth at the church, and Alice was doing some work at the free clinic. They barely had time to see each other but always made time to pray and have a bite to eat together. Alice was the romantic one. She would leave notes of encouragement for Alex when she knew he was having a difficult class and was being challenged. However, Alex was thoughtful, too. He would do the laundry and wash dishes when Alice was cramming for a test as well.

Dr. Davis had kept his promise and made phone calls to all of Alice's professors, letting them know that once she graduated from medical school, she would return to Georgia and go into practice with him. He was so proud of her. and talked with both of them often.

Pastor Taylor was not going to let Dr. Davis outdo him when it came to supporting the kids. He made it known to the school that Alex would be over the entire youth ministry when he graduated. Both men were beside themselves when it came to Alex and Alice. This didn't hurt their healing marriages either. Their wives knew God had worked a miracle. From this a new ministry was birthed called Coat of Many Colors. It dealt with racial issues, differences, unity, and most of all showing the love of Christ.

None of them could believe God used all of their family issues to start a ministry, but the very first meeting was a packed house. So many hurting people came talking about how they were treated because of the color of their skin or because of how they dressed, their hair, or even a handicap. People were opening up, and Pastor Taylor was becoming very busy. Dr. Davis was also doing a lot of research on biblical colors. He wanted to know everything there was to know. God was using him, and he was okay with that.

Sean and Michele decided to visit Alex and Alice. It would have to be a very short visit because they had news they wanted to share with them. A lot had happened during the course of the Thanksgiving Holiday. Sean and Michele hadn't seen their friends since Thanksgiving Day, but they had heard about Dr. Davis's conversion and were overjoyed that both families had been reunited. This would make their news and the question they had for their friends so much easier to discuss.

Alice ran to the door when she heard the knock. She and Michele hugged like they hadn't seen each other for years. The men just laughed, said hello and sat down. A college football game was on, and Alex had a front and center seat on the sofa.

The ladies took their conversation to the bedroom. They talked about midterms, Thanksgiving, Christmas shopping, decorations, cooking, and, of course, their favorite conversation, the men in their lives. Alice saw something in Michele that she hadn't noticed before in her, what Alice would call womanly experience. She said, "Michele, what is going on with you?"

Michele smiled and said, "What are you talking about?"

Alice was blunt and said, "Have you and Sean been sleeping together?"

Michele looked at her friend and dropped her head. She couldn't lie to her best friend. They had known each other too long. Alice knew by her friend's expression that it had happened. She didn't want to be too hard on her, but they'd have to stop before it got out of hand. What was she thinking? It was already out of hand.

Their very testimony was at stake. Alice jumped up, grabbed Michele by the hand, and went right into the living room. She turned off the television and said, "Alex, Sean and Michele need to tell us something, and we will need to counsel them."

Alice hadn't given her friend a chance to explain anything. She just assumed she knew what was going on.

Alex looked at Sean, who looked at Michele who then looked at Alice. Alex said, "Don't everyone start talking at once."

Alice said, "Sean and Michele have been sleeping together, and it is wrong. It's a sin, and we need to address this issue right now."

She was a little perturbed at Sean and he knew it, but he knew it would be okay, too.

Sean said, "That is why we wanted to talk with the two of you before we go back to Georgia in a few weeks. We have some news for you."

Before he could finish his statement, Alice jumped in, saying, "See I knew it! You're pregnant, aren't you? Oh Lord! Now what? The Judge is going to kill you, Sean, and Michele, your mom and dad are going to be devastated. Our little community will have a heyday with this news. I'll have to get my dad involved. He will know what to do."

She was still talking when Michele gently put her hands over her mouth and said, "Shhhh, please. No, I'm not pregnant, and yes, Sean and I have been intimate, but that was after his father married us over the Thanksgiving holiday! We didn't want anyone to know yet. It was a very small and quick ceremony. It was my parents, Sean's parents, Mr. and Mrs. Johnson and their son Wes. Did you all know he was a musician? He's really really good. He played the wedding march, my dad gave me away, the Judge married us, and Mr. and Mrs. Johnson were our witnesses."

Alex and Alice were stunned. They didn't see this coming at all. Sean and Michele were married, and they didn't tell anybody. Especially not them! This was a little hurtful to both of them. They were best friends and didn't keep anything from one another.

Alice spoke first. "I thought your parents didn't want you to get married until you finished law school?" she said. What she said had a little bite to it as though she was a little angry. Alex could see the hurt. He was hurt, too, but didn't want to blow it out of proportion. This could get ugly really fast. They'd just gotten their family back. He was not about to lose their best friends

Sean spoke next. "Please forgive us for not telling you, but there is so much more to this story. Let's sit and I will tell you how this all came about."

They were all standing after Alice barged in the room. They sat down and Alex held Alice's hand and gently massaged it to comfort and calm her down.

Sean said, "Remember what happened with Mr. Dobson and how Alice and Mr. Johnson got hurt? After that I called and talked with my dad. I told him that life is just so short you never know when something bad could happen to me or Michele. I explained to my dad that I didn't want to wait to marry Michele after law school. That is six years away. My dad said that if I felt that way and Michele felt that way, I needed to call Michele's folks and talk to them. We both talked with them, and they gave us their permission to get married. Michele and I want to honor God with our lives, and we've had a couple of close calls where we could have made a huge mistake, but we didn't, so we knew with the time that we spend alone and the feelings we have for one another it was only a matter of time before something would happen and we wouldn't be giving God our best."

They could hear the sincerity in his voice.

Michele said, "We wanted to ask you, but while we were making plans and getting ready to call and ask you to be our witnesses, we got news about Alex's dad, so we couldn't very well ask you all to leave the hospital to come be our witnesses. Instead we asked Mr. and Mrs. Johnson."

Michele looked straight into Alice's eyes and said, "You've been my best friend since kindergarten. Do you really think I wouldn't want my best friend by my side as my matron of honor?"

Sean looked at Alex and said, "Same here, man. You know I would have wanted you there, but we could not barge in on you. It's a good thing we didn't. Look at what God did. Please don't be disappointed in us, and please don't be angry."

This took the sting completely away. Alex and Alice knew they needed to ask for forgiveness immediately because of their attitudes. They had jumped to conclusions, and they were completely wrong.

Alice said, "Sean, I'm sorry for accusing you of being less than honorable to Michele, and I apologize to both of you for thinking the worst of you and the situation. Please forgive me."

Alex said, "Yes and forgive me. I had almost written off our friendship, knowing that without the two of you, Alice and I would never have carried off a plan to get married in secret. So please forgive us."

Sean and Michele both said, "Of course! That is why we are here. We have some more news to tell you or ask you would be the more appropriate way to put it."

Michele said, "Now that we are both married but didn't get a wedding, I was wondering if you would want to have a double wedding with Sean and I on Christmas Eve night, during your father's evening church service. Before you say no, we've already spoken with your dad, not about you but about us, and he has agreed. I thought if you wanted to, you could call your dad and tell him that you and Alex would like for him to remarry you, too. That way he gets to walk you down the aisle and your mom gets to fluff your veil and we both get the wedding we've always wanted. I didn't have a wedding dress. I got married in the dress I wore to your ceremony, and Sean wore his suit."

"If we do this, it will be the wedding of all weddings. Since your mom is an interior decorator and my parents own a catering company, it's all covered. Alex's mom can do our flowers. I think we have it all covered."

Alice's eyes were wide, and the wheels were turning. She was thinking about finals. The drive back was a two day drive and they would be tired, but she so wanted a wedding.

She looked at Alex, and he knew what he needed to say. "Yes babe, let's have a wedding."

Alice spoke with both her parents, who were over the moon about the idea. Her mom said she would fly down this weekend and go dress shopping with her.

Alex knew his mom would want to be involved, too, so he called his parents. They too were over the moon and their mothers were on their way.

It was settled. There was going to be a wedding in about three weeks. There was lots of work to be done. In the meantime the couples were ecstatic to know that they would forever share a special day together. Even if it wasn't their original day of marriage, it would become their day going forward. They were all so thrilled that God was working things out.

It was late and Sean was tired. They decided to spend the night but not at Alex and Alice's apartment. They wondered if the little bed and breakfast across the street from Mr. and Mrs. Johnson's house was available. They called and sure enough there was room. They left their friends and headed to the bed and breakfast. They barely made it to their room before Sean reached for his wife, and she gladly submitted to his warm and loving embrace.

CHAPTER TWENTY EIGHT

Finishing Touches

Finals were over. They packed up and were ready to leave. Alex's dad said the two days of driving would be way too much and would take away from the time they needed to put the finishing touches on the wedding plans. Therefore, he paid for first class, round trip tickets for the two couples. They planned to meet Sean and Michele at the airport and leave their cars there.

They arrived early in the afternoon, and all the parents were at the airport waiting. The moms had just been to Oklahoma a week ago helping Alice and Michele pick wedding dresses. They were amazed at all the different styles of dresses. The mothers couldn't agree on which dress looked best, strapless, long sleeved, chiffon, taffeta, ball room gown, or thin spaghetti strap.

Michele and Alice knew exactly what they had in mind. They had been planning their weddings since they were little girls. Also, secretly they went one Saturday morning together and chose their dresses. They didn't tell their moms and swore the owner of the bridal boutique to secrecy. They explained that they really didn't have a lot of time, but they needed to make a decision and that the dresses they had chosen would be the very last dress they tried on. They just wanted their moms to have the experience. The shop owner totally understood and thought it was very thoughtful and loving of the girls to go ahead and try on dresses to please their moms.

Alice chose a sweet heart ball gown with floral beaded embroidery. It was perfect for her. When she tried her dress on, her mom smiled with tears and said, "Alice, that is the dress."

Alice smiled. She knew her mom would approve of the dress but having her approve of the price tag was an entirely different matter. She smiled and said, "Mom, this dress is expensive. I can choose something else."

Her mom looked at the price and didn't blink. She said, "This is the dress. Your dad told me to tell you that love has no price." Alice was happy. She would have the wedding of her dreams.

Michele's dress was totally different. She chose an off the shoulder, feathered, fitted organza gown with sequined tulle with a feather detailed train. Her mom had the same reaction regarding the cost of the gown. Both gowns were exquisite and individually matched the girls' personalities.

They were excited to be home. The couples had agreed the men would stay at their parents' homes and the ladies would stay at their parents' homes. They wanted this wedding to look and feel as much like a real wedding as possible, so they were going back to how things would have looked had they not already been married. It was back to the basics for them.

Alex and Sean went directly from the airport to the tuxedo shop to be sure their tuxedos fit. Then, they needed to help decorate the church and fellowship hall. Since the wedding was Christmas Eve, they didn't want to have to leave for a reception. Everyone would be at the Christmas

Eve and wedding service. Those that wouldn't be there were either out of town or truly weren't friends of the families.

The guys were amazed at the details these moms and dads had gone to in making sure that their wives had an amazing wedding day. The ladies were at a special bridal shower tea that had been planned by Alex and Sean's moms. Since they didn't have daughters, they wanted to do something for their new daughters.

The tea was held at one of the prestigious country clubs. Again no money was spared. The ladies were showered with everything from expensive perfume to furnishings for their new homes. They had an amazing time.

At one point Alice whispered to her friend, "How will we get all of this back to Oklahoma? Since we flew, what in the world will we do?"

Michele said, "I'm sure our parents will either ship everything to us or volunteer to bring it to us." Both ladies laughed because they knew it was true.

The bridal shower fit for two queens ended several hours later. Alice and Michele were exhausted to say the least. They were picked up and driven home in a limousine as a gift from their dads.

When Alice arrived home, her dad was in his office working on his Sunday sermon. She had only got to kiss him at the airport. Then, she and Michele were whisked off to the bridal shower. She knocked at the door, and her dad looked up with a smile. "Looks like you are deep in preparing your sermon for Sunday," she said.

Her dad responded with a smile and said, "How were your grades this semester? There was a lot going on, and then you threw in a wedding."

Alice said, "To be honest I don't know. I think I did okay, but you just never know. I studied and did my best, and worst case scenario, I didn't get all A's. I'm good with that though."

Her dad said, "I have all the confidence that you knocked it out of the ball park."

She said, "I hope so because you know I'm on scholarship and I have to keep a certain grade point average or I could lose my scholarship."

"That is not going to happen, so don't even say it," he said.

She was truly tired and started to yawn. "I'm sorry. I'm just tried."

He said, "Go to bed and let me finish my sermon, missy."

She chuckled and made her way to her room.

Alex was calling as soon as she slipped into bed. "Hello, beautiful," he said.

"Hello back, handsome, I miss you. This sleeping arrangement feels funny to me. I'm used to being in your arms at night. Now all I have is a pillow to hold onto," Alice said.

"I know, I feel the same way, but we really have to do this for our parents. They deserve to be honored this way, really they do," Alex said.

Alice knew he was right. She wasn't upset that they had made the arrangements; she just missed him.

They said goodnight, I love you and miss you, and hung up. Alice was asleep before she could hang the phone up. She was still exhausted when morning came. She could hear her parents giggling, and she knew they were being romantic. After all these years they were still in love. She hated that her decision to marry caused friction in their marriage. That made her teary eyed, but everything was okay now. In her heart if she had thought it through and had known things would have been as rough as they were, she was not sure she would have gone along with the plan, but then she thought about her father in law's conversion and knew this was God's plan.

Alice smiled as she thought one more day and she would officially again be Mrs. Alex Charles Davis. Since the wedding was tomorrow and her and Alex's birthdays were the next day, she thought she would go birthday shopping for him. She hadn't spent much money on Christmas shopping either. She needed to finish.

It was still early, but the shops opened early since it was two days before Christmas. Time flew by. As though it could read her mind, the phone rang.

"Hello," Alice said.

"What are you doing?" the other voice on the phone asked. It was Michele.

"I'm getting ready to do some serious Christmas and birthday shopping," Alice replied.

"I'll pick you up. I'm dressed and can be there in ten minutes." Michele's parents lived directly across the street, but she knew Alice was not ready. She drove across the street, honked three times, and Alice came running out the door.

"To the mall," they said, and off they went. Their little town didn't really have a big mall, so they traveled the hour to Savannah and did some serious shopping. They had all day and only today to get it done!

Alice and Michele were able to purchase gifts for everyone. Many times through their day they went in different directions to purchase gifts for each other individually as well as for each other as couples. They literally shopped until they dropped.

Michele was glad she took her dad's SUV because they needed it. Alice looked at Michele and said, "How much money did you spend? I hope you spent more than I did."

Michele said, "I'm not that worried about it. My aunt whose cottage I stay in gave me a nice check and told me to spend it how I wanted to. So I spent it loving on my family and friends."

Michele continued, asking, "What did you get Alex for his birthday gift?"

Alice smiled and said, "I wanted to get him a watch like my dad's with engraving, but they couldn't get it done before Christmas. I found a book on the history of ministry that my dad has. He is always studying from it. I also bought him gift set of my favorite cologne for men," Alice said "I purchased him a wedding gift, too."

Michele said, "Great minds think alike! I purchased Sean a wedding gift, too." They sat silently in the car for a few minutes before Alice said, "I wouldn't want to share my wedding day with anyone but you and Sean. I know Alex feels the same way."

Michele had tears streaming down her face. She was too choked up to respond. She just grabbed her friend's hand tight.

They had a bond and there was no doubt that the scripture iron sharpening iron was talking about them.

Michele helped Alice carry in all of the bags and boxes. They took them to the attic, because Alice knew no one would dare go there. She also had all of her wrapping papers, scissors, tape, bows, and bags there. That was her space, and everyone knew it.

Alice then ran across the street to help Michele. She didn't have an attic space, but she had a closet within a closet that was huge. They stored her bags there. Alice hugged her friend and across the street she ran. It was late, and she had only spoken with Alex a few minutes to say I love you and I'll see you tomorrow. She sent kissing sounds through the phone and hung up.

As Alice came into the house, her mom was sitting in the living room reading. She walked over and kissed her on the cheek. Her mom looked up and said, "What is that for?

This is going to be the greatest wedding Georgia has ever seen."

Her mom smiled and said, "You know this was not done by me only. Alex's parents contributed quite a lot of money too, as well as Judge Brooks and his wife, not to mention Michele's parents. We just want you four to be happy. There were lots of mistakes made at the beginning, and God has truly given us a chance to give him honor with our attitudes and actions by giving back to each other as parents as well as friends. We've known each other for so very long, we have always felt like family, but you, Alex, Sean, and Michele have shown us with your friendship what that truly looks like."

Alice said, "I'm so tired, but I need to wrap all of these gifts!"

Before her mom could volunteer her help, Alice said, "No, you may not help me. There are gifts I don't want you to see, so you can't help this time."

Her mom made a pouting mouth and then smiled. Alice left and headed to the attic, where she wrapped gifts until three o'clock in the morning. When everyone woke up, her gifts were under the tree, meticulously wrapped as if they had come from a department store. It was just one of her many talents.

When her mom entered the family room where the Christmas tree was standing, she smiled and said, "My baby has been hard at work. Today is her day." Then, she prayed, "Lord, today is Alice and Michele's special day. Not only are they doing this to honor their parents, but they all got married first to honor you. They aren't perfect, but these young people need your guidance in their marriages. Bless them, Lord. Provide for their every need as your word says you will. I know you love them more than we do as their parents, and we trust you with them. I'm asking you let this day be a blessing to Alice, Michele, Alex, and Sean. Allow us as their parents to set a Godly example tonight as they say their vows. Be with my dear husband as he not only walks Alice down the aisle but as he performs this very special ceremony tonight. Be with me, Lord, as his Help Meet and the other wives and fathers, too. I love Jesus. I glorify your name, and I ask you to get glory out of this entire day and our lives. In your name I pray. Amen!"

She had done what she was supposed to do. She had gone before all of them and prayed. She knew that the prayers of the righteous availeth much! She was humming a tune, and when her husband came into the room. she was still staring at the Christmas tree. He looked at the meticulously wrapped gifts and said, "Alice." He knew his daughter well, too!

CHAPTER TWENTY NINE

Wedding Blessings

The day went by so fast. It was Christmas Eve. Alice sat in her bedroom waiting for her mom to say it was time to go. The wedding would start at six o'clock sharp. Her dad would perform the normal Christmas Eve service at four o'clock, and those who were participating in the wedding would stay. Then, they would give them time to take their places for the ceremony.

Alice heard a knock on the door. "Yes," she replied.

It was her dad. "May I come in, Pumpkin?" he asked.

"Yes, daddy," she said softly.

He said, "It's two o'clock, and we need to get ready to go, but before we go I have a little gift for you."

He handed her a small box that was exquisitely wrapped. Alice knew that neither her dad nor mom had wrapped this gift. That was not their talent.

She slowly opened the gift and discovered a beautiful necklace. It was a gold locket with a small diamond cross in the center. At the bottom of the cross were the initials ATD-Alice Taylor Davis. On the back it read, "To my Pumpkin, love Daddy."

She opened the locket, and there was a small picture of Alice, Alex, her dad, and mom, and Alex's parents that was taken right after Alex's dad left the hospital.

Alice said, "Daddy, this is so beautiful. I love it! When did you get this done?"

"I had it made right after you called and asked your mom and me if you could have a wedding with Sean and Michele. I wanted you to have something special when you walk down the aisle tonight," he said.

Her mom joined them and said, "Aww, you gave it to her."

"Mom, have you seen this?" Alice asked.

Her mom replied, "Yes, I was with your dad when he had it made. It's really beautiful. Would you like for me to put it on you?"

Instead Alice wanted her dad to do it, and he couldn't quite get the clasp in his fingers, so his wife helped him. This was a moment that would be sketched in her mind forever.

They arrived at the church at three o'clock. Neither Alice nor Michele had seen the sanctuary or the fellowship hall decorated for a Christmas wedding. Instead the two were ushered off into separate rooms to get ready for the wedding. They would be able to hear her father preach the Christmas Eve service over the intercom system, but they needed to get dressed. There were two of everything, two hairdressers, two professional makeup artists to do their makeup, two personal assistants to get them whatever they needed, two photographers to take candid pictures of each of them, and their moms were with them. Alex's mom and Sean's mom were with them as well. The men would take care of their sons, but they wanted to be with their new daughters and so they were.

Alice slipped into her dress. She immediately looked like a beautiful queen. She wore a tiara in her thick black hair that had been twisted into a French roll with curls falling around her face. She wore the necklace her dad had given her, which was her new. Her something old came from Alex's mom, a beautiful gold and diamond comb for her hair to hold her French roll. Her something borrowed came from her mom, which was her earrings and tennis bracelet. Her something blue came from Michele's mom, a laced blue handkerchief to dry her tears.

Michele's scene was much the same. When she came from behind the curtain, her mom stood there and looked for a while. Michele was a vision of beauty with her dark auburn hair that had been twisted into a roaring twenty style. Cascading curls fell in the back. She looked like a portrait standing there. Michele's mom handed her a beautifully wrapped box. When she opened it, there were diamond tear drop earrings, necklace, and bracelet to match.

Michele looked at her mom and said, "You and daddy have spent way too much on this wedding. I can't take this! It must have cost you a fortune!"

Her mother looked at her and said, "This is not just from me and your dad. Judge Brooks and his wife also paid for this. It's from all of us."

Then, Mrs. Brooks came into the room. Michele had tears in her eyes. Mrs. Brooks embraced her new daughter and said, "Michele, we are so very happy that Sean chose you. When you were interning for my husband, he told me that he thought you were the one for Sean. I told him not to say a word because that would make Sean not talk to you or think of you in that manner. We prayed that God would put the two of you together, and he did."

"I'm so glad you like your jewelry. Now you need something old."

A knock came at the door, and a bag from Alice was handed to them to give to Michele with a note attached.

"This is your something old. I love you. See you soon."

When Michele looked in the bag, it was the other half of their friendship ring. Michele thought she had lost hers a long time ago, but over the Thanksgiving holiday Alice found it in the attic. She took it to the mall to have it polished, and it looked brand new. Michele was overcome with love for her friend. She now had her something old and new but she needed her borrowed and blue.

In came Mrs. Taylor with her borrowed and blue. She handed her a beautiful handkerchief that was blue. It had been a gift from her beloved husband a few years back. She wanted Michele to borrow it. After all, Michele was like a daughter to her.

The women were set. They had their something old, something new, something borrowed, and something blue, and they both said no pennies in our shoes. Instead they sent one penny each to the men to place in their shoes. It was exciting for everyone.

The men seemed to be more nervous than the women. Alex was pacing the floor. His dad came into the room.

"What's wrong Alex?" his dad asked.

"I'm not sure. I've got a knot in my stomach, my mouth is dry, and I feel like I'm going to pass out," Alex said.

His dad said, "You're just nervous and that is to be expected. There are a lot of people out there waiting to see you and your bride. Do you realize that many of these people don't even know you and Alice are already married? I know for a fact none of them know that Sean and Michele are married. So this is actually the real deal."

Alex said, "Have you seen Alice?"

His dad said, "Let's sit down, son."

He began with, "I love you, Alex, and again I'm so very sorry for the heartache my actions caused you and Alice. I now know that this is God's will. I know you're nervous because of the crowd of people here, but remember all of these are here to celebrate you, Alice, Sean, and

Michele. Your obedience to Christ will speak volumes to other young people who desire to follow Christ."

Alex knew his dad's transformation was real. He was thankful that God had given him back that dad he grew up with, but this time his dad had a little something extra called compassion. He had never known this man but longed to get to know him better.

Alex said, "Thank you so much. You just don't know how much it means to me for you to be here and be my best man today."

They hugged and his dad said a silent prayer thanking God for allowing him to repent and see God's favor on his and his family's life.

Sean entered the room with his dad, Judge Brooks, who said, "It's time for us to take our places, gentlemen." He would be Sean's best man today.

The men took their places. When Sean and Alex entered the sanctuary and saw Mr. Johnson, their hearts were full. He had made another trip within weeks to be there to officiate their wedding, and they both were filled with joy.

Once they took their places at the front of the church, a song began to play. They noticed some other familiar faces. Wes Johnson was getting ready to sing, Mrs. Johnson was at the piano, David Brown, Alex's college friend and house counselor, was playing the saxophone, and the one that threw them off the most was the police officer, Beaux, who was playing guitar. The song was called, "Now What."

Wes began to sing, "Now what sweet Jesus, please tell me what to do, now what sweet Jesus, please help me follow through, oh tell me what to do, help me follow through."

As he was singing the mothers of the brides and grooms were being seated in their proper places. The lights were dimmed and the wedding march played.

Alice was the first to enter with Pastor Taylor holding her steady. He whispered "You look so very beautiful. I'm so blessed to walk you down the aisle to a man I love and respect and most of all a man that loves Jesus. I know this is your destiny from God. I love you."

Alice replied "Thank you, Daddy, for all of this. The decorations, my dress, all of the things I truly wanted in a wedding you've given me and so much more. I'm so grateful and blessed to have you as my father."

Pastor Taylor said, "Shall we walk?"

Alice nodded her head and down the aisle they went.

Alex couldn't take his eyes off of Alice. He was no longer nervous and his father noticed the transition of confidence in his son. This further gave him confirmation from God that Alice Elizabeth Taylor was the woman God wanted his son to marry. Alex met Alice and her dad at the end of the aisle and took her hand. They moved to their position making room for their best friends.

It was Michele's turn to walk down the aisle. As she stood at the back of the church with her dad, she was overwhelmed with the beautiful decorations of gold, silver, white, and clear lights strung throughout the sanctuary. It looked as though she was in a winter wonderland globe that she had seen in a store window one day. However, this was her wedding day, shared with family and her closest friends. Her dad was the most soft-spoken man of all the fathers.

He said, "Michele." He had to say her name twice because of his soft voice.

She turned to him and he said, "I want you to know how very proud I am of you. You waited on God's best for you in a husband, and I couldn't be more proud of you and Sean. I know you'll be happy. I thank God for the blessing of a Godly son in law and Godly in laws. I'm overwhelmed today with all the blessings God has bestowed on my family."

Michele knew her dad had been praying for her all of her life. She grew up with his soft spoken spirit and his commitment to serving God.

Michele looked at her dad and said, "I love you so much. Thank you so much for being the standard of the man I'd want to marry one day. Sean has all of those qualities. He's gentle, kind, giving, and wise when it comes to finances and following Christ. He is a man that I want to submit to, just like I submitted to you when I was growing up. You made it easy with the love you showed me and mom."

Her dad had to wipe his eyes before they started down the aisle.

Sean was waiting on his wife/bride at the end of the aisle. He held out his hand for Michele's, and her father placed her hand in Sean's. The couple took their place, and Mr. Johnson started by saying a prayer and talking briefly about each couple and his experience with them. He talked about forgiveness, love, forbearing one another, mistakes, misunderstanding, moving forward, and allowing God to have his way in your children's lives, even when you aren't sure about the direction they may be going.

He told the congregation that Mary had been overcome by the Holy Spirit and was pregnant with a child, but Joseph had to trust that when the angel Gabriel came to him, that it was from God. He went on to tell them that even though Mary and Joseph knew what had happened, many people did not know. He spoke so eloquently that he himself was surprised at the words God was placing in his mouth. These were not these words he had prepared.

He stared at Alex and Alice as he gave them the command of God regarding marriage. They repeated their vows, and he asked for the rings. Alice was amazed when Alex slipped a diamond ring onto her finger. She thought they would use their same wedding bands. However, as a wedding gift, his dad had taken him shopping and told him to buy Alice whatever he wanted her to have. The princess cut one carat diamond ring their original band that had been changed a little with diamonds on it as well was so beautiful. Alice almost couldn't contain herself. Alex too was surprised when Alice slipped a different ring on his finger. This ring had a cross on it and on either side had an "A" with a diamond in the center of each. The A's were for Alice and Alex. He smiled at her and gave her a wink of approval.

Mr. Johnson moved on to Sean and Michele. As they said their vows they, like their friends, had surprised each other with new wedding rings. Michele was given a heart shaped diamond ring that had a matching band with hearts all around it. Sean's ring looked much like Alex's ring. It had a cross with their initials on each side.

It was now Mr. Johnson's turn to say the magic words, "Gentlemen, you may now kiss your brides."

Their kisses were short and sweet. The crowd stood and clapped in approval. The couples turned to face the crowd, and Mr. Johnson said, "It is my privilege to introduce to you on my left, Mr. Alex and Alice Davis and on my right Mr. Sean and Michele Brooks."

The couples made their way down the aisle, where the wedding coordinator escorted them to the fellowship hall to begin their reception.

They entered a room that took the couples' breath away. They knew that Mrs. Taylor had worked really hard to make the fellowship hall look like one of the finest country clubs in the state of Georgia. The tables had white linen table cloths with centerpieces of a different nativity scene. The place settings were gold chargers with plates, flatware made of gold, and crystal that shimmered and looked like diamonds. The lighting had been replaced with chandeliers. The chairs had coverings of white with gold sashes with their initials on them.

They stood in the room silently to take in all that was done for them. Truly they served a mighty God.

Sean said, "Did you all hear the song, "Now what?"

They all said yes. He said, "Did you know that Wes wrote that song for us because we are always saying now what?"

Alice said, "I didn't get to hear it all, but what I heard was beautiful."

They all agreed. The coordinator asked them to sit at their designated tables so that the guests could join them. They needed to remember it was Christmas Eve. They wanted to be respectful of their guests and had requested that everything end by 10:00 p.m. so their guests could get home to rest to celebrate Christmas.

Their reception was as it should be with lots of well wishes, hugs, kisses, and prayers. The guests started to leave after they all enjoyed a light but filling mix of Christmas hors d'oeuvres, appetizers, and snacks. Everything from wedding cake to small quiches shaped like Christmas trees and small ham, turkey, and chicken sandwiches was served. Once the last guest left, the couple looked at their parents who were all at one table including Mr. and Mrs. Johnson and said, "Now what?"

Everyone in the room started laughing. Pastor Taylor looked at Mr. and Mrs. Johnson and the other guests from Oklahoma and said, "You have made such a sacrifice to leave your homes for Christmas. Please come and spend the holiday with my family."

Mr. Graham, Michele's dad, said, "I'm sorry, Pastor Taylor, but you know that little cottage down the street from us that was for sale?"

Pastor Taylor said, "Yes, I know the place."

"My wife and I purchased that property about a month ago. We thought if Michele decided to come back this way, we would gift it to her and Sean. However, right now it's vacant, and my wife, along with your wife and Mrs. Davis, has decorated the place. The Johnsons and their guests will be staying there. We've stocked it up with Christmas food and that way they can have Christmas as though they were at home," said Mr. Graham.

Pastor Taylor shook his head and said, "No one tells me anything anymore."

Meanwhile the happy couples had started to clean up the fellowship hall. All of a sudden Mrs. Taylor yelled, "What do you think you are doing? We've paid someone to come in, pack up the leftover food, take it to the children's shelter, and clean up the church for us. So please sit down or get out!"

They all started laughing.

CHAPTER THIRTY

Christmas Question

The couples woke up on Christmas morning still reeling from the wedding of a lifetime. They were staying at the Country Club Lyonsville Hotel. Their parents had reserved them the honeymoon suite. To their surprise, this hotel hosted several honeymoon suites. Alice and Alex were on the 8th floor and Sean and Michell were on the 12th floor.

The couples stayed to themselves on Christmas morning and left the hotel at noon to join their families to celebrate Christmas. Although it was Alex and Alice's 19th birthdays, they were still consumed with wedding bliss.

Alice looked at her husband and said, "Your parents or mine first?"

He said, "Let's start with mine and end with yours. We'll leave our things at the garage apartment on our way to my parents' house. How does that sound?"

Alice smiled and said, "That sounds like a solid plan, husband of mine," She was happy. God had answered her prayers.

Dr. Davis answered the door when Alice and Alex came.

"Merry Christmas and Happy Birthday to my newlyweds," he said with a huge grin and a bear hug to boot.

They were excited as well to see him. Alex's mother came and ushered them quickly into the family room where Alex's two sisters and brother in laws were waiting. The family opened gifts, but first they wanted to give them their birthday gifts. Before they could begin, the phone rang.

Of course Alice knew her dad's voice. He said, "I take it they are there?"

"Yes, they are in my study with me and Joan. Is Dianne there with you?" Charles asked.

"Yes she is," Pastor Taylor said.

Charles began, "We know that you two are very comfortable in Oklahoma going to school. We also know that Alice has a full ride and Alex you don't. Now hear us out. We have a proposition for the two of you. As your parents we just can't stand that you are so far away. Of course your plans are to come back to Lyonsville to live once you finish with your studies. Is that correct?"

They both nodded yes.

Then Pastor Taylor said, "Alex, I spoke with the board of directors and you know that our youth minister has accepted a new position in Dallas, Texas. That leaves me in quite the bind. Since you're going to be a pastor, I've asked the board to approve paying the difference of your tuition if you'd come on board part time as the youth pastor while you're in school, and once you graduate, the position will be yours full time. The other part of this is that we will pay for your insurance."

Alex said, "That sounds great, but what about Alice? I can't be here in Lyonsville while she's in Romans."

His dad said, "That is just the first part of the proposal. The second part is I've asked South Care Medical University if they'd honor your scholarship. Anything that is not covered, the hospital has agreed to cover if you agree to come into my practice as the new pediatrics resident. It's all in place if you want to move back home once you finish your year in Oklahoma."

Alice and Alex both looked at each other.

Alex said, "Can we have a few minutes to talk? This is a lot to consider. We do need to talk first before we give an answer."

The parents agreed to give them some time. Alex's dad said, "The other gift will have to wait until we find out your answer because it won't make sense."

They joined the other family members, exchanged gifts, and ate Christmas food. Alex and Alice couldn't eat much because they still needed to go to her parents' house.

They said their goodbyes and told his mom and dad they'd have an answer tomorrow. They arrived at Alice's parents' house right at six p.m. Alice's dad's greeting was pretty much the same, "Merry Christmas and Happy birthday to my newlyweds."

The conversation was light, and her dad had promised his wife he wouldn't push them to make a decision. He'd let God do his bidding for him. They exchanged gifts, laughed, and played games. It was quiet at Alice's parents' house, and she personally was thankful for that, especially after the last few days of running. She was ready to settle down.

Her mom said, "I freshened up the attic for you for tonight." Alice was sad to have to tell her that they were going to stay at the garage apartment for the rest of the time until they went back to Oklahoma. However, her mother completely understood and was okay with their plans.

They said their goodbyes for the second time and drove to the garage apartment. Alex's sister and brother in law had refurnished the apartment. It had a fresh coat of paint and really looked nice.

Alex thought it would be fun to carry Alice over the threshold but almost fell. She quickly jumped out of his arms so they wouldn't get hurt. He forgot from time to time that his leg was still weak, and he couldn't do everything he used to do. They laughed it off, settled down in the living room, and both were quiet for a while.

Alice spoke first. "So what do you think of the proposal from our parents?"

Alex looked at her and said, "It's a good opportunity for me to grow closer with your dad and learn firsthand what it looks like to be the youth pastor for a large church. But I also think that God sent us to Oklahoma. What are your thoughts?"

Alice said, "I feel the same way. While I would love to work in your dad's clinic and learn from him, it feels as though God commissioned us to be in Oklahoma."

Alex said with a heavy sigh "Now what?"

Alice said, "I know the now what. We need to pray and ask God to make it crystal clear what we should do."

Alex took her hands and said, "Let's ask Him what we should do."

They bowed their heads and Alex prayed, saying, "Lord, we've followed you from the very beginning, and we are not going to stop now. This offer our parents have placed before us is an amazing offer, but everything that glitters isn't gold. If this is not your will, then it could all go south quickly. Also, our families have just been mended, and if we say no, they may feel like we are rejecting their love and kindness. We don't want that to happen either. Therefore, please show us what to do, and we'll be sure to follow through by obeying you. In your son Jesus' name we pray. Amen."

They were tired and just wanted to sleep. They knew God would give them an answer. It may not be the answer they wanted, but certainly they would get an answer.

It was early afternoon when their wedding partners came banging on the door. Alex looked out the door. There stood his friends with bags in their hands. Alex opened the door to let them enter. By that time Alice had joined them in the living room with a tired smile on her face.

"Hey guys, what time it is?" she asked.

Michele smiled and said, "It's one o'clock in the afternoon."

Alice said, "Are you kidding me?" Alice couldn't believe she had slept so late. She was always a morning person. However, she remembered all the things she had done in the last month.

Alex said, "How did you know where we were? Did we tell you?"

Sean said, "No, Michele went to Alice's parents' house thinking you stayed in the attic apartment, and her mom said you were here. We thought we would bring you some breakfast/lunch. We had no idea you would still be sleep. Anyway we have some news to share with you."

Alice said, "Let me clean up really quick, and I'll help Michele get the food set up. Then, we can all talk. We have some information to share with you, too."

They sat at the table and prayed before they ate. Sean said, "Yesterday my dad had a few friends over for Christmas brunch. One of the men has a pretty big law firm in Savannah. His law firm has offered me and Michele a position when we finish law school. The blessing is if we move back here and go to school at the Southwestern School of Law, they will pay for our entire education."

Alice smiled and said, "Have you made a decision yet?"

Michele said, "We didn't want to give a knee jerk reaction, so we prayed and asked God to please lead the way for us. Yes, we'll be closer to home and we are guaranteed a job, but God can do all of that too if we say no. I know we'll have the cottage to live in that my dad purchased for us, but it just has to be God's plan, too. It would be so good to be close to our parents, but I we want God's will."

Alex said, "We were offered something similar to that last night from our parents as well."

Sean said, "Have you made a decision yet?"

"No," Alex said. "We prayed last night, and we are waiting on God to give us an answer."

The couples sat in silence, knowing in their hearts they would love to come home in the spring, but they also knew they must wait for God to direct them.

CHAPTER THIRTY ONE

The Answer is Clear

It was a few days before the couples needed to go back to school. The New Year had come and gone. Neither couple had a clear answer yet. They were praying every day. It was frustrating, yet they knew they must wait. Their parents were being very patient with them, knowing that they'd need to wait on God as well.

Alice and Michele had arranged to spend time together before they left. When Michele arrived, she looked pale to Alice.

Alice said, "Michele, what is wrong? You look like you don't feel well."

Michele said, "I don't feel well at all. I have gone to the doctor and they don't know what is going on either. I've been tired for a long time, but I thought it was just all the things that were going on, with cramming for finals, the wedding, and other things. I'm taking vitamins, but I'm not getting better. I'm so irritable, and my moods are up and down. I've lost like fifteen pounds in a few months, and I'm not trying to lose weight."

Alice said, "Sit down. She then called her father in law. He answered immediately, thinking they had an answer for him.

She said "Dr. D., this is Ali. I have an issue, and I need your help."

He said, "Sure Ali, what is going on?"

She gave him the run down on what was going on with Michele. He advised her to bring her to his office immediately. Once she and Michele were at the office, she called Alex and told him that he and Sean needed to come to his dad's office.

Sean was nervous. He kept saying what could be wrong. He came up with pregnancy to cancer and everything in between. Once they arrived, Alice brought them into Alex's dad's private office. He was still examining Michele when they got there.

Dr. Davis came in and then Michele joined them. Dr. Davis said, "Let me say that Michele will be fine. However, she will need to change some things in her life, diet, exercise, and stress level to name a few.

Sean looked at Dr. Davis and said, "What is wrong with my wife, Dr. Davis? Please tell me."

Dr. Davis said, "I told Michele I would let her tell you."

Michele cleared her throat and said, "I have type one diabetes. I don't know a lot about it, but I know that my grandmother had it when I was growing up. She passed away when I was in middle school."

Dr. Davis said, "There is no reason why Michele can't have a normal life. I will start her on medication and refer her to a diabetic specialist. Today I want her to go home and rest, stay off the sweets and carbs, and focus on more vegetables and water. I have a booklet for you to take home and read."

Michele looked sad, and immediately Sean said, "Michele, with God all things are possible. We will learn everything about this disease. We can take classes and do what we need to so you'll live a long, healthy life." He meant every word.

They left Dr. Davis's office and headed home. Michele and Sean needed to go talk. She was scared, and he was, too, but he knew God had a plan. They headed to her parent's house and shared the news with them.

Michele's mom said, "Oh honey, I know you are scared but it's okay, I have type one diabetes, too. I'm very careful with my diet, and I make sure I keep my weight down so I stay healthy."

Michele looked at her mom and said, "Why didn't I know you had this?"

Her mom responded, "I didn't need to tell you. I am fine. I could have shared it with you, but I didn't think it was an issue. I can also say I thought you knew. I will help you with this."

Michele said, "How can you help me if I'm in Oklahoma and you're in Georgia?"

Sean didn't hesitate. He said, "This is our answer. We will finish our semester in Oklahoma, and then we'll come home. How does that sound?"

Michele smiled and said, "Sean, are you sure? You loved living in the row houses on campus."

Sean said, "You do remember that I would be moving from the row houses when we get back anyway and moving to the cottage with you."

Michele smiled and said, "All right, then we'll move back home. I guess we need to call your dad's friend and tell him we will accept his offer."

Sean said, "I'll talk to dad before we leave."

Alice was sitting on the sofa praying for her friends.

Alex came in from visiting with his sister and brother in law. He had been sharing what went on with Michele. They were all concerned but it wasn't a life threatening disease if handled well.

Alice said, "I'm concerned for Michele."

Alex said "I know you are, and I'm concerned, too, but I believe she'll be fine."

Michele laid down for the rest of the afternoon and slept. Sean didn't leave her side, napping with her. When she opened her eyes, he was looking at her and stroking her hair.

She smiled and said, "Whatcha doing handsome?"

He smiled and said, "Looking at my beautiful wife and loving you more today than the day I met you."

Michele said, "We need to tell Alice and Alex that this will be our last semester in Oklahoma. They need to know. Not that this will affect their decision to go or stay, but they need to know."

They agreed to go the next day and visit with their friends!

CHAPTER THIRTY TWO

Going Forward!

Alice woke up and was staring at the ceiling when Alex rolled over and said, "Good morning, Mrs. Davis."

She didn't respond, which made him think she was angry with him. They had talked with Sean and Michele who shared with them that after this semester, they would be returning to Georgia.

In light of Michele's diagnosis, it was best for her to be closer to her mom. Meanwhile since she was newly diagnosed, her mom would come and stay a few weeks out of the month until it was time to move back to Lyonsville. They had already planned to fly her home. Sean, his dad, and Michele's dad would pack up the cottage. Then, Michele's dad would drive her car, and Sean and his dad would drive his SUV and get it packed up. It was all settled.

Michele was adjusting to her new diagnosis and researching everything she could to know more about her condition. She realized that millions of people were living with type one diabetes, and a lot of them were also under twenty years old.

Alex leaned on one elbow facing her and said, "Okay, Ali. We've got to talk this out or it's just going to fester and cause more issues for us down the road. We've always said we would never let the sun go down on our anger." He was quoting the scripture from Ephesians 4:26. "Be angry, and sin not: let not the sun go down upon your wrath."

Alice was very familiar with this scripture. She knew he was right, but she didn't want to accept his decision.

Alice said, "You can't tell me if the shoe were on the other foot and this was Sean that you wouldn't want to stay in Lyonsville and help him get through this, or to even help Michele as well!"

Alex responded, "You are right. I would want to, but that doesn't mean I would do it. We both know that Michele has plenty of support. She has her mom and dad, Sean's parents, and my dad who has set her up with one of the best endocrinologists in the country, not to mention your mom and dad who are like second parents to her. She doesn't necessarily need you here. I know you want to be here, but is that what God has told us to do?"

Alice turned her head in defiance. She knew Alex was right, and she also knew to continue this argument would mean she wasn't trusting the direction God was leading her and Alex. She had promised to submit to his authority as the head of their home, which would build him up as a Godly husband, and she knew that if she fought this, God would not be pleased. She started crying and Alex held her in his arms.

"I love you so much, and I'm very sorry that at this time God hasn't given us permission to stay here in Lyonsville. You really don't know how much I wanted to jump at the chance to work with your dad in his church. It's growing so fast and the opportunity is so amazing, but until God says move. We must return to Romans and continue our journey there," he said.

Alice simply said, "I know."

Their day was busy. They needed to say their final goodbyes and head to the airport where they would meet Sean and Michele. It wasn't easy saying goodbye to their parents. They had had the difficult conversation for which God hadn't given them an answer; therefore, they had no answer to give them.

Alex said, "I'm speaking for both Alice and myself when I say we'd love nothing more than to work side by side with our parents in ministry and medicine, but right now God has not given us a green or red light. Pastor Taylor, I remember a sermon you preached where you said when you don't know how to move, stand."

Pastor Taylor nodded his head in approval. Dr. Davis said, "We love you two whether you're here with us or somewhere else. We wanted to hear the word yes, but more than anything we want God's will for your lives."

They were both so relieved with the conversation. Once again Alice's fears were put to bed. No one was angry, maybe a little disappointed, but no one was angry.

Sean and Michele were already at the airport waiting for them. When Alice saw Michele, she still looked weak to her, and Alice teared up. Michele approached her and said, "We need to talk."

Alice agreed. They found a little corner, and Michele began, "I know you've been fighting with Alex about not moving back to Lyonsville. You want to be here for me. We've always shared our lives. No matter what was going on, we were there for one another, but Alice, I'm not alone."

She held up her left hand and wiggled her ring finger, displaying her beautiful heart- shaped wedding ring.

"I have a wonderful, Godly husband in Sean, parents and in laws who love me too, and most of all I have Jesus. I hope you haven't forgotten about him. I am fine, and I will be fine. You will always be with me whether over the phone, in letters or text messages, or in person. We carry each other in our hearts," Michele said.

Alice knew her friend was right. She only wanted to support her, and Michele loved her for it.

They landed at the airport and shared their usual hugs. The men watched their wives cry like they were never going to see each other again although they were only forty five minutes away from each other. The men just didn't understand it, but they thought it was quite cute. They had to pull them apart as always.

Alice was silent on the way home, and Alex respected her silence. He knew she had to process everything that was going on. Classes would start on Monday, so they had the today and tomorrow to settle in and rest up for this semester.

Alice busied herself cleaning their little apartment. A knock at the door stopped her in her tracks. Ever since the incident with Mr. Dobson, her heart would skip a beat when someone unexpected came to the door. Alex sprang into action and answered. He looked through the tiny peephole to see Rhonda and David standing there. He opened the door and welcomed them in.

"Welcome back newlyweds," Rhonda said. "I made you dinner for tonight. I knew you would be tired from your trip, and I'm sure Alice doesn't feel like cooking."

Alice turned to her and smiled, saying, "Rhonda, you are the best. Thank you so very much for thinking of us."

Rhonda replied, "It's not much. I just made a tuna noodle casserole, salad, and for dessert I made my homemade German chocolate cake."

Alex had a huge grin on his face and then said, "Do we need ice cream?"

Rhonda smiled and said, "You know I didn't bring that, but you and David can run and get some if you would like."

The guys headed to the store while Alice and Rhonda got everything set up for the guys.

"Okay, out with it," Rhonda said with her hands on her hips.

Alice turned to her and said, "It's that obvious?"

"Yes," Rhonda said.

Alice sat down on the love seat, and Rhonda followed. Alice explained the situation with Michele and her desire to stay in Lyonsville after this semester and how Alex didn't want to do that.

Rhonda said, "Alex didn't say he didn't want to. He said God didn't say you could. There is a big difference between wanting to do something and waiting on God for approval. You know that. I'm sorry you're struggling with this, but until you get peace with God, you're going to be going through the motions. Eventually Satan will use this to place a wedge between you and your husband, and you don't want that."

Once again God was speaking to Alice through wise counsel. She had a decision to make either; obey God or disobey by having a grumbling spirit of discontent.

Rhonda prayed with Alice while the men were gone. They weren't aware that Alex was having his own conversation with David. It was very apparent that Alex wanted to give in to his wife's desire to move back home.

David said, "As husbands it is our duty to follow Christ. This is how our wives know they can trust us if we follow him. You said God hasn't given you a green light or a red light. That means wait, man. You need to wait, but while waiting, pray for Alice. She loves her friend and wants to be near her. The other thing you can do is every opportunity you have to get her and Michele together, do it. She will see your support in that. I would also advise you to make sure Alice hears you praying for Michele. She needs to know what is important to her is important to you even though you can't give her what she wants right now."

They prayed and made their way back to the food.

Alice took the rest of the weekend to get peace about their decision to stay in Romans, Oklahoma, for the time being with the plans to return next semester as well. Classes started, and it was a race for time. They both were carrying full loads. They received their final grades and

Alice was surprised to see she had straight A's. Alex was just as surprised to see he had done the same.

They made it through the week when they got a message from Sean that Michele was in the hospital. She became weaker once classes started. Her mom was on her way to Harmony to be with them.

Alex drove Alice to the hospital to be with her friend, and they decided to spend the weekend in Harmony. Michele looked weak, but she was resting comfortably. Sean said the doctors said that she was extremely dehydrated and had a urinary tract infection. This was all common with having diabetes, especially type one.

Michele wanted to talk with Alice alone, so the men excused themselves.

"Alice, I need you to do me a favor."

"Okay," Alice said.

"Listen to me closely. Stop worrying about me! I'm fine. This is just a disease that you have to stay on top of. I have to get lots of rest, drink plenty of fluids, and watch my diet. Once I got back here, I felt okay, so I slacked up a bit. This is just God's way of saying get back on track. I'm not going to die, Alice, so stop it. This crying and calling me every other day, girl you have got to get a grip on yourself. You are not my God, and I'm not yours either, so stop. Actually if I didn't know any better, I'd think you had no faith at all, and you've always been the stronger one when it came to quoting scripture and knowing what the word of God says," said Michele.

Alice was so surprised that Michele had spoken so candidly and that she wasn't very nice about it. However, she wasn't mean; it was just a matter of fact. Then, Michele sat up in the bed a little straighter. The nurse came in and gave her her medication and asked if she was hungry.

Michele said, "Actually I am."

The nurse gave her a menu, and Michele ordered baked chicken, a salad, and some strawberries.

The men came back in the room, and for some reason Michele looked healthier. They had no idea what had happened, but both women were back to their old selves and were laughing and talking. Alex and Sean shrugged their shoulders and went along with this new atmosphere of peace.

They parted on Sunday, but there was no long crying spell at all. Alice hugged Michele and said, "I'll see you in a few weeks."

Michele was being released from the hospital, and the college had agreed to send her work home. She could do the work from her home until she felt like coming back to class.

As they drove home, Alice turned to Alex and said, "Al, I'm sorry I've been so difficult these past few days. Please forgive me?"

Alex took her hand as he drove and said, "Thank you for that, but you're always forgiven. I've been praying for you and Michele both. I know she's your best friend/sister, and I hold that dear in my heart, believe me I do, but we must follow the path God has laid for us. Otherwise, we don't get his best for our lives."

They knew how important it was to stay on the same page with one another. A marriage divided would fall, and that was not what either of them wanted. Alice settled her spirit and knew God would take care of her friend. She remembered Romans 8:8, "And we know that all things work together for good to them who love God to them who are the called according to his purpose." She knew she could rest in this scripture for Michele, herself, Alex, Sean, their families, and friends.

She was ready to move to move ahead because the answer was clear now! She had gone through a now what crisis, and the answer was simple--not now--and she was okay with that.

CHAPTER THIRTY THREE

He Works In Mysterious Ways

It was official. They had finished their first year of college. They headed home to Lyonsville to be with family and friends. Sean and Michele were already there. They had left a couple of weeks earlier to get set up in their new home, the cottage with which their parents had surprised them.

Alice laughed. A cottage? All right, it was more like a mini mansion.

Alice knew things were falling right into place. She would be working with Alex's dad in his clinic and in the hospital while Alex would be working at her dad's church and his sister and brother in law's youth center. They moved back into the garage apartment for free. This was a sweet time. They were with family and friends once again.

Alice's first week at the clinic proved to be very hectic. Everyone was nice, and she was definitely going to learn a lot. Medical school was a ways off, and she was blessed to be getting all of this experience ahead of that time. Alex felt the same way.

Once a week they had one set of parents over for dinner. The tiny garage apartment couldn't hold more than that. When they all wanted to get together, they would go to one of their parents' houses or his sister would host it at hers. They all came back to Pastor Taylor's, church believing that a family that prayed and served together stayed together.

Dr. Davis had become a deacon in the church and served any and everywhere he was needed. He just wanted to be used by God. Sundays had become special to him because all of his family was with him at church and then a huge dinner afterwards. Usually they didn't leave until the evening, and that was okay by him and his wife Joan. They loved having the family over.

However, this particular Sunday was Mother's Day weekend, and they were having both families at their home. Pastor Taylor and Dr. Davis decided that they would grill and have the girls bring sides. The mothers didn't have to do anything. Joan and Dianne loved this because they knew they would be treated like royalty.

Alice loved being at the grill with her dad and father in law. She grew up grilling with her dad. He called her his assistant chef, and she loved it. She brought all the seasonings to him and watched him season his meat just right. He grilled the corn on the cob as well. She was right there in the thick of things. It had been unusually hot in the south, so she made sure she was drinking lots of liquids, too.

She was heading back outside to the pit to help with bringing in some meat when she felt lightly faint. She didn't think anything of it, so she just kept going. The food was done, and they all gathered inside to eat.

Alex and Alice presented their mothers with their framed college grades from their first year. They also wrote each other's mom a personalized letter saying how grateful they were for their support and love this past year. It was touching. Mrs. Davis's daughters called Alex a suck up, saying you know she'll like your gift more than ours since you're is so sentimental.

Everyone laughed. They started calling him baby boy, which was what Mrs. Davis called him until he went into middle school when he asked her to please stop calling him that.

Alice's head had started hurting, so she didn't eat much. She got up from the table but felt dizzy again, and this time Dr. Davis noticed it.

She politely excused herself, and when no one was watching, he waited outside the restroom. When she came out, he startled her and she jumped.

"I'm sorry, Dr. D.," she said, which was short for Dr. Dad.

"Alice what's wrong? I've noticed today you aren't yourself. You haven't been very steady on your feet. Are you okay?" he asked.

"Yes, I think it's the heat," she said.

He said, "Young lady, why don't you and I head down the hall to my office and let me do a quick examination?"

She tried to protest, but he gave her that loving, persistent fatherly look, and she agreed.

He said, "If it's nothing and just the heat, no harm done, but if it is something, then we can get a handle on it."

Alice said, "They'll be looking for us and get suspicious."

He said, "Watch this," and winked at her.

He yelled down the hall "Hey everyone, Alice and I are going into my office to go over some work things. We'll be back in a few."

They all yelled back, "Okay."

He smiled and knew they wouldn't bother them because they thought they were working. He thoroughly examined her, and when it was done, he smiled and said "Alice, have a seat. You have a low grade temperature, but you're also pregnant. I would say you're about four weeks if my calculations are right."

She looked at him and said, "Oh no, I can't be. We've been really, really careful, Dr. D. This will ruin everything. I can't have a baby. I'm only in my second year of college. I haven't even started medical school."

She was sobbing now. She continued, "How I could be so stupid? Also, the doctors said because of my endometriosis I probably couldn't conceive anyway." She looked at her father in law and said, "Are you sure absolutely sure?"

He said, "Alice, it's Sunday, and this will be our secret until we get all of the tests back, but my preliminary findings are that you are pregnant. Tomorrow come to the office an hour early, and I'll examine you again, and we'll send off the blood and urine tests to make sure. Then we'll know beyond a shadow of a doubt."

She agreed, still with tears.

He said, "Come on now, wipe away those tears, or we'll have to explain why you've been crying."

They stayed a little longer in his office and then came out. Everyone was having such a good time, they didn't even notice her little blotchy face except Alex.

He came to her and said, "Hey, are you okay?"

Before she could answer, his dad said, "She's got a low grade fever and she may need to go home and lie down. It is hot outside, and she's been running back and forth. I've asked her to come into the office tomorrow a little early so I can run a few tests to make sure she's not coming down with something."

Alex bought it hook, line, and sinker.

They said goodbye to the others, and everyone said, "We hope you feel better, Alice. We love you."

They made it home, and Alice didn't want to talk, so she took a quick shower and went right to bed. She was scared. She had already lost one child. She didn't want to go through that again.

"Oh Lord, please if I'm pregnant, let me carry this baby to term and protect this child. I know you know what's best, but this was not done intentionally. What will happen with my hopes and dreams of becoming a doctor and Alex becoming a youth pastor? We don't have the resources for a baby, but I want this baby if I'm pregnant. Please, Lord, help me. Let your will be done." And with that she was asleep.

She arrived at the clinic an hour early just as her father in law had asked. He performed the tests and sent them to the lab. They put the name Jane Taylor on them so no one would know, and Dr. Davis asked for a rush to be placed on it. It was early afternoon when his nurse bought the sealed lab results to him. He thanked her and then read them. POSTIVE! He smiled, thanked the Lord, and prayed a silent prayer of protection over his grandchild and daughter in law who he had learned to love.

The office was closing, and Alice hadn't heard anything from Dr. Davis. She thought to herself no news is good news. Maybe it was a false positive. That happened all the time when she worked in the ob-gyn department, so she knew it could happen. She was about to leave, so she stuck her head in Dr. Davis's office to say goodnight. He was on the phone and beckoned for her to come in and shut the door.

He hung up the phone and said, "I have your results."

She looked at him and his face didn't show any sign. He slid the lab results over to her. She read the results, positive for pregnancy. She dropped her head and tears flowed freely.

He came from behind his desk and held her in his arms, thinking how in the world could he ever have had any type of hurtful feelings toward this gentle and beautiful woman God had blessed his son with? It was a fleeting thought, and he knew that was behind him.

"Alice, it's going to be okay," Dr. Davis said.

She looked at him and said for the first time, "How you can be so sure?"

He smiled and said, "Because we serve a mighty, awesome, forgiving, and loving God. I know he makes no mistakes, Alice, and this baby is a gift. God will show you and Alex what to do next. Yes, this is a now what moment, but so what? Life is filled with now what moments, and we just have to let God give us the answers."

She was concerned for her health, school, Alex, money, and health insurance. All of this was on her mind and she just wanted to run away. She felt as though now she had become a burden to Alex, not a benefit. She wanted to have children one day but not now, and certainly not her sophomore year of college. She didn't know what to do and how to tell Alex. He would be so angry and yet he would act happy. This was more than anyone should have to bear, a wife who had become a financial liability.

As though he read her mind, Dr. Davis said, "I tell you what, why don't you call your parents and invite them over to my house for dinner Friday night? You hold on to this information, and you and I are going to bathe this in prayer. Friday morning you and I will tell Alex together and then we'll tell Joan and your parents Friday night. We will come up with a plan. Right now I'm going to prescribe you some prenatal vitamins that you can leave them here in my office and take when you're here. Once Alex knows, you can take them home."

She agreed with the plan but knew it would be hard to keep it from Alex.

The week seemed to move so slowly for Alice, but Friday morning proved to be even more difficult as she had to deal with her first bout of morning sickness. She was trying to vomit quietly but she couldn't. Alex heard her and came running into the bathroom. Her hair was damp, and she looked as though she had the flu.

"Alice, what's wrong? Do you need to go to the hospital?" he asked.

"No Alex, I'm fine. I think I may have eaten something that didn't settle well with my stomach."

She tried as quickly as she could to get out of the house without vomiting again. She got half way down the street away from their apartment and ha to pull her car over.. She did this several more times before getting to work. By the time she arrived, she was very tired. Dr. Davis saw her from his window. He knew immediately she was having morning sickness. He also knew they couldn't keep this information from Alex any longer.

He met her at the door and ushered her into his office. "Morning sickness, huh?" he said.

"Yes, in the worst way. I only had it once the last time. It wasn't this bad," she said.

He sat her down, giving her a few saltine crackers. "Eat these. They will help settle your stomach. I'm going to give you the day off with pay, and as soon as you think Alex has left the apartment, I want you to go home and go straight to bed, understand me?" he said with a loving smile.

She smiled but had tears in her eyes again. Dr. Davis lovingly hugged his daughter in law, reassuring her that everything would work out. He walked her to the car and slid a note in her hand and told her to read it after she was comfortably in bed.

Once Alice got home, she showered again and went to bed as instructed by her father in law. She opened a note that read, "Dear Alice, my sweet God given daughter, I'm so proud of you. I want you to know you are a gift to my son and my family. I know with everything in me you'll be okay and so will my grandchild. I know that you are scared, but you don't need to be because I will be right by your side, of course along with my loving son Alex. I just want you to rest in Jesus and know everything you need to be a great mom and one day a great doctor is inside of you. I won't let your dream of becoming a doctor die. I will help you in every way I can to reach your dreams. Please rest and I'll see you tonight. Love Dr. D."

Alex picked Alice up after he left the church. She had phoned him to let him know she was home. They drove in silence. Alex had a lot on his mind. He thought Alice was keeping something from him and didn't like that. He wanted them to always be honest. However, he also knew that in her time she would share with him. He always wanted to be the first to find out something was going on. He also knew that she worked with some nice looking doctors who were successful and had more to offer her than he did. His insecurities were talking to him, and he was trying really hard to fight those thoughts.

Alice was nervous. She didn't know what Alex would think when he found out she was pregnant. She wasn't sure if he would be angry or think she got pregnant on purpose. However, she had to calm her nerves. When they arrived, his dad was getting the mail and waited until they reached him. They all entered the home together. Mrs. Davis was in the kitchen cooking. Alex went straight to the family room, removed his shoes, and sat on the couch. He was emotionally and physically tired. His dad joined them and said, "Son, how was your day?"

Alex said, "It was okay, but I'm a little tired. How was your day?"

Alice was very nervously wondering how in the world they were going to get to the conversation at hand. She didn't need to worry because all of a sudden Alex said, "Did Alice tell you she was vomiting this morning? I'm concerned about her, and she's not telling me everything. I know she's hiding something, and I need her to tell me the truth. If she's sick, we need to deal with whatever it is."

Now it was out there, he thought, wondering how Alice was going to respond. However, he didn't expect her response. She started crying. He felt horrible. He didn't think she would start crying. He thought she would come out with what was going on. His dad was a doctor, and they seemed to have such a great relationship now.

Instead it was his dad who sat next to Alice and said, "Tell him, Alice. The time is now."

Alice reached into her purse and handed Alex the lab test that said she was pregnant. He looked at the paperwork and read it Positive! At first he didn't understand what that meant. Then, his dad pointed to the word pregnancy.

Alex looked at his wife and said, "Are you sure? How? I thought we were being careful and besides the doctor said we couldn't have children, remember?"

He really wasn't asking her a question; it was more of a statement. Alice wouldn't look at him until he moved to sit right next to her.

"Look at me, Ali." She looked up into his beautiful green eyes that were glistening from tears. "I'm not crying because I'm angry. I'm happy that we're going to have a baby. God is going to give us a family. Mr. Dobson didn't take anything from us." Then he quoted Psalms 84:11. "No good thing will be withheld from those that walk uprightly."

Alice fell into his arms, and he showered her with kisses and hugs.

Just then her parents walked in the door. They knew something very special had happened and they couldn't wait to hear what it was. Alex's mom joined them in the family room.

Once everyone was seated, Dr. Davis spoke. "We serve a mighty God, a good God, an awesome God, and we serve a God of forgiveness and second chances. I'm a witness to that, and you all know it to be true. I was a mean, self-serving, prideful man, and I am blessed and happy to say I'm not that man anymore. That's the power of a Heavenly Father that loves us so much. He'll meet us right where we are if we allow him to."

He then looked at Alice and Alex and continued. "These two kids, our kids who we raised to love the Lord and honor him with their lives, have done that in spite of our shortcomings. We fought them on it because of our ignorance and pride. Because we are the parents, we thought we knew better, but what I've learned that young people can teach us so much if we're willing to listen to them. With that said, let me give you the news. We are going to be grandparents!" he said it with a huge smile and tears.

Alice's parents were stunned. They immediately started asking about school, finances, and all sorts of things that were overwhelming for both Alex and Alice. However, Alex knew he had to get a grip on things before they got out of hand and Alice certainly didn't need the stress right now.

"We just found out today, or at least I just found out. My dad and Alice suspected it on Mother's Day but wanted to be sure, so they kept it quiet while my dad ran further tests to make sure. They planned to tell us today. Alice and I have not had a chance to talk this through and find out what God would have us do yet, but certainly as soon as we know we'll let you know," Alex said, and he said it with authority but respectfully.

Pastor Taylor liked that Alex was Alice's husband and he was learning to handle these sometimes overstepping but loving parents. He said, "Thank you, Alex. We will be waiting to find out how we can assist. We certainly don't want to overstep our boundaries."

Alice was so proud of her dad. She saw his growth in the Lord as well. He always had told her that he was growing every day in the Lord and that when God couldn't teach you anything anymore, you would soon be Heaven bound.

Their dinner was short but sweet. Alice and Alex needed to go home and talk. He knew she would want to share more of the details with him in private.

They opened the door to their garage apartment and sat looking at the ceiling. Then, Alex turned to Alice and said, "I love you so much!"

He then touched her stomach lightly. "Hi, I'm your dad," he said to her stomach. Alice smiled and said, "Yes you are."

They sat on the sofa in silence, each praying that God would lead them to do what was right for their little family. Once again they were in a now what moment in life and needed guidance.

Morning came quickly, and they didn't have to go anywhere. Saturday was their favorite day. This was a special Saturday since they were going to be parents. Alex lay next to his wife watching her sleep. She looked so peaceful. As if God had spoken out loud to him, he went to Ecclesiastes 3:1-8.

Alice found her husband praying and thanking God for all he had done for them. He said, "I have an answer from the Lord, Alice, do you want to hear it?"

She sat down, prepared to submit and go in the direction God had shown him.

"We are going to move back home to Lyonsville."

Alice sat there stunned. She was prepared to go back to Romans, Oklahoma, with the possibility of coming home and having the baby, but she certainly didn't think this would be the decision.

Alex looked at her and said, "Are you okay with that, or did you have something else in mind?"

Alice said, "Oh no, I had nothing in mind. I was prepared to follow you. I've learned that God loves us both and that our marriage works best for us when I follow your lead. I know you love me and would never place me in danger on purpose. I also know that you'll make mistakes because you are human. We are both growing and learning how to trust God and be married all at the same time."

They prayed, dressed, and decided to go talk to their parents. The parents agreed that it was best for Alex and Alice to move back home. They could stay in the garage apartment until the baby came and then move to a bigger apartment.

Pastor Taylor and Dr. Davis had a surprise for them. They would have received the gift at Christmas except they decided to go back to school in Oklahoma, so the parents placed the announcement on hold.

Pastor Taylor looked at Dr. Davis and said, "Do you want to tell them or should I?"

Dr. Davis said, "Tom, you know you want to do it so go ahead." He rarely called Pastor Taylor by his first name, but this time they were in a family atmosphere so it was okay.

Pastor Taylor said "You don't need to stay in the garage apartment and then have to move again when Alice is so far along in her pregnancy that she is miserable trying to move. Once our family had mended, Charles and I were golfing, and we came across a cute little house that was for sale. It's just down the street from Charles and Joan on the corner. It needed a little work done to it, so Charles and I hired a contractor to fix it up and our loving wives were kind enough to head that project for us and get it decorated for you."

Alice was getting ready to say something before she was cut off by her father in law. "It's not furnished, but your moms have purchased you a gift certificate to several stores to furnish it however you want. These are things you would have gotten eventually had I not been such a...." Dr. Davis said. He started to call himself a bad name but after a conversation with Pastor Thomas, he just left if alone and said "Well, you know."

Once again their kids were speechless, grateful, and truly humbled that God would provide in such a way. Then, Alice's fears kicked in and she said, "What if I lose this baby? What if I'm not meant to be a mom? What if Alex and I are being punished for sneaking off and getting married?"

Alice's mom came over and knelt beside her and said, "If that happens, we will deal with that as a family at that time. Right now let's just be happy with the blessing that you are pregnant, and we'll leave the rest to God. What have I always told you about worrying?" Then she quoted, "Worry is taking on responsibility that God never meant for you to have in the first place." She couldn't remember where she had read this quote, but it was true.

Alice knew her mom was right. Moreover, she wanted to believe everything was going to be okay, but she knew life just wasn't like that. She and Alex had already been through so much. They were forbidden to see each other, their parents wouldn't talk to them for a long time, and Alex's dad disinherited him. She had lost a baby already and had been attacked by a crazy man. People still didn't agree with interracial marriages, and they received crazy looks from people who judged them. There was a list of things that had gone on in their young lives. Now there was a baby. She sighed to herself now what?

CHAPTER THIRTY FOUR

It's Time!

It wasn't long before Alex and Alice had told the family about their news of having a family. They had a private conversation with Sean and Michele and asked them to be their child's godparents, and of course they were over the moon about it. They moved into their new home. They had to make the difficult phone call to Mr. and Mrs. Johnson to tell them they would not be returning to Romans, Oklahoma. However, through a tearful conversation, the Johnsons totally understood and knew that they had a bond that would never be broken.

Alice invited both sets of parents to come with her and Alex to find out the gender of the baby. Once they were in the ultra sound room, the tech stopped short and said, "I need to get the doctor. Alice became frightened and so did Alex, but Dr. Davis saw it clearly on the screen. He said nothing nor did he allow his face to tell it either.

Alice's obstetrician came in the room and looked at the ultrasound. She was a wonderful woman Alice knew her from when she worked in the clinic as a unit clerk. Dr. Grace Pruitt was a kind and gentle soul. She was what they called a little person. She only stood about 4'10", but she was confident and she knew her stuff. When Alice and Alex got married and had so many issues, Dr. Pruitt took Alice to the side one day at the clinic before they first left to go to school and said, "Let me tell you something, Alice. I've been different all my life, and it's obvious no one will ever love you like Jesus. Did I want to be born with dwarfism? No, but this is how God made me. I had to learn to live with the ignorance and prejudices of people. Many times my feelings would be hurt. I would go home and tell my mom and dad I couldn't take it anymore just wanted to die. Both of average sized parents told me that great things came in small packages and that God had a plan for me. However, I was responsible for how I found out what his plan was. One day I prayed and said, 'God, I believe you have a plan but please show me and help me be the best me I can that you get glory out of my life.'"

It was then that God gave her a passion for medicine. At one of her doctor's appointments, and there were many, she was talking to her doctor. The doctor asked her, "Do you know what you want to be when you grow up?"

Grace laughed because she was already a freshman in high school and the phrase "grow up" threw her for a loop. She knew what the doctor meant, however.

Grace said, "No, what can I be?"

She looked me straight in the eye and said, "Anything you want to be." It was then that she decided she was going to become a doctor!

Alice never forgotten their talk and knew when she became pregnant who her obstetrician would be. Dr. Pruitt looked at the ultra sound. Then, she turned and looked at Alice and Alex. Seeing the fear in their eyes, she said, "Relax! I have a bit of news for you." She sighed and said, "Alice and Alex, you are having twins."

Alice said, "Twins? Are you kidding me? You have never mentioned this in any of our appointments."

Dr. Pruitt said, "I didn't know myself for sure. In your last appointment I suspected it but wasn't sure, so I thought I'd wait."

She showed them both babies on the ultrasound.

Alex said, "Can you tell the sex of the babies?"

Dr. Pruitt took over the controls of the ultrasound, moving the device across Alice's tummy, and said, "Yes, you are having a boy and a girl."

The grandparents were hugging, laughing, and crying. Everyone was on cloud nine except for Alice. She was overthinking again, and Doctor Pruitt was on it.

She said, "These babies are healthy and fine from what I can tell. Stop worrying right now, do you understand me?"

Alice knew she meant business. She smiled and said, "Yes ma'am, I'm sorry."

Doctor Pruitt explained, "I know you have endometriosis, but these babies are not affected by it. Stop worrying about something that you have no control over anyway. It's my job to take care of you and these babies. Please understand I'm going to do just that."

Because of her height she had had a special step stool made. It gave her just the height she needed to reach over and hug and kiss her patient and say, "Congratulations, little mama, you'll be just fine."

The news was overwhelming, but they knew it was a blessing. They also knew they may not have any more children, so God was giving them both at the same time. They were back in school and working. Alice had to go part time to school because her pregnancy was considered high-risk. She worked two days a week at the clinic and went to school two days a week. Alex did all of the house work and only occasionally allowed Alice to cook a meal or two. She was never on her feet much and she hated it, but knew it was best for her and the babies.

It seemed her nine months went fast. She really wasn't sure exactly when she became pregnant, but the doctors had decided the babies were coming either late December or early January. In Georgia it didn't really get cold, but it was chilly that day, and she was cold. Her back was hurting, and she didn't want to complain. It couldn't be labor pains. It was only November. Besides, Thanksgiving was in two days. She needed to keep quiet and call her doctor. They were friends, so she wouldn't mind.

Alex had gone to the grocery store, so she could talk candidly and didn't have to whisper and worry him. She made the call

"Dr. Pruitt, this is Alice" she said in a soft voice.

"Yes, Alice, what's wrong" Dr. Pruitt asked in a concerned voice.

"I've been having some pain in my lower back for a couple of days, but I don't think I'm in labor," Alice said more like a question, not a statement.

Dr. Pruitt knew with her high risk pregnancy anything could be going on, but she didn't want to alarm Alice so she said, "You don't live far from me, so I will run over and take a look. Is that okay?" Her tone showed no urgency, so Alice didn't feel any alarm.

They hung up and Doctor Pruitt headed to their house. Alice met her at the door. She asked Alice some questions and then examined her. Alex arrived shortly after Dr. Pruitt had examined Alice. Alex was surprised to see Dr. Pruitt there but wasn't going to get alarmed for no reason.

He greeted Dr. Pruitt and placed the groceries in the kitchen. When he came back to the bedroom, Dr. Pruitt said, "I was hoping you'd get here. Alice is in labor. It's early labor, but she is in labor. I'd like for you to drive her to the hospital, and we'll get her checked in. Once we've gotten her comfortable, then you can call your parents."

Alex had some concern on his face but didn't say anything.

Dr. Pruitt said, "She's fine and the babies seem to be fine, too, however, I'll know much more once we get to the hospital."

Alice didn't want to go to the hospital. It was two days before Thanksgiving, and she didn't want to ruin it for everyone. She knew her thinking was off, but she wanted everyone to have a great Thanksgiving and not be worried about her. When they arrived at the hospital, Alice checked into the new labor and delivery rooms. They looked like little hotel suites. Her mom and mother in law had packed her bag a while ago, saying you never know, so we'll be prepared. Alice didn't mind. She knew they knew more than she did, and now that the time had come, she was elated she let them.

Dr. Pruitt examined Alice, and it was official. She was in labor; however, Dr. Pruitt said the babies could come today, tomorrow, or even on Thanksgiving Day. She was adamant that Alice would be in the hospital until the babies were born.

Alice was having small contractions but nothing major at this time. The parents arrived shortly after Alex called them; then, Sean and Michele came. They were all talking, laughing, and watching movies. Alice was calm and resting with Alex at her side holding her hand. They exchanged small talk between the two of them. Then the question no one had asked came up from Sean.

"Do you have a name for these babies?" he asked.

Alice said, "We've discussed some names, but we haven't come to a final conclusion on any name yet. We thought we had more time."

Sean smiled and said, "Sean is a good name, don't you think?"

Alex said, "Yes it is, but we are not naming our son Sean. Sorry buddy, love you but no."

Everyone in the room laughed. Michele was laughing, too. She said "I've been telling him for months that you weren't going to name your baby Sean, but he didn't believe me."

It was getting late, and Dr. Pruitt came in and ordered everyone out except for Alex. They hugged and kissed them both, and told them they were praying for them and to call if anything changed. They promised they would.

Thanksgiving morning came and still no twins. Alice's contractions were inconsistent. They would start and stop, then start again and stop. She thought at one point Doctor Pruitt would let her go home, but she said, "No, you've dilated too far to leave. These babies have a mind of their own; they will come when they are ready."

Alice was a little sad that she couldn't eat the turkey and dressing. The family had called and planned to come later to visit. Alex had run to the cafeteria to grab a bite to eat. They were having Thanksgiving food at the hospital. Although it wasn't his mom's or Alice's mom's food, it would do. He left when Alice fell asleep. The wet bed woke her up, and she called for a nurse. After the nurse checked her, she called for Dr. Pruitt who came in, examined Alice, and then smiled. "Your water just broke, Alice. We are going to have babies today," Dr. Pruitt said with a huge grin.

Alex walked into the room, and Dr. Pruitt informed him of Alice's condition. Her contractions were coming quite frequently now, and she was very uncomfortable. She wanted her mom, and Alex made the call. Alice requested that only her mom, Pastor Taylor, and Alex's mom and Dad come right now. Once the babies arrived, they could call everyone else. Alice's mom agreed.

Their parents arrived at the hospital at the same time. Alice's labor pains were more intense, and she was doing her best not to cry. Her mother could tell that Alice was in a lot of pain, but she was scared, also. She had never been through anything like this. The only experience she had was having her tonsils out at age ten and even then her mom almost had to go into surgery with her.

She went straight to her daughter's side. "Mom, it hurts a lot and I mean a lot. No one said the pain would be this intense. I really didn't know what to expect. I have watched a few videos, but I thought the women were just over the top. No, this is real!" Alice said while wincing in pain.

Alex was sitting on the side of the bed, holding Alice's hand. He had no idea what to do, and it hurt him to see her in so much pain. He looked at his dad and then at Pastor Taylor. They knew they needed to talk to him fast.

Pastor Taylor walked over to the bed and leaned down close to his daughter's ear and said, "Pumpkin, I love you more than my brand new tennis shoes."

Alice smiled at her dad. She knew he would make a joke to make things a little easier on her. She then whispered, "I love you more than my brand new house."

He winked at her and said. "That a girl. You've got this. We are going to take Alex out and pray with him for a few minutes. Mom and Joan are going to stay here with you. Is that okay with you?"

She could only get out, "Okay," and then another contraction came.

As the men left, Dr. Pruitt was coming into the room. She looked at Alice and said, "I think we are close. Let me check you."

The mothers moved so that Dr. Pruitt could close the curtains to give Alice some privacy. She checked Alice and said, "Let's go have some twins."

As Alice smiled, she was looking for Alex. Dr. Pruitt said, "I passed him in the hall with your dad and Dr. Davis. We can pick him up on our way to the delivery room?" Alice nodded yes.

Dr. Davis and Pastor Taylor knew Alex was feeling bad. They needed him to know this was what all men went through watching their wives labor to bring their children into the world.

Dr. Davis said, "It's difficult to see your beloved in so much pain when there's nothing you can do, isn't it?"

Alex said "Yes sir, but what I do?"

Pastor Taylor said, "You pray and reassure her that you love her, that she is beautiful, and that she is the most important person in this world to you, even more important than those babies she's carrying. She has to know that you understand if it wasn't for her, none of this would be possible."

Alex said "Pastor T., I'm doing my best. I feel like I'm no help to Alice at all."

They were about to give more advice when Dr. Pruitt came around the corner with her team and Alice on their way to the delivery room.

She looked up at the men and said, "New daddy, let's go. We're about to bring these twins into the world. Do you want to join our party?"

Alex leaped to the task, grabbing hold of Alice's hand, and they made their way to the delivery room.

"One, two three, push; one, two, three, push," were the words from Dr. Pruitt. "I can see the head. One more good push and baby number one is out!"

She pushed hard and baby girl Davis came out, crying loudly. Dr. Pruitt said "It's our girl. We have one more to deliver, and we can take care of mom."

Alice was trying to see what they were doing with the baby, but Alex said, "We've got more work to do."

She smiled and said, "I'm tired, Alex."

He smiled and said "I know, but you can do it Alie. We can do it."

Dr. Pruitt, standing tall on her stool, looked at Alice and said, "Let's get him out, one, two, three, push; one, two, three, push."

Alice was pushing, but baby boy Davis wasn't moving. Dr. Pruitt said to give him a minute because he was being stubborn. She took her hand and massaged Alice's stomach a little bit. Then, she hit it as if she were spanking him, and he started down the birth canal.

"I need one last huge push, and you'll be done."

Alice pushed with all of her might, and out came a little blonde headed boy. He wasn't crying. Instead he had his thumb in his mouth and was pouting as if to say leave me alone.

The nurse swooped up baby number two while other nurses began to take care of Alice. She was tired but wanted to see the babies. Dr. Pruitt moved to the top of the bed and said, "They are healthy babies. We will have the weight and length in a few minutes. How are you doing, Alice?"

"I'm fine," she said.

Dr. Pruitt looked at Alex and said, "You've done a great job being a support to Alice. I'm very proud and impressed with you."

The nurse came over and said baby girl Davis weights four pounds six ounces and is eighteen inches long. Baby boy Davis weights five pounds eight ounces and is twenty one inches long.

Alice smiled. "No wonder he didn't want to come out. He wanted to eat some more," she said.

The nurses brought the babies to them, Alice held her son while Alex held his daughter. It was all surreal to them.

Dr. Pruitt went to tell the parents everything went fine. Alice, Alex, and the babies were doing great. She asked that they give them about an hour, and she would take them back to Alice's room. She then turned to them and said, "Happy Thanksgiving, grandparents!"

The grandparents were so excited, looking through the window at the Davis twins. They hugged and kissed and hugged and kissed one another. They had not yet called family and friends. They wanted to talk with Alice and Alex first and see who they wanted to call personally. They were learning boundaries.

Alice was moved to a larger room that could accommodate more people. She was tired and was still in some pain. Alex sat next to the bed watching Alice as she slept. He was amazed at their journey but more amazed at the strength of who she was as a woman. He understood they were young, yet he felt older and more mature than the young people their age. Yes, they had had lots of help, but that didn't come without a price. He knew God had sent them on a journey but it took faith, obedience, commitment, prayer, and love. He knew they had no idea if their parents would ever come around and that they might have lived their entire life without their support. He then looked upward and thought, but God! He was teaching them all lessons in love, faith, forgiveness, obedience, guidance, and yes, of course, listening to God through his word.

Alice opened her eyes. She knew Alex was either praying or he was thinking about their new family. He was already in the planning stages of their children's lives and they were only hours old, but that was who he was. He was a planner. He didn't like things to catch him off guard. This entire two year now what experience had taught her that God is God, and he just wants her to trust and obey his direction. Things didn't look anything like she thought they would. They looked better. God had turned a situation that started out tumultuously into a blessing for everyone. She looked upward and said, "Thank you, Jesus, my sweet loving Jesus. Don't ever take your guidance and protection away from us. Thank you so much." Although the prayer was silent, she knew he heard her.

Alice touched Alex's hand; he looked toward her and gave her hand a gentle squeeze and said, "I love you, Ali."

She said, "I know. I love you, too"

She smiled and then he said, "What are we going to name the twins?"

She said, "I've been mulling that over in my mind, and I think have the names figured out. If you don't like them, please tell me. This is our decision. Promise me if you don't like them you'll say something?"

He promised. She said, "I think we should name our daughter Amber Dianne after my mom and your mom."

Alex's mom's middle name was Dianne, but she didn't spell it the same as Alice's mom's first name. Their daughter would carry both mom's name.

Alex said, I like that, and I think our moms will like that, too, but why Amber?"

Alice said, "Remember when your dad was in the hospital and he was calling for me but was saying Amber?"

Alex said, "Yes, that name is the color God spoke about in Ezekiel, meaning the glory of God."

Alice and, "It also marks a very meaningful time in your dad's life. Did you know he can tell you everything about colors from a biblical standpoint? He has studied it closely."

Alex was so very happy that Alice and his dad had developed such a close relationship. Sometimes he thought his dad preferred her company over his but knew it was their love for medicine that drew them together. His dad had a huge respect for Alice. He told Alex that she was smart as a whip and picked up on things that most miss. He was so proud of Alice.

Alex then said, "What should we name our son?"

That was an easy one for Alice. She said, "His name should be Thomas Charles Davis, after my dad you and your dad. What do you think?"

Alex smiled and said, "That is exactly what I thought. We can call him TC for short."

She looked at him and said, "By the way, where are the new grandparents?"

Alex said, "I'm sure they are at the nursery."

It wasn't long before they came rushing into Alice's hospital room with grins on their faces. Alice's mom went straight to her daughter's side, asking how she felt and if she was okay. Alice assured them all she was fine.

Her dad looked at her and said, "You look tired, but I know that is par for the course. If you want us to leave and give you and Alex more time alone, we can do that."

Alice said, "I'm fine, really I am. Besides, we've named the twins and want to share that with you."

They were all standing at the foot of the bed wide eyed. They had just been talking names and what they thought their children would name the babies. They really had no clue. All the names they came up with were names of grandparents and friends of Alex and Alice. They were sure that they would name their daughter after Michele even if they used it as her middle name, and they were certain Alex would name his son after Sean because of the close friendship and support.

Alex looked at Alice and said, "Okay, you tell them our daughter's name, and I'll tell them our son's name."

Alice said, "Our daughter's name is Amber Dianne. We wanted her to be named after both of her grandmothers who have stood by our sides. Alex and I couldn't have made this journey without the two of you loving us and supporting us even when our dad's were still angry with us. You placed a lot of stress on your marriages because of us, and we truly are sorry."

Alice had tears in her eyes thinking of the struggles they all had been through. Mrs. Taylor and Mrs. Davis both were now crying. Alice continued and her first name is Amber because it means…." Before she could finish the sentence, her father in law interjected, "the glory of God."

Alice smiled and said, "Yes sir! I wanted to honor your new relationship with Christ as well as our family being reunited together." Charles was so honored. Again God was showing him what true love looked like and what an amazing daughter in law he had gained.

It was now Alex's turn to share their son's name.

He looked at all of them, took a big breath, and said, "Our son's name is Thomas Charles Davis after his two amazing grandfathers. We love you and we are so blessed to have such giving, caring, loving, and supportive parents in our lives. We will call him TC as a nickname."

The granddads were now standing taller with their chests stuck out, so to speak. The men were elated and proud to have their first grandson named after them. The nurse entered and asked Alice if she wanted them to bring the twins in the room.

Alice said, "Of course! I only got to look at them a little bit in the delivery room. Yes, please bring them in."

The babies were sleeping. Alex held his son while Alice held their daughter. Alex thought both children looked just like Alice, while Alice thought the very opposite. They both had sprigs of blondish hair, and their complexion was whitish red. No one knew for sure what skin tone these children would grow up with, and no one cared. The babies were healthy and would grow up with all the love, support, and guidance their parents, grandparents, and godparents could give them.

Pastor Taylor asked if he could hold his grandson, and Alex handed him over. Then, Dr. Davis reached for his granddaughter. Both men started singing Amazing Grace in unison. Everyone joined in.

Once the song was over, Pastor Taylor prayed, "Heavenly Father, we do give you honor and praise for a Thanksgiving filled with love and the blessing of our new grandchildren. May you hold Amber and little TC in your loving care. Teach them to love you, honor you, and obey you in all they do. Lord, give my daughter and son in law the guidance and direction they need as new parents. Teach us as grandparents to know our role and not over step our boundaries. Lord, continue to keep our family together. When we do disagree, give us a strategy to come back together in forgiveness. Help us leave a legacy of you to these children. Lord, give them good health and sound minds and teach them respect for your word and for family and friends. Lord, we love and praise you, and it is in Jesus Christ, your son's name we pray. Amen!"

There was not a dry eye in the room, and they all said, "Amen!"

CHAPTER THIRTY FIVE

Present Time!

lice had been sitting in her car thinking. It was TC knocking on her window that brought her back to reality. "Mom, Mom!" he said with his big voice. He looked a lot like Alex with his tall lean body and sandy blondish hair. Alice rolled her window down and said, "TC, why are you banging on my window?"

"Because you've been sitting out here for a while and Amby and I need to get dressed for our graduation pictures. The photographer will be here in a while and YaYa, Papa, Mimi, and granddad are here, too." They referred to Alice's parents as Ya Ya and Papa and they referred to Alex's parents a Mimi and Grandad.

TC, like his dad, was a planner, while his twin sister Amber was a thinker. She really liked to be more adventurous. She was the leader, and Alice was always having to reel her in.

TC opened the car door for his mom, who still had on her white doctor's coat. He reached down and hugged his mom, towering over her. "I love you," he said.

Alice smiled back "I love you too, but why do you love me so much, TC?" Alice asked. She knew her son had something up his sleeve, and she was waiting for him to asked for something that she and Alex would say no to.

Amber met them at the door. "Mom, what took you so long to get out of the car?" she asked with a little concern but more irritation. She needed her mom to hurry to help her to pick out the right outfit. Mimi and YaYa had helped her do her hair. It was long, curly, and sandy blond with a hint of auburn when the sun hit it just right.

Alice said, "Amby, is your dad home yet?"

Before she could get the question out, Alex met her at the door with a tall glass of iced tea. It was May and getting hot.

"Hi, Doctor Davis," Alex said to his wife.

She said, "Hi, Pastor Davis. How was your day?" He shrugged his shoulders and Alice knew that meant nothing new.

Alice entered her home. It was so different from the home their parents had purchased them almost nineteen years ago. Alex was now the Pastor of Alice's dad's church. Her dad had semi-retired, and Alex ran all the day to day functions of the now mega church. Alice was the director of pediatrics at the Hospital where she started as a unit clerk when she was in high school. After they moved back to Lyonsville, she had worked with Alex's dad in his clinic while going to college. Once she finished medical school, she did her residency at the hospital and was asked to stay once she graduated. She promoted quickly and now at thirty six years old was one of the directors. They had done quite well. They had this house built in a new subdivision that sat half way between both of their parents' homes.

Their parents both had moved to the new retirement homes on the golf course. It was amazing to see her parents older and how she had taken their place. She thought about the circle of life. Soon TC and Amber would take her and Alex's place.

Alice saw her dad sitting in the big recliner and she smiled. "Hi, Daddy!"
He said, "Pumpkin, how was your day?"

She smiled "It was fine." She reached her mom and mother in law, hugged them both, and kissed her father in law on the cheek. "I need to run upstairs to change my clothes. I know the photographer, Michele, Sean, and the kids will be here soon, and I don't want Michele to be stressing about me not being ready yet," Alice said. She rushed up the stairs to get dressed. The family knew Alice was the late one, and they all laughed.

The door front door opened, and they heard Sean's voice. "Hey, family! The Brooks are here!" he said loudly.

Michele and Sean were now attorneys. They had started out in Savannah, Georgia, at a law firm while they were still in law school as interns. Much had changed for them as well. They had moved back to Lyonsville and had built a house right across the street from Alex and Alice. They had purchased the lots as soon as they came on the market. They had two children as well, but they were younger than Alice and Alex's children. Their son was a junior in high school and their daughter was a freshman. They had waited with their daughter so Michele's body could recuperate. It was more challenging for her, but Michele stayed on top of her health and for the most part she was fine. Their son was SJ, Sean Junior, and their daughter's name was Clara. She was named after Mrs. Johnson. Mr. and Mrs. Johnson both had passed away in a car accident a few years after their son graduated from college. They were still very close to Wes Johnson, who was now a huge song writer and composer in Nashville.

Michele asked immediately, "Where is Alice?"

Everyone said in unison, "Getting dressed."

Michele knew her friend would be late, but that was who she was.

Alice came downstairs, and it wasn't long before the photographer arrived. Sean's dad and mom entered along with Michele's parents.

They were not only getting high school graduation pictures but also a family portrait. It would respresent nineteen years of trials, tests, and temporary assignments sprinkled with a lot of now what moments of life—moments full of joy, purpose, passion, forgiveness, and most of all love of family, friends and God!

The photographer had the couples strategically placed next to their parents and the grandchildren sitting on the floor in front of the adults. He took several family photos and graduation pictures as well. Although they would see the finished photos later in the week, the photographer showed them some proofs that day. Alice stood back with a photo of all of them in her hand and thought about all of the things they had gone through. Look at them now. They were stronger than they had ever been.

Alex saw her face and moved closer to her, looking at the photo in her hands, and they both whispered, "NOW WHAT?"

Now What?

Alice an Alex sat in their living room reading a letter from their daughter Amber. She and her twin brother had chosen to go to school in Missouri! Alice had challenged the choice because they were far too young to be so far away from home. Yet her husband Alex reminded her that they had secretly gotten married before they graduated from high school. If this was the journey God had their children on, they needed to move out of the way and let it happen. Alice was protective, yet she knew her husband was right.

They flew to Missouri to take the children to school instead of driving the twelve hours. They knew they would be in good hands. Their former college friends David and Rhonda Brown lived in Missouri and were both on staff at the college. Rhonda was a professor of psychology and David was dean of student affairs. Mr. and Mrs. Johnson's son, Wes Johnson, was still writing music for many well-known music artists in Tennessee. He could do that from anywhere in the world, and he and his new wife Melissa had moved to Missouri to work at a university where he was head of the music department. Their friend Beaux was living nearby in another suburb of Kansas City, where he was the minister of music at their church. His wife Christine was a nurse at one of the local hospitals.

Knowing their children were surrounded by such a cloud of witness, they could rest a little easier. Alice read a letter from her daughter.

"Dear Mom and Dad, TC and I like Missouri. We are meeting lots of new friends and our studies are going well. I have a couple of classes with Professor Rhonda Brown. She is a sweet lady, and I've become very close to her son DJ (David Jr.). He's a great guy and very smart, too. He is a journalism major, too.

TC is doing okay, although I don't really care for the crowd he's chosen to hang out with! He says he knows what he's doing, so I'm leaving that alone. I have told Dean Brown about my concerns, and I think he's talked with TC, too. However, I can't keep track of your son aka my brother. Sometimes I feel responsible for him while other times I'm just angry that he doesn't see the danger right in front of him.

For the most part we are doing okay. College is not as easy as I thought it would be. You really have to apply yourself. I've overdrawn my checking account and would appreciate your putting a few dollars in it for me please. (smile) Sorry. I will make sure I look closer to that situation. I know we have a few more months before we can come home, but I would like for it to get warmer here. It's October and the temperature has already dropped to 30 degrees. Some of my friends have said wait until it snows, but I'm not looking forward to that. I'm going to close this lengthy letter and say I love you and miss you both. Love Amby."

Alice looked at Alex and said, "Have you talked with David Brown about TC?"

Alex had to confess he had heard from David but didn't want to alarm her. He knew she would want to catch the first flight to Missouri to check on TC.

Alice said, "Alex, how could you withhold information about my son from me? We promised early in our marriage that we would be honest, up front, and tell each other the truth. When you withhold things like this, important things, it makes me wonder what else you've been holding back from me."

She was angry, and Alex knew she would be, but he wanted to process what David had told him and then tell her.

"Come on now, you know I'm not holding anything from you. I was going to tell you, but I was praying about this and trying to process it myself. It appears that TC has been hanging around with some guys who are known to start some trouble. David said he spoke with TC and told him that if he's going to be effective in medicine, he needed to make sure he kept his grades up. He also emphasized that who he chose as friends should be upright people as well. David thinks TC listened to him, but he's not sure. I thought I'd call TC myself before I burdened you with all of this," Alex responded.

Alice picked up the phone and called her son, but there was no answer. She knew she needed to hear from him in a few days or she would be on a plane Missouri bound.

Alex asked about Amber's checking account being overdrawn. Alice said she had no idea why, although they both knew their daughter could spend money like drinking water. They would have to pay close attention to that.

Alice said, "She didn't call Papa or granddad because they wouldn't just sent her some money. A lecture from both of them would have been her fate. Since she didn't want the lecture, she thought she'd just tell us." Alice laughed and said, "I don't blame her."

Sean and Michele were at the door. The couples were having dinner. While at dinner, Michele mentioned that her daughter Clara was having some issues with bullying at their school. Although it was a private school, that problem was everywhere. Michele wanted to pull her from the school, but Sean insisted that she couldn't run away from problems. Clara needed to face them head on. Their son, who was now a senior, was dating a young lady who they didn't approve of. Sean said she came from the wrong side of the tracks, so to speak. He had investigated her and her parents and found that her dad had just been released from prison and her mom had just gotten out of rehab for drug use. The young lady had been living with relatives near them, and that is how she got into the private school.

Alex and Alice shared the letter from Amber and they all just dropped their heads and said, "Now what?"

They knew that their children would face trials and tests just as they had. They hoped that as parents they would have the wisdom to seek God and not play God in their children's lives, but now they saw the challenges that their parents had faced trying to help almost adult children make right decisions but knowing you really have no control over the decisions they make. Their children were hundreds of miles away and they can't put their hands or eyes on them. This was a different time than when they grew up, and there were different rules. However, they hoped their children would hold fast to the concept of the scripture in Romans 15:4, "For whatsoever things were written aforetime were written for our learning, that we through patience and comfort of the scriptures might have hope."

They hoped they would look at the many lessons God taught them and would apply those lessons to their lives and not have to be chastised by God because of their disobedience. However, they knew there were just some things that they would have to learn on their own. They prayed as parents they would keep their wits about them and not overreact to the challenges that their children were going through. They all knew one thing they could trust was God!

They started humming the song, "Now What." "Now what sweet Jesus, tell me what to do. Now what sweet Jesus, help me follow through. Tell me what to do, help me follow through, tell me what to do Sweeeeeeet Jesus. Tell me what to do help me follow through."

This was the now famous song composed by their friend Wes that was played at their wedding. They knew the lyrics to this song were true for them as well as for their children. Jesus needed to tell them as well as their children what to do and how to follow through or obey, in other words. They knew now what moments would come to their children, and they would not be able to always solve their problems. They bowed their heads and prayed. "Lord, please help us trust you in the now what moments in our children's lives."

After they prayed, Alex said, "This is the most we can hope for just as our parents prayed and hoped for us. Would we ever have thought we'd be where we are today? I would never have imagined we would be the parents of twins or that I would be senior pastor at Ali's dad's church. But God works in mysterious ways. I know our children will be okay, but they'll have to learn some very hard lessons that only come from now what situations."

Sean interjected, "I know that we want to protect them from the snares of the Devil. I'd love nothing more than to go up to that school and fight Clara's battles, but she won't know what God can do if I do that."

Michele said, "While I'm not happy with SJ's choice in a girlfriend, I think of you, Alice, and how Dr. Davis didn't like you and thought you had all but ruined his family. This young lady can't help what her parents have done, and we can't judge her for that. I just hope she isn't in SJ's life because she thinks he comes from money."

It was clear they were getting ready to face some now what moments in the lives of their children. The question they were facing now was—are they ready?

Now What?
A LOVE STORY

Meet the Author: Roz

Roz is a native of Missouri, where she has lived all of her life. This is book number five for her, but it is her very first novel. She's excited, to say the least, and has poured her heart into this book.

Roz would be the first to say she wears many hats, as mother, grandmother, author, conference speaker, lyricist, blogger, spiritual mother to many, and minister of women's ministry at her home church. She loves teaching and spending time in the word, although in her words she says, "I don't spend nearly enough time at his feet as I desire and need to."

Roz is a collector of old Bibles, shoes, and pajamas of all things. She enjoys spending time with her closest of girlfriends. They can talk for hours sharing in God's word and supporting one another in ministry and family. At heart she's a loner although you would not believe it to meet her or to hear her teach. She's becomes a people person during those times, desiring women to know and love her Jesus just as she does. Her favorite scripture is Matthew 5:16--Let your light so shine before men that they may see your good works and glorify your Father which is in Heaven.

ROZ SPEAKS ON A RANGE OF TOPICS!

If you desire Roz to speak at your next event, go to **http://therobinsonagency.com/Brown-Roz.**

You can read Roz's blogs at **https://inspirationsbyroz.com**

To order books by Roz Brown go to **http://imperiumpublishing.combookstore**